# The Transition

# The Transition

**Luke Kennard**

4th ESTATE • *London*

HarperCollins
PUBLISHERS
Since 1817

4th Estate
An imprint of HarperCollins*Publishers*
1 London Bridge Street
London SE1 9GF

www.4thEstate.co.uk

First published in Great Britain in 2017 by 4th Estate

1

MIX
Paper from
responsible sources
FSC
www.fsc.org
FSC® C007454

For Zoë

# The Transition

# 1

**WHENEVER KARL TEMPERLEY** felt that he couldn't endure another moment he would imagine that he had just run over and killed a child. The shock of the impact, the screech of his too-late emergency stop, the tiny body in the gutter, a parent – sometimes the mother, sometimes the father – running towards him as he stood by the bloodied bonnet of his wife's Fiat Punto. This imagined, he returned to his real world and its trivial sorrows with relief and gratitude.

'… your marital status notwithstanding …' the notary public was saying.

Lately though, facing fifteen months in jail for fraud and a tax infraction he still couldn't quite fathom – neither what he had done or neglected to do, nor how exactly he had accomplished or overlooked it – he found himself spending longer and longer at his inner roadside.

Karl Temperley wrote consumer reviews of products he had never used and bespoke school and undergraduate essays as 'study aids' for ten pence a word. It was a lowly portfolio career, but such was his determination to do something literary with his education: he had read English and taken a Master's degree in the Metaphysical Poets. It had cost him £78,000, an amount which seemed impossible and therefore easy to ignore.

His employers were email addresses who signed off with different names, but their tone was warm and jovial enough and he was well thought of – of this they assured him – for his ability to write essentially the same thing as if it were being said by ten different people. Where some saw a carbon-fibre laptop case, Karl saw a Russian novel.

His wife, Genevieve, taught at a local primary school. An enviable demographic once known as Double Income No Kids and yet, once the rent and bills were paid, their debts serviced, Karl found that he had to think twice about buying a pair of shoes when his old ones wore through at the sole. The rent kept going up. He was aware they brought some of this on themselves; they had expectations. Every day they drank flavoured coffees the size of poster tubes, which cost as much as the baristas serving them would earn in an hour. They loaded supermarket trolleys with snacks and treats which could largely be consumed on the way home. In the last week of every month they were inevitably down to the wire, so he would put a week's shopping on his credit card. Then a return train fare. The pair of shoes he needed. A birthday present for Genevieve. Dinner. The bank was happy to increase his credit limit, increase it again and, instead of increasing it a third time, to offer him a temporary loan to consolidate his debt, so that the double-capacity credit card went back to a tantalising £0.00. Karl decided he might start taking advantage of the daily invitations to take out more credit cards, credit cards with banks he hadn't even heard of, cards in every colour of the spectrum, cards with limits of £300 which he could use for small purchases, cards with limits of £5,000 with which he could chivalrously pay for a new head gasket when Genevieve's car got into trouble and, the following week, take her on a five-star mini-break to Paris when she turned thirty-two (her thirtieth had been marred by a minor psychotic episode, and her thirty-first was not much better, so he felt the need to compensate). Finally, there was one beautiful, transparent credit card which shimmered like a puddle of petrol and had a limit of £11,000. He used it to pay off some of the smaller credit cards and make the minimum monthly payment on the middle-sized ones. Whenever this one needed servicing he would take out another bantamweight card or a short-term advance.

Genevieve knew nothing of his seventeen-card private Ponzi scheme. As far as she could see, both she and Karl worked damn hard all week then collapsed, exhausted, and spent all weekend either asleep or streaming complete seasons of American dramas to get back to full strength. Whenever they had some time off they both came down with head colds. It never occurred to her that they might be living beyond their means and it took three years for Karl to finally max out his most copious line of credit, the rat queen of his nest of cards. After that, letters printed in red ink started to arrive. Statements with lateness penalties, interest on the lateness penalties, penalties for exceeding the credit limit and lateness penalties on those penalties, punitive rates of interest and demands for final settlement. The double dose of sleeping pills he was taking with a tumbler of mid-priced brandy to silence the grinding gears of his incipient ruination stopped working. He was getting crotchety with Genevieve and it was upsetting her. His very *raison d'être* was to not upset Genevieve; it was, so he told himself, the reason he'd got into so much debt in the first place and yet it had led to him upsetting her anyway.

*Maybe I should kill myself?* he thought, looking at his face in the communal bathroom mirror one winter morning, his cheeks covered in shaving foam. He pressed the five-blade Ultra Smooth Advanced Wet Shave System safety razor to his left wrist and shaved a Parmesan-thin centimetre of flesh. Blood appeared like a watermark. It really, really stung. *Maybe not.* He put his watch on over the top of it.

The tiny abrasion tingled and throbbed sporadically throughout the day. It made him laugh. Karl thought of a story he'd once heard about a would-be martyr in the third century who was on his way to the capital with every intention of being tortured and killed for his faith. He had to break his journey and a monk put him up in an old barn and, in the morning, asked him how his night had been. He complained about the draught and the flea bites, and the monk told him that he probably wasn't ready to face martyrdom.

Karl knew what to do. He wrote to his anonymous employers. Anyone he had ever worked for, all eighty-two email addresses. He needed more work, better work, urgently, whatever it was. He got only one reply, from someone called Sot Barnslig, offering to make him supervisor for two click-farms, enlisting people from around the world to generate fake traffic for websites, paying them out of the same reserve from which he would draw his own fee. The work was menial and morally dubious, but the pay was better than his fake copywriting and he started to make a dent in the most pressing credit cards.

Actually, said Sot Barnslig – after Karl had been successfully paying down his seventeen debts for a fortnight and was starting to get some rest again – actually, the click-farms were a front for an enormous skimming operation. Sot Barnslig confessed that he was stealing tiny amounts from thousands of different accounts and credit cards, amounts too small to be noticed by their owners, and Karl was unwittingly assisting him.

Karl emailed Sot Barnslig: *Why did you tell me that?* and carried on.

Unfortunately Sot Barnslig had either been compromised by investigators or had been an undercover agent all along. Karl was required to give up his laptop and, in desperation, he called his old university room-mate, Keston, an accountant, told him everything, and tried not to cry during their preliminary conversation.

'*Oh*, K-Pax,' said Keston. 'You've got yourself in a right pickle, haven't you? That gross yellow one.'

'Am I going to prison?'

'This is where being male, middle-class and white comes into its own,' said Keston. 'Nothing but safety nets. And you've touched the hem of the right garment.'

Keston organised a lawyer, who failed to adequately demonstrate Karl's ignorance and now it seemed that Karl was going to have to spend some time in a low-security prison.

★ ★ ★

The young, owlish notary public had been talking for some time. The only representative of Spenser and Rudge currently willing to talk to him pro bono, he was telling Karl it was neither the best- nor the worst-case scenario. Did he know, by the way, that the origin of the phrase *worst-case scenario* was not legal, but in fact military? Karl said that he didn't. It's a strategy, the notary public told him. Before a manoeuvre you must always imagine the most awful thing the contingent world might throw your way.

There was a strong antiseptic smell in the notary public's office. He must have injured himself somehow.

'It's a good product, Mr Temperley,' said the notary. 'The Transition. It's worth considering as an alternative. Your accountant is working out the finer details. He agrees it's a good product.'

Karl pictured a pearlescent turquoise ball bouncing into the road between parked cars and he imagined slamming down the brake and the clutch at the same time, but he was doing almost forty because he was a terrible, negligent driver. What is the first thing you say to the parent? It doesn't matter. You're *so, so sorry?* Well, that's just great. Real voices, official voices with their assurances, codes and timbre would take over at some point. Voices like that of his notary public, who had just said,

'I appreciate this is probably not what you were expecting.'

Such was Karl's distraction that by the time he realised that the notary public was offering him a place on a pilot scheme called The Transition in lieu of fifteen months in jail, he said yes without asking for further information, without calling his wife to discuss it with her, without pausing for breath.

The notary public blinked twice and handed him a thick, glossy brochure, saying that he might like to read it over before making up his mind. The cover depicted the blueprint for a house, but the rooms were designated things like EMPLOYMENT, NUTRITION, RESPONSIBILITY, RELATIONSHIP, BILLS, INVESTMENT, SELF-RESPECT. A semi-transparent overlay had THE TRANSITION embossed in capitals.

'Your accountant was actually the one who drew our attention to it,' said the notary public.

'Keston,' said Karl.

Aside from the online fraud, Karl's tax infraction went back several years – a thread that snagged and unravelled the whole of his self-start marketing operation – and it was going to cost him and his wife a lot to pay it back. On top of Genevieve's car payments and the credit card Karl had been using for groceries for the last six months, they were in a tight spot. And they were two months in arrears with their rent. Genevieve had texted him just before the meeting with the notary public and the text read only *Eviction. Next Week :(*

It was unseasonably hot for March. It was hot in the notary public's office, and although Karl was only wearing climbing shorts and a red Cookie Monster T-shirt, the sweat was running sunblock into his eyes. He peeled open the brochure and scanned the first page but couldn't take the words in.

*Piaget defines the cognitive task of adolescence as the achievement of formal operational reasoning …*

He looked up at the clock, at the maroon leather book spines, at the notary public's suit jacket baking in a shaft of sunlight and mingling a distinctly sheepy smell with the TCP.

'Can you summarise it for me?' he said.

# 2

**KARL WALKED HOME** through the Thompsons' suburb. The last decade had seen the professionalisation of the amateur landlord. Entire terraces were bought up, the houses divided and divided again. *Is it not time, finally, for the government to curb this rampant greed which is draining our country's resources and disenfranchising an entire generation?* an editorial would occasionally ask. In fact three administrations had tried: a certain percentage of property portfolios had to be dedicated to social housing, to key workers, to people in their thirties, but the sanctions only made the landlords, who had inherited their property portfolios from their parents, put up their rents to cover their losses. They felt their losses. Karl's own landlord, an affable man with toothbrush hair who always wore a grey Crombie, impressed this upon him. They had school fees and gastro-holidays and multiple mortgages to pay. Families spent their money raising their children and, as the years went by, savings became the preserve of the shrinking caste who already owned several houses. The average age of leaving the parental home drifted into the early forties. For Genevieve, raised by her grandparents, several years deceased, and Karl, who was the youngest child of an older couple, his father now convalescing in sheltered accommodation, this wasn't an option. They were living, with their two-bar heater and all-in-one toaster oven, in the former conservatory of a Victorian semi-detached villa, a shared bathroom on each floor and a sense in both their minds of having made a bad decision at some critical juncture. The conservatory's Perspex ceiling had been wallpapered, but it was peeling at the corners and let in a nimbus of brilliant light.

Well, whatever. The fact remained they had running water, supermarkets, cinemas.

'I mean for goodness' sake, we're still wealthier than ninety-seven per cent of the world's population,' said Genevieve, whenever Karl complained. 'We're still a three-per-cent leech on the side of the planet, sucking most of it dry. And you have a cold half the time. You could be the richest man in the world and you'd still spend most of the day blowing your nose and moaning about your sinuses.'

Karl sniffed.

If their generation were waiting to have kids, or perhaps electing not to have kids at all, that was all for the better. It wasn't as though the world might run short of people. The development of a safe male contraceptive device, a tiny chip implanted in the thigh (occasionally, and in Karl's case, without spousal accord; the doctors never asked), had its part to play in this, for sure. 'Does any man ever really *want* to have children?' its inventor asked, palms upward at a press conference. This was met with some derision. 'Yeah, because I've hit a nerve,' he said. 'Mark my words: the languor and fecklessness of the male gender will be the salvation of the human race. There are plenty of orphans if you want to adopt.'

Karl crossed the road between two yellow sports utility vehicles and walked by the Ravencroft Community Centre which had been converted into eleven luxury condos by the Thompsons.

The Transition was founded, the notary public had explained to him, because there had been a steep increase in cases such as Karl's. A generation who had benefited from unrivalled educational opportunities and decades of peacetime, who nonetheless seemed determined to self-destruct through petty crime, alcohol abuse and financial incompetence; a generation who didn't vote; who had given up on making any kind of contribution to society and blamed anyone but themselves for it.

So Karl ignored the pamphleteer, a young white guy with dreadlocks who stood by a cracked bathtub on the communal green with a stack of statistics about the Thompsons' neglect of their 700 tenants. Fronting for the Socialist Workers Party. *Thompson Slumlords Extraordinaire.* But as far as Karl could see, the Thompsons' tenants had it pretty good. Fixed contracts, solid walls and ceilings.

'I'm fine, thanks.' He kept his hands in his pockets.

'You're not fine,' said the pamphleteer as Karl walked on, 'you've been conditioned into total indifference.'

'Same thing, innit?' said Karl.

# 3

**GENEVIEVE PUT HER** hair up with an enormous tortoise-shell hair-clip and wiped her eyes. Ten minutes before, when Karl had told her he was off the hook, she had cried and hugged him. Then she read the Transition brochure while smoking three cigarettes with increasing speed and intensity. Karl made two cups of tea in someone else's mugs from the shared kitchen. Everything else was packed. One of them, a shiny black mug, bore the motivational slogan: *Don't fear the future. Be the future.* It was supposed to be heat-activated, but something had gone wrong so that when Karl poured boiling water into the mug the only words visible were *fear the future. Be*

He was stirring one sugar into Genevieve's tea when he heard her give a long, low howl. Not quite a howl, he thought, as he tapped the spoon on the side of the mug and threw it into the sink. It was too flat and unemotional to be called a howl. It was more like the cry of an animal in the jaws of a predator when it resigns itself to its fate. Karl pictured himself driving along a suburban road ... He walked towards the sound.

Genevieve was lying on her side, like a shop-window dummy knocked over.

'I'm so angry,' she said, quietly.

'I know it's …' said Karl.

'It sounds absolutely bloody awful,' she said, sitting upright and closing the booklet. 'Couldn't you have just gone to prison?' Karl put the cups of tea on the floor next to Genevieve, sloshing a little over the side so that it scalded his hand. 'I'm joking,' she said. 'It does sound dire, though. So don't try to pretend we have any choice.'

'The way I see it is it's like a speeding course – you take the points on your licence or you give up a day for re-education.'

'Yeah,' said Genevieve. 'Except your wife has to go with you and it's six months.'

'No rent,' said Karl, shuffling down to the floorboards next to her.

'So we get to live rent-free in a loft apartment – that's great, Karl. Maybe I'll start painting again.'

'It's more like lodging.'

'I can see it's more like lodging,' said Genevieve. 'Except the landlords don't get paid. So they resent us. Even more than normal landlords.'

'Well, the programme pays them,' said Karl, taking a sip from his tea, which was still too hot, 'but they're not really doing it for the money. The notary said it was more like jury service.'

'You know I don't take sugar,' said Genevieve.

'What?'

'My tea.'

'I thought you—'

'Only in coffee. It calls them "mentors". I don't like the idea of having mentors.'

'So we put up with it,' said Karl. 'It's supposed to help us and, you never know. It's a pilot scheme; they haven't ironed out the kinks yet, so it might actually be more helpful than they mean it to be.'

'It's patronising.'

'That's true.'

'It says it's a "fully holistic approach to getting our lives back on track". It says they give us advice on being married. As well as the financial stuff. We've been married four years! It's enormously patronising. And what about privacy?'

'I'm not trying to argue that this is a good thing, G.'

'It's humiliating.'

Karl looked at her. Saying he was sorry seemed redundant.

'You've read this?' said Genevieve, flicking to the fifth page. 'There's a section on healthy eating. There's a section on how to vote. *A generation suffering from an unholy trinity of cynicism, ignorance and apathy*,' she read. 'That's you and me, honey.'

'It's certainly me,' said Karl. 'You're just getting dragged down by the rest of us.'

'And who *are* they, anyway? Are we randomly assigned? Is it like a dating website?'

Karl looked at his feet. They had already been allocated mentors. Once he'd agreed to the terms and signed and dated two documents, the process had been seven mouse clicks on the other side of the notary public's desk.

'Do they pick us out like puppies?'

'We meet them tomorrow,' said Karl.

'Oh God,' said Genevieve. 'What are their names?'

'Stu. Stuart Carson. And Janna Ridland.'

'Janna,' said Genevieve. 'Janna. The name sounds half empty.'

'You're doing this to keep me out of prison. Do you need to hear me say how much I appreciate it?'

Genevieve turned and kicked her legs over his. She shuffled closer.

'This is what I don't like, Karly, we're –' she put her head on his shoulder – 'we're going through the same ups and downs young couples have always gone through, and they're treating us like we're an aberration.'

Karl took a sip of his tea.

'I'm thirty-four,' he said. 'When my father was thirty-four he and Mum already had my two sisters. And a Ford Escort. They owned a house. They went on holidays.'

'When my father was thirty-four,' said Genevieve, 'he had my mother sectioned, dropped me and Nina at Granny's and drank himself to death in Madrid.'

'Madrid?' said Karl.

Last time it was Berlin and, now that he thought of it, he was certain that Genevieve never mentioned the same city twice.

# 4

**IN THE COUNCIL CHAMBER,** every room looked like a waiting room, lined with low oblong benches and school chairs, one strip light flickering. It was hard to get up from the deep spongy bench when their mentors came through the double doors of 151.

Karl's first thought was that they didn't look any older than him or Genevieve, but then maybe there was only a decade or so in it. He had expected an aura of age and experience: authority figures, the way teachers looked when he was a pupil. Janna was angular and pretty, a white blouse tucked into a black leather pencil skirt. Her mouth was very small, like a china doll's. Stu at least looked weathered. He was wearing black jeans and a black T-shirt with a lightning bolt on it. He had a black and purple Mohican, four inches tall, five spikes.

'God, this place is depressing,' said Stu. 'Sorry they made you come here.'

'Don't get up,' said Janna, once they were up. They exchanged air kisses.

'You probably weren't expecting us to look like this,' said Stu.

'Oh, what, the Mohawk?' said Karl.

'The Mohawk actually wore a patch at the base of the skull and a patch at the forehead,' said Stu. 'This is closer to an Iro.'

'Do you have any ...' said Genevieve. 'Indian blood, I mean?'

'Genevieve,' said Stu, 'I am merely an enthusiast.'

Stu busied himself collecting four flimsy cups of coffee from the machine in the corner. The two couples sat opposite one another over a pine and clapboard table too low for the seats.

'Drink,' he said. 'It's terrible, but, you know, ritual. Everything feels better when you're holding something warm. You're a primary school teacher, I'm told?'

'That's right,' said Genevieve.

'That's brilliant,' said Stu. 'You're one of the most important people in the country. And Karl?'

'You know those fliers you see stuck to lamp posts that say *make £1,000 a week online without leaving your house?*' said Karl.

'You stick those up?' said Stu.

'No,' said Karl. 'I make a thousand pounds a week online without leaving my house. Except it's not really a thousand pounds a week. I suppose it could be if you never went to sleep.'

'So you're self-employed,' said Janna. 'But what's the work?'

'Search-engine evaluation, product reviews,' said Karl. 'Literature essays for rich students. It's actually duller than it sounds.'

'A fellow middle-class underachiever,' said Stu.

'You know the type.'

'I *was* the type. Look, you don't need to rush into anything, but this is a chance to do something with your life. The Transition isn't a punishment, it's an opportunity.'

He took two thick, stapled forms out of his shoulder bag, and a blue pen.

'You'll be living with us as equals – we eat together, talk together, leave the house for work together. Or, well, Karl, in your case you'll be staying in the house to work, but you get the point.'

Genevieve and Karl, who had never read a contract in their lives, both turned to the final page of their forms, wrote their names in block capitals, signed.

'The thing is, with the hair, it's a lightning conductor,' said Stu. 'People think, oh, the guy with the hair. Or they think, in spite of the hair, he's quite a nice guy. Any opinion that anyone ever holds about me is in the context of my hair. It's the equivalent of being a beautiful woman.'

'To be fair, it *is* the most interesting thing about him,' said Janna, giving Stu a friendly but very hard punch on the shoulder, which he rubbed, pouting. 'The removal team are picking up your stuff now, so that's taken care of. We'll see you for the general meeting in the morning, okay?'

Stu folded up their contracts and slipped them back into his shoulder bag.

'Tomorrow, then,' he said. 'The Transition will send a car. Eight thirty.'

They stood.

'We want you to know that we don't judge you,' said Janna.

'Oh,' said Genevieve. 'Thanks.'

'What she means,' said Stu, 'is that we don't expect you to be grateful for this … situation. But we hope you'll be nicely surprised by the set-up tomorrow. We hope you have as brief, as useful and as mutually pleasant an experience as possible.'

'Okay,' said Genevieve. 'Thank you for … Thanks.'

'What made you sign up to this as mentors?' said Karl. 'If you don't mind my asking. What's in it for you?'

'We love this company,' said Janna. 'We're proud to work for The Transition.'

'A few years ago my generation kicked the ladder away behind us,' said Stu. 'This is our chance to teach you to free-climb.'

'Oh, God, always with the analogies,' said Janna. 'It's so embarrassing.'

'Besides which, and I'm going to be honest with you,' said Stu, 'only crazy people lie; we never wanted children—'

'We never wanted babies,' said Janna.

'Right, babies,' said Stu. 'Or children, really. Or teenagers. Plenty of our friends did and I can't say it appealed.'

'But sometimes we'd be talking and Stu would say, what if we'd had kids?'

'What if we'd met each other at, say, twenty, and had kids?'

'What would they be doing now? And it just got me thinking, *what would my grown-up kids be doing now?*'

'What kind of advice would we give them?' said Stu.

'But you can't adopt a thirty-year-old,' said Janna.

'Until now,' said Genevieve. 'Well, if it's the only way out of the fine mess my husband's landed us in, consider yourselves *in loco parentis.*'

And Karl was surprised to see his wife put her arms around Janna who, a little disconcerted, patted her on the back, lightly and rapidly as if tapping out a code.

# 5

**THEY SPENT THE NIGHT** painting over Blu-Tack stains with Tipp-Ex. Then Genevieve scrubbed the floor with a hard brush and a cartoonish bucket of soap suds and Karl asked her why she was bothering.

The next morning a black 4x4 was waiting for them outside their eviscerated bedsit.

The driver leaned out.

'Transition?' he said.

It felt like they were gliding over the potholed roads. It was an auto-drive, so for the most part the driver sat with his hands behind his head, watching the blue orb move up the map. Now and then he took the little steering column to fine-tune the car's decisions, or put his foot down to override its obedience so that a stern female voice said *speed limit exceeded*. They were driven through urban clearways and bypasses, across double roundabouts and out-of-town shopping centres which had been absorbed into the town, past the football ground.

They were entering a rougher part of the city, but the high-rises had been freshly painted porcelain white. They looked at them and thought of a tropical island hotel rather than Findus Crispy Pancakes and canned cider; although Karl disliked neither, now that he thought of it. A building site promised a forthcoming swimming pool and multi-gym.

'All that,' said the driver, 'that renovation – paid for by The Transition. I grew up around here.'

The car turned before a railway bridge and crunched over a gravel drive before entering an industrial estate. Corrugated-metal warehouses with big numbers and little signs. They passed a car mechanic's, a boxing gym, a company called Rubberplasp whose name bounced around Karl's auditory centre. Further in, the lots turned hipster: a craft brewery, a Japanese pottery, a vanity recording studio. Karl expected The Transition's headquarters to be another identical shack, but when they rounded the last corner they were at the foot of a hill from which emerged four shiny black obelisks connected by footbridges, a letter H at every rotation. Each obelisk was roughly as tall as an electricity pylon, but only broad enough to contain a couple of rooms.

As they stepped out of the taxi the shiny black surface of the four towers turned blue, and brightened until it almost matched the sky. A film of a flock of birds flew across it, disappearing between the towers, which faded to black again.

'This is ...' said Karl. 'Wow.'

'Hmm,' said Genevieve.

A young woman was standing at the door of the first tower they came to. An earpiece stood out against her short, fair hair. They gave their names.

'You're married – that's so sweet!' she said. 'Everyone is on the mezzanine. Floor 8. Here are your tablets.'

She gave them each what looked like a giant After Eight mint: a very thin square touchscreen computer in a protective sleeve.

'Pretty,' said Genevieve.

'I was told this was a pilot scheme,' said Karl. 'It looks …'

The towers went through the sky sequence again.

'… fairly well established. We've been going for eleven years,' said the woman with the earpiece. 'We try to stay under the radar.'

The lift opened on a wide balcony full of couples. Instantly shy, Karl stood to admire a giant hyperrealist painting of a pinball table, Vegas neons and chrome. He stared at the electric-pink 100 POINTS bumpers and the matte plastic of a single raised flipper. He felt Genevieve take his hand. She did this rarely.

'What a waste of a wall,' she said.

'I like it.'

'You like pinball? You like bright colours?'

'I like the painting.'

'You're such a boy. Boys love bright colours. Like bulls,' said Genevieve. 'That's why underwear is brightly coloured. Do you remember that bag I had, the one with the Tunisian tea advert with the sequins? Grown men stopped me on the street to say they liked my bag. I told Amy and she was like, what they mean is *I like your vagina.*'

Karl paused to make sure Genevieve had finished her train of thought. She had barely said a word for the last two weeks, but today she had opinions, theories. It was like she had been recast. It had taken him three years of marriage to learn that it was best to let her recalibrate without too much comment. Get a little depressed, then a little high in inverse proportion. Balance the ship.

He looked at the reflection of the pinball table's garish surface in the painting of the large ball bearing that dominated the right-hand side of the canvas. It was so convincing he expected to see a reflection of his face peering into it. As you got closer you could almost make out the fine brushstrokes.

'I just think it's incredible anyone can paint something that looks so much like a photograph,' he said.

'Yeah,' said Genevieve, 'but on the other hand so fucking what, you know?'

A brushed-silver bar served free cappuccinos and muffins in three flavours: banoffee, apple and cinnamon or quadruple chocolate.

'Quadruple? I can't choose!' said Genevieve.

'Have one of each,' said the barista.

Handsome boy, thought Karl. Slightly wounded expression. An RSC bit-player face.

'*Really?*'

'Three muffins, Genevieve?' said Karl.

'Don't listen to him,' said the barista.

'I never do.'

She sounded too grateful. But then everyone Karl could see wore the glazed, winsome expression of the all-clear, the last-minute reprieve. The hundred or so young couples, the other losers who had accepted The Transition in lieu of some unpayable fine or term of incarceration, looked up from checking the impressive spec of the free mint-thin tablets they'd been handed at the door to admire the sun-dappled view over the city from the 360-degree window: *Really?* And they looked at each other, too. A preponderance of attractive, well-adjusted young people of every creed and orientation. They were athletic or willowy, at worst a kind of doughy, puppy-jowled fat which spoke of donnish indolence rather than profligacy. Inconspicuously smart or very casual – torn jeans, neon T-shirts – because they were good-looking and could get away with it. The couples were casing the joint, talking, making one another laugh. You wanted them as trophy friends. Thirty-somethings who could pass for teenagers.

Gradually, the lights dipped.

'It's getting dark,' said Genevieve.

The stage held a glossy black podium and a large glass screen. There were rows of designer chairs. The chairs were spindly, improbably supporting fleshy orange pads which, when you pressed them, took a while to reshape, like a stress toy. Karl sat down, expecting to feel hung on a strange apparatus, but it was more like a hug. As the orange pads cupped his buttocks, moulded to the small of his back and pressed his shoulder blades he realised he was sitting in a modern classic: *Eames meets Brutalism in contemporary Norway, an alien catcher's mitt.* He drafted five-star reviews in his head; it was unusual to actually experience the product first.

Genevieve sipped her coffee.

★   ★   ★

The rows filled in around them. A man sat on the corner of Karl's anorak and didn't notice, pulling Karl slightly to the right. Karl leaned towards him, then back. His coat was still trapped. He cleared his throat. He tried to make eye contact with Genevieve, who was eating her apple and cinnamon muffin. He leaned in again. He couldn't look at the man's face without putting himself uncomfortably close to it. He looked at the man's shoes. Brogues, a slight residue of shoe polish. He stared ahead at the empty stage. Now he had left it too long to do anything about it. If he pulled the corner of his anorak out, the man would wonder why he hadn't done so immediately. *You actually sat there for two minutes without telling me I was sitting on your coat? What's wrong with you?* Karl tensed his right shoulder and cricked his neck so that he appeared to be sitting more or less straight.

'It's Stu,' said Genevieve. 'Karl, it's Stu.'

'Yep,' said Karl, looking up to see a tall man with a Mohican approaching the podium.

'Why is it Stu?'

'Shh.'

'Is he the boss or something?'

'Genevieve, shh.'

Stu put his hands on the lectern, cleared his throat and looked at the big glass screen which was hanging to his right, seemingly without support. It flickered and a white oblong, off centre and barely a quarter of the size of the overall screen appeared. It was a clip-art image of a man with a briefcase taking a big step. Stu looked at the screen. Slowly the words WHAT'S STANDING BETWEEN YOU AND SUCCESS? appeared in Comic Sans by the side of the clip-art businessman, who had a perky smile. There was a wonky blue parallelogram behind him.

'What's standing between you and success?' said Stu.

Karl, to his surprise, felt disappointed. To the extent that he yanked the corner of his anorak free from his neighbour, who looked startled. It doesn't matter how you dress it up and how good the free coffee is, the medium is the message and the medium is fucking PowerPoint. It was a dismal feeling, like the moment when a delayed train is finally cancelled.

But then the lights went out completely and the clip-art businessman smeared and flickered into a dance of glitches up the glass screen. Karl's knee-jerk delight at something boring going wrong was hijacked by an orchestral overture via invisible speakers, and a long, low cello improvisation. As the soundtrack dissolved into electronic pops and gurgles, the image left the screen, a jagged mess of pixels, and bounced over the panoptic window, bursting into smaller copies of itself, a screensaver taking over the world; it covered the whole room, morphing into clip-art houses, clip-art office cubicles, cups of coffee, ties and cufflinks, clip-art strong, independent women, clip-art harried-looking commuters. The seats by this point were vibrating and Karl's laughter was distorted, like a child in a play fight. The images seemed to peel off the glass and float along the rows. The room was swimming in obsolete icons and logos, slogans and mangled business-speak – push the change, be the envelope – clip-art Filofaxes and aeroplanes, shoes and computers duplicating, fanning out like cards, whirling and distending, blittering into fragments. The cello piece was melodic, abrasive, fearfully attractive, and the windows resolved into operating systems and programs Karl remembered from childhood, a museum of dead technology, single ribbons of green text, and then the music stopped and darkness was complete – until a spotlight picked out Stu adjusting the point of the second spike of his Mohican.

'Sorry about that,' he said. 'Bit gimmicky.'

Karl was one of the first to start clapping.

'All right, all right,' said Stu. 'There's no getting away from the fact that this is a lecture, and I know there's not a single couple in the room who's chosen to be here so you can't blame me for falling back on special effects. I don't know if you've had a chance to talk to anyone else yet?'

Silence. Aside from discussing the scene with their partner, none of the couples had exchanged more than a resigned nod, a hello which could have been a hiccup.

'You all have something in common,' Stu smirked. 'I'm kidding. It's true, though. You're all feeling a little bruised, I'm assuming. You're all here under duress, expecting to count out the minutes, endure the insult to your intelligence. You were probably expecting …' He rubbed his right eye. 'You were probably expecting something like a speeding awareness course, right? I know what they're like – I've been on three.' He looked at the floor in mock contrition then glanced up. A ripple of laughter. 'Well, I'm biased because I love this company, but it's more like being given a new car. Take out your tablets.'

A mass shifting in the orange chairs. Karl slipped the computer out of its fur-lined pouch. It was a black sheet of glass, eight inches square. The words *HELLO, KARL!* in the middle. He looked at Genevieve, who was already moving a glowing white orb around hers with her index finger.

'Your copy of the Transition handbook is on there,' said Stu. 'It has everything from the FAQ – constantly updated – to the history of the scheme, to the complaints procedure, which we hope you won't be needing. But aside from that, you just write on them like a slate. Try it. Write *Hello Stu.*'

Clusters of *Hello Stu!*s appeared on the screen behind him.

'Good,' he said. 'We're going to look at three articles. Use your tablets and just write down your reactions. Whatever comes into your head. Be completely honest.'

The screen faded into a photograph and a long headline. A young woman in an old-fashioned floral-print dress posed by a spiral staircase. The headline: WHEN THIS DESIGNER'S FAMILY GREW SHE BOUGHT THE APARTMENT DOWNSTAIRS AND MADE THEIR HOME A DUPLEX. After ten seconds she was replaced by a man with a beard stirring an orange crockpot: HOW GREG'S POP-UP RESTAURANTS BECAME A PERMANENT CHAIN AND MADE HIM A PROPERTY MAGNATE. Next a shiny man who looked about twelve adjusting his tie in the mirror: WHILE PLAYING WITH HIS TWO-YEAR-OLD DAUGHTER, THIS TWENTY-SIX-YEAR-OLD HAPPENED UPON AN IDEA WHICH REVOLUTIONISED THE WAY WE SEE PUBLIC RELATIONS OVERNIGHT. All three appeared together with their headlines.

'I remind you that this is a completely anonymous process,' said Stu. 'We're interested in your frank, knee-jerk opinions. You have ten seconds.'

Gradually the magazine clippings disappeared from the screen and a selection of comments scrolled across the glass and around the windows:

I want to kill them all.

## HOW A PRIVATE INCOME AND MASSIVE INHERITANCE MADE ALL THESE ASSHOLES' DREAMS COME TRUE!

oh fuck off just fuck off fuck off fuck off

seriously a designer who can make enough to buy TWO FLATS fuck you what does she design nuclear weapons?

'Good,' said Stu. 'This is all good.'

Karl watched as his own comment – *what kind of a monster would bring a child into this world?* – performed a loop-the-loop off the screen and landed on the window to the east.

'Okay,' said Stu while the last of the two hundred comments disappeared into a spiral behind him, as if going down a plughole. 'I'd like to welcome to the stage Susannah, Greg and Paul.'

The trio walked onto the stage in unison, dressed exactly as they had been in the projected magazine articles. Susannah's dress, Karl noticed, actually had a Russian-doll motif. They stopped in the middle of the stage and turned to face the audience, who were quiet. Karl shook his head. Genevieve had put her hand on his knee. The bearded chef folded his arms and looked up, bashfully. The designer and the PR man smiled with a hint of defiance. Karl's temples pulsed. A lone voice yelled 'BOOOO!' which caused some brief, relieved laughter, shared by those on stage.

'Susannah, out of interest, what *do* you design?' said Stu.

'Patterns for mugs and tableware,' said Susannah.

'And maybe you could tell the ladies and gentlemen of the audience what exactly you were doing two years ago today?'

'This time two years ago,' said Susannah, pointing into the crowd, 'I was sitting in that chair, that one, fourth row. I was sitting in that chair writing shitty comments about the three people onstage because they were more successful than me.'

'We know what it's like out there,' said Stu. 'The landlord puts the rent up every six months. We know. Let alone saving, it's hard to meet the bills and reduce your debts once you've stumped up the rent. We *know*. You never expected to be earning the salary you're earning, but on the other hand you never expected to have to think twice about whether you could afford a new pair of socks this month. You're trapped. The debts keep growing. We know. You're overqualified for everything except a job that doesn't actually exist – a historian or something. We *know*. This is the most expensive house in London.'

A moving image of a hallway covered in dust and rat droppings appeared behind Stu. The point of view tracked inwards towards a grand, sweeping staircase with moss growing on it.

'Uninhabited for twelve years. A giant, house-shaped gambling chip. None of this is fair. We *know* it's not fair. There's no changing that. So what can you do? You can throw in the towel, eat cereal straight from the box, watch internet porn and wait for death, if that's what you want.

Or you can be part of the solution. You can get into a position of power and wield it with a little more responsibility. That's what this is about.'

# 6

**JANNA AND STU'S** house was the second in a row of four
Georgian terraces, elegant sandstone buildings with high
ceilings and multi-pane windows. The cherry tree in the
front garden was in early full blossom. Karl was used to
seeing such houses occupied by the offices of accountants
or solicitors. It was a secluded street culminating in a
Gothic Anglican church, apparently deconsecrated – there
were no noticeboards or signs – but well maintained. Even
the paving slabs felt antique, broad as tombstones, a 'superior sole-feel'. Karl and Genevieve stood in the shade
with their rucksacks and looked up.

'I could just sit at the window writing long letters to my
detractors all day,' said Karl.

'Why did they choose us?' said Genevieve. 'I mean really,
of all the couples we saw yesterday …'

After Stu's overture they had been separated into
breakaway groups and had to share their origin story –
how they became Bankrupt Man, Fraud Girl – and then
their aspirations. Karl said he wanted to write video games.
Genevieve said she'd only ever wanted to teach, but that
she'd like to be solvent enough to have children. Although
Stu had warned the groups that all the disclosure might

feel a bit American, Karl had found it strangely cathartic to hear from other bright young things who'd used loan sharks to pay off loan sharks, or shoplifted cheese, or owed tens of thousands in council tax, or got busted for growing hydroponic weed in their attics. There was a free buffet lunch: big dressed salads, grilled fish, roasted vegetables and complicated breads. Janna gave a final speech, practical stuff. They learned there were to be six meetings in the Transition HQ, one per month of the scheme. The rest of the time the young couples would live with and learn from their mentors without formal intervention.

A single petal fell from the cherry tree now and landed at his feet.

'I don't know that we're any worse than the rest,' said Karl. 'Maybe they liked my face.'

'*Your* face,' said Genevieve.

'I have a very symmetrical face.'

'Are you two just going to stand there?' Janna leaned out of the first-floor window. 'The door's open – Stu's made drinks.'

'Stuart,' said Genevieve.

'Stu,' said Stu.

They were sitting in the first-floor living room with gin and tonics. The upper branches of the cherry tree touched the windowpanes. It was beautiful.

'Stu. Are you and Janna *in charge* of The Transition?'

'Oh no, no, no,' said Stu.

'Ha!' said Janna.

'We're lieutenants, at most,' said Stu. 'Department heads. All of the mentors have a managerial role within the institution – keeps things democratic. We take turns doing the talks. I just like the sound of my own voice, so …' he shrugged.

'So is there, like, a CEO?' said Genevieve. 'Who's in charge?'

'There's a committee,' said Stu. 'If you mean who thought up the whole concept it came out of a think tank called Bury the Lead. That was twelve years ago. It started very small. There's a chapter in the book about it. It's on your tablet.'

'I'll read it,' said Genevieve.

'It's an interesting history,' said Stu. 'Not without a few skeletons in the closet, but we're in a good place now. We've managed to avoid attention, thanks to the whole confidentiality thing – we don't allow our graduates to acknowledge the scheme in interviews. Why should they? You earned it – The Transition is just a leg-up. Most of them end up successful enough to be interviewed, which is the important thing. Generally they're only too happy to move on – they've earned their right to a fulfilling life, we just gave them the means to start the journey. All we ask is you keep in touch, maybe come back to talk to a future year group.' He got up. 'Come on, you must want to see your quarters.'

Karl and Genevieve's attic was not completely self-contained – cohabitation was stipulated in The Transition's terms and conditions – but Stu had installed a small but luxurious bathroom with grey granite fittings. The shower head was the size of a frying pan.

'Ooh, it's like a hotel!' said Genevieve. She tried the taps. The bevel was gentle and heavy like a volume knob and the water poured out with calm insistence.

They weren't labelled.

'Are you just supposed to know which is hot and which is cold?' said Karl. 'I can't live like this. I have no memory for things like that.'

The rest of the attic had been divided into three rooms, one with a double bed and a small flat-screen TV on top of a chest of drawers; one with a sofa, a side table with a bowl of oranges and a print of Klimt's *Forest* framed on the wall; and the last was a study with an old school desk and a new office chair, based on the audience seats in The Transition's mezzanine. A little bookshelf had already been stocked with Karl and Genevieve's library of twentieth-century fiction and poetry, the only possession The Transition's removal service had had to contend with. A tall, bronze anglepoise lamp lurked in the corner like a prop from a steampunk movie. Next to it a blue Wi-Fi router blinked fitfully.

'This is actually really thoughtful,' said Karl, propping the second cardboard box of clothes on top of the first.

'No more damp,' said Genevieve. 'I'll have my fur coats taken out of storage.'

Each room had a Velux window and the view from the bedroom was of a tree-lined green with a wrought-iron fence and a locked gate. The four tall houses overlooked six parallel streets of Victorian terraces, the ornate and defunct public baths, a cordoned-off area of scrubland promised years ago to a major supermarket, and a hill with a busy road that wove down to the valley. Standing behind Genevieve, Karl put his hands on her waist and rested his chin on her shoulder.

'We'll manage, won't we?'

He started working her skirt up and she pulled it down again.

'I think so.'

By the end of the scheme, as long as they carefully followed the financial regimen, the young couple should have saved enough for a five per cent mortgage deposit on one of the new-build estates that sponsored the pilot scheme, as well as having developed the skills and responsibilities necessary to meet repayments. He kissed her neck.

'You don't even notice the Mohican after a while,' said Genevieve.

They lay on their new bed, a firm mattress that yielded just enough to make you feel like you were lying in mid-air when you closed your eyes. The bed in their flat had felt like a giant bag of spoons and Karl was accustomed to arranging his internal organs around them when he slept. He lay on his back, speechless, while Genevieve took her square tablet out of her rucksack. She started to read the History.

'"Everything was temporary,"' she read. '"Because they could be moved on at any time, nobody felt like a stakeholder in their community, so the very idea of community had started to erode. Once, we gathered round the piano in the pub or the town hall to sing songs together in harmony; now we sang *at* one another in cold-lit karaoke bars, a lonely imitation of the fame we felt was our only possible escape." That's by Hannah Eldridge – she was part of the think tank ten years ago.'

She stopped reading out loud and Karl closed his eyes. Both of them were drifting into sleep when they heard Janna at the foot of the stairs.

'Um … guys? Food's ready.'

Dinner was roast squash, pumpkin seeds and rocket leaves with fresh bread and yoghurt. Stu explained that they weren't vegetarian, but that they only ate meat twice a week. Janna opened a bottle of Rioja.

'He only ever buys wine wrapped in a wire cage,' she said. 'He thinks that's how you tell if it's good. Look, we'll talk through some basic rotas and stuff tomorrow, but tonight let's just have a drink. We're very happy to have you here. Cheers.'


**'THEY SEEM REALLY LOVELY,'** said Genevieve. 'I think we're very lucky.'

They were drunk on red wine, lying in each other's arms.

'I think we're going to be okay,' said Karl. 'This could actually be the best thing that's ever happened to us.'

Very suddenly, Genevieve started snoring.

Karl slept lightly and woke up at what his tablet told him was 4:26. He could hear a faint, uneven squeaking noise. It sounded like a pulley being operated.

'You awake? You hear that?'

'I've been listening to it,' Genevieve whispered. 'It's crying.'

'What? No, I mean the squeaking noise.'

'What do you think *I* mean?'

'It isn't crying.'

'It's coming from the next attic. Someone in the attic next door is weeping.'

Spooked, Karl turned on the green glass library lamp on his bedside table.

'It's a creaking sound.'

'It's crying.'

'It's pipes or something.'

'Someone,' said Genevieve, 'is crying.'

'Let me get close – OW! Mother*fucker*!' said Karl, falling back onto the bed, holding his foot. 'What *is* that?'

'Poor thing,' said Genevieve. 'You've stubbed your toe.'

'I think they're broken,' said Karl. 'All of them. Who installs a fucking metal buttress in the middle of their floor?' He went down on his hands and knees and inspected the silver girder he'd dashed his foot against. Difficult to miss, now that he saw it. When his toes felt better he tried to get his ear flat to the low wall, but whatever the noise was, it had stopped.

# 7

'**OH, HEY, LOOK** at this. Look. How did you sleep? It's telling me precisely how I slept. These are the points where I was dreaming. This is where it brought me out of a dream that seemed to be upsetting me. I'm not sure how it does that. Did you have any bad dreams? Karl? Karl?'

Karl woke up. He was not hungover. There was no crust in his eyes. Genevieve was sitting up playing with her tablet. The smells of fresh coffee and bacon drifted up to the attic.

'I'm a "full disclosure" kind of guy,' said Stu. He poured them both a cup of coffee from the stove pot and pushed a jug of steamed milk towards them. They were sitting at the black granite breakfast bar. 'Anything we do that pisses you off, you tell us, okay? Everything out in the open. Even if it seems really petty. If I come back from kiteboarding and trail wet sand through the house—'

'Which he does every bloody week, so good luck with that,' said Janna.

'I want you to tell me. If Janna intimidates you with her coarse language and aggressive personality, I want to know about it. Don't let it bottle up and explode.'

'We'll do the same,' said Janna. 'There's nothing more poisonous than pretending everything's fine when it's not. Okay?'

'Okay,' said Karl.

'You're being so lovely,' said Genevieve, stirring her coffee. 'You don't need to be so lovely.'

'Genevieve, the loyalty you've shown in joining your husband on The Transition; and Karl, the guilt you'll be feeling about that … we understand this is a strange situation for you both. I promise you, it'll be over before you know it, you'll have a permanent residence and you'll be doing the job you always dreamed of. How do you want your eggs? Poached?'

'Poached is great.'

'Right answer.'

'This is how we start,' said Janna. 'Tomorrow is Monday and you go back to work as normal. We share every duty – we have a rota – it's on your tablets so you'll be reminded when it's your turn to cook or clean up. You don't have to pay anything – that's part of it. Not just rent, but bills, food, travel to work – we'll have a Transition car drop you off and pick you up. It's all covered.'

'See it as a complete break from ordinary life – a total anaesthetic while the operation takes place.'

'Ick,' said Janna. 'But you don't have any money either. So it's a kind of economic house arrest for the first couple of months. We know that's … patronising.'

As per the contract, Karl and Genevieve's wages were paid straight into The Transition's holding account. Half of Karl's income went towards paying off his outstanding debts and fines. The rest accumulated and would eventually become their down payment.

'But in losing your economic freedom you'll gain something you didn't even know you were missing: time.'

'The language you've always wanted to learn, the weight you wanted to bench-press. All the things you've been putting off,' said Janna.

'I always wanted to learn Italian!' said Genevieve. 'Or Spanish, or maybe French!'

'Pick *one*,' said Janna. 'You're learning Italian.'

'*Molto bene!*' said Genevieve.

'I don't actually know what a bench press is,' said Karl.

'You'll be surprised how quickly you take to it,' said Stu. 'And you'll be surprised how quickly it makes a difference. To everything.'

Karl looked at Stuart's thick and gladiatorial torso. He seemed like a different species, or at least a fantasy – what Karl imagined a man to be when he was growing up.

'I *have* been thinking about getting in shape,' he conceded.

'But the first thing we want to talk about,' said Stu, 'and this may surprise you, is actually that lesion on your face, Karl.'

'It's an ingrown hair,' said Karl.

'Is that what it is?' said Stu.

'Whatever it is,' said Janna, 'it's clear that you're not leaving it alone to heal.'

'I don't even realise I'm doing it,' said Karl, scratching his cheek to illustrate.

'I've tried to get him to stop,' said Genevieve. 'For, like, a year.'

Karl felt his face flushing.

'Mindfulness,' said Stu. 'You may wonder why we're focusing on something so small, especially in the first lesson, but think about your face, Karl. Think about *the face* in general. It's the first thing people see, before they even start talking to you.'

'We believe that that mark on your face is a microcosm,' said Janna, 'of everything else you're doing wrong with your life.'

'Wow,' said Karl.

'Oh, do me,' said Genevieve. 'What do my split ends mean?'

This particular ingrown hair had followed the plot of a never-ending police procedural, with Karl the brilliant but obsessive detective on the trail of an ingrown-hair-stroke-serial-killer who might or might not even really exist; digging and gouging the same spot on his cheek night after night; thinking he once caught a glimpse of it, long ago; taking the drastic and controversial decision to stop shaving altogether for a fortnight; insisting that it was there, finding nothing, alienating his co-workers; letting it scab over, then going at it again too soon.

- *I'm calling in the tweezers.*
- *Every time you call in the tweezers without a warrant you set our department back five years of good practice.*
- *I want the tweezers goddammit.*
- *Take some time off. See your family.*

'Karl?' Genevieve called.

'Yep?'

'I hope you're not fiddling with your face again.'

Karl's hand shook as he turned off the shaving light.

'You know what?' he said. 'I think it's maybe just a spot after all.'

# 8

**ON MONDAY KARL** woke up to find that Genevieve, Stu and Janna had already left for work. It was half past nine. His tablet displayed a chart of his time spent in REM sleep. There was also a text message from Keston. Stu had showed them how to re-route everything through the tablet. Karl had already bagged up their mobile phones to send to a mail purchasing service, which ought to make them a couple of hundred pounds in emergency funds.

   – How's the prisoner?

Karl thought about it, stretched, put a jumper on over his Garfield T-shirt and replied.

   – This is a joke, right? I'm a petty criminal and I'm being treated like a long-lost son.

Keston replied while Karl was buttoning the fly of his jeans.

   – Safety nets, broseph.

While the prosecution had moved for Karl being banned from the internet altogether, his livelihood still depended on fake consumer reviews and essays and his lawyer had been able to prove this was a basic human right. On his first day working alone in the house Karl stayed within his quarters, writing five-star reviews of a new orthopaedic desk chair for eleven different office-product sites. 'It goes way beyond health-neutral!' he wrote. 'This chair should be prescribed before you even know you have a back complaint.' After 3,500 words of copy he felt bored. This wasn't his internet connection, and he was on best behaviour. That he had used it so far solely to check his emails and search for information on the human spine was an act of discipline in which he took an almost ascetic pride. Perhaps this was The Transition working subtly in him already. He went to the little oak bookshelf he and Genevieve had shared since they were students.

He took out his copy of Machiavelli's *The Prince*, opened it in the middle, flicked through it from the beginning and dropped it. He frowned. He took out Walt Whitman's *Leaves of Grass* and did the same thing, dropping it on top of *The Prince*. This was perturbing to Karl because he kept a Polaroid photograph of Genevieve sleeping naked in his copy of *The Prince*; formerly he'd kept it in *Leaves of Grass* until they heard a radio documentary about *Leaves of Grass* and Genevieve said she'd like to read it. She hadn't shown much interest in any form of intimacy over the previous months, which he supposed was probably understandable, but it was getting to the point where she got dressed and undressed hurriedly, irritably, as if on the beach, and the Polaroid had become an increasingly treasured possession.

He started going through each of the paperbacks in turn. When he got to the first book on the second shelf, Hartley's *The Go-Between*, a MasterCard with the name MRS GENEVIEVE TEMPERLEY landed face up on the carpet. Genevieve had apparently judged *The Go-Between* the novel least likely to appeal to Karl or to Janna or Stu in the event of a spot check. Well, whatever. He felt happy that she had a secret. What was she going to use it for? A work do? Clothes? It was harmless.

What if she decided she'd had enough and got on a train? What if she skipped town? What if she caught the train to the airport? What if she skipped town, fled the country and didn't take her medication? God, he loved her. He wanted to look at the photo.

He searched every book on the shelf, but it wasn't there. Maybe Genevieve had found it. Had found it ages ago, hated him for it. Maybe it was a fairly innocuous thing to have by most people's standards, but the fact remained he had taken the photo, four years ago, while Genevieve was asleep, two T-shirts wrapped around the camera to muffle the sound of the shutter, and some of the frisson of looking at the photo came from her unawareness of its existence. A betrayal. A seedy little voyeuristic betrayal. Is that why … No. He had last ogled the photo when they were packing a few days ago, while he was loading the books into a cardboard box, while Genevieve was out of the room. He distinctly remembered slipping it back into *The Prince*. Fucking hell.

Karl put Genevieve's credit card back in *The Go-Between*, decided to say nothing and sadly went back to reviewing the chair. He took breaks in the kitchen to make tea or coffee and eat chocolate digestives, which he consumed at the rate of a hyperactive child. For lunch he boiled an egg and baked a tomato and garlic flatbread he found in the fridge. It was a Smart Fridge. He had read about them, reviewed a couple of models. The back of the fridge was a locked metal door which opened directly onto the back-street and it got replenished every four days by an auto-mated delivery service. You didn't even need to order anything unless you wanted something special.

After overeating he went straight back to his work.


**THIS RESPECT FOR** Janna and Stu's privacy lasted until that afternoon, when Karl made a reconnaissance of the ground floor. The dining room had feature wallpaper depicting a storybook woodland. Karl cracked a walnut by throwing it against the tiled floor. In the living room two unblemished white sofas sat in an L shape. A vast flat-screen TV faced a large abstract painting on the opposite wall. It was grey, black and white; the paint looked like it had been slathered on with a trowel and could have been taken for a DIY process abandoned part way through. Karl didn't like it, but he liked that Janna and Stu liked it. He liked that there were things in the world people loved which he didn't understand.

When he turned he noticed a low emanation of yellow light between the black-painted floorboards by the living-room door. Some kind of underfloor lighting? The light vanished, and Karl imagined the click of a switch, although he heard nothing. Then the light appeared again, for a moment − as if someone had forgotten something and returned temporarily to retrieve it – then off again. Karl lay down and tried to look between the floorboards, but the gap was too narrow. 'Hello?' he said. He got up, brushed the dust off his face and stamped on the floor. It sounded hollow, but this meant nothing – the usual cavity under the floorboards. What he had seen, presumably, was the glow of a light fitting mounted in a ceiling beneath the ground floor. He walked to the hallway and stamped on the red tiles, which felt solid. He unlocked the front door and walked into the street. The front garden had a cherry tree and pale Hepworth-like stone. There was no indication that there might be a cellar. He tried the door of the understairs cupboard. It was locked. It had a big Chubb keyhole, which was a bit much for a cupboard. He looked in the little wooden key house by the front door and it didn't contain any likely keys, which only cemented his notion. Something else was wrong, something askew, but it took him a while to identify it.

'There are no *books*,' he said to Genevieve, that night. 'Unless you count the Blu-ray manual.'

Genevieve shrugged.

'They're not readers,' she said. 'Don't be a snob.'

The next day he decided to explore the first floor. He let himself fall backwards onto Janna and Stu's king-size bed. It felt pliant and firm, like lying in plasticine, but then it moulded to his form. He looked upwards at the black metal chandelier – a silhouette. In the corner there was what looked like a trapeze – a chrome bar hanging from a ceiling reinforcement on two wires. Behind it a framed print, white on red in large block capitals:

# GET
# THINGS
# DONE

From their bedroom window you could see the neighbours' gardens. The one on the left was dominated by a trampoline, but its flower beds were very neat, with lines of bedding plants and a large fuchsia. Janna and Stu's garden was a well-maintained vegetable allotment, all the way down to the garage. When did they have time to work on that? In contrast the garden to the right was completely overgrown with brambles, taller than the fence and thick as snakes; some fresh and livid green, some dead grey husks. There was a bald patch in the middle of the wasteland, and Karl was surprised to see a single, gnarled foot and the beginnings of a grey-haired shin gently kicking. He craned his neck, but this only revealed a little more of the shin. Crazy old man sunbathing in his bramble forest.

He felt a prickle on his hand and looked down to see a tiny brown spider crawling over it. Karl recalled hearing something about Lyme disease being transmitted by ticks which looked like small spiders, so he flicked it onto the windowsill and crushed it with a corner of his wallet. The spider curled up and was still twitching when he took the wallet up. You have to really finish the job, reduce it to something non-sentient, a paste of minerals. He used his thumb. Karl noticed a silver key propped up in the corner of the windowsill, a substantial little Chubb key. His brain lit up as if he had picked up the key in a computer game. It had to be for the locked cupboard. He grabbed it and ran down the stairs.

The door to the understairs cupboard chocked open when he turned the key and in the darkness Karl could make out a bracketed shelf holding a pot of screws and a torch. He picked up the torch and a square of card fluttered to the ground. He knelt. It was the photo of his wife, lying on her side, eyes closed, a half-smile, one arm folded under her breasts. It felt like someone had hit a mute button in his head.

He put the photo in his pocket and was about to turn on the torch when he heard the jangle of a bunch of keys being dropped on the front doorstep and Janna swearing. He just had time to close the cupboard, lock it and pocket the key before Janna's key was in the front door. When she came through he was walking down the corridor and turned, as if surprised.

'Oh, hi Karl,' she said, brightly.

'You're back early,' he said. 'Tea?'

'I work from home Tuesday afternoons. I'm fine, thanks,' said Janna. 'Is Genevieve at work?'

'School, yep. Inter-tutor football tournament, actually.'

'Oh, that's fun.' Janna sat down on the hallway chaise longue to take off her shoes. 'Although I can't really imagine Genevieve with a PE whistle.'

'Ha. No.' Karl had wandered back into the hallway with the full kettle. 'I really like your chaise longue,' he said.

'Oh, thanks,' said Janna. 'I reupholstered it, actually. Evening class.'

'Wow. That's ace.'

Was ace something he said? Was it something anyone said? Was the general consensus that *ace* was an acceptable term of approbation?

'Karl?'

'Yes?'

'Does your wife like me?'

'Yes, of course.' Karl passed the kettle from one hand to another. 'Really. I mean we've only just met you, but she really likes you, yes.'

'She said something odd to me yesterday.'

'What did she say?'

'It's not really ...' Janna took out her tablet and started tapping on it. 'It doesn't matter, actually. Is that just for one cup?'

'Um,' said Karl. 'It is. Sometimes she says odd things. I wouldn't think anything of it.'

'Don't boil the whole kettle for one cup, okay?'

'Sorry.'

Janna put her tablet down, walked up to Karl and put her hand on his cheek. He tensed all over.

'And stop apologising all the time,' she said. 'You're making me feel bad.'

Back at his desk Karl wrote 500 words on lumbar support. It was only in the wake of his arrest that Karl had diversified into the shady world of bespoke essay writing through an online database called Study Sherpas©. Wealthy students, canny enough to fear plagiarism-detection software, could use the fairly expensive service to commission bespoke essays, written by actual educated human beings. An essay would never be reused – it became the customer's intellectual property the minute they paid for it. Study Sherpas© was covered in disclaimers pointing out that it was intended as a study aid providing model answers in a variety of subjects and that collusion was an offence punishable by expulsion from any given institution, but that, nevertheless, their product was one hundred per cent undetectable provided it was used with basic common sense. You could request a particular grade: if, for instance, you were an un-brilliant student who needed to complete a module for whatever reason, you could request a 2:2 in postcolonialism and your Sherpa would do their best to deliver just that. Within three marks of the target or the fee was halved.

The site took the majority of the fee, but even at its most paltry there was a better per-word rate than the average journalist or book critic received and this more than made up for the dubious morality of facilitating lie after lie in the lives of a growing pool of strangers with undeserved degrees. It was dishonourable work, but he was getting paid for doing what he loved in a competitive economy, and how many people really got to use their degrees in the real world? Karl had already provided five 2,000-word essays for A-level coursework and six presentations and papers of various lengths for undergraduate students, and was now working on a 12,000-word dissertation on elliptical technique in Henry James, a plum job he'd scored thanks to his five-star rating in the English/Comparative Literature section of Study Sherpas©. He read his most recent customer review and flushed with pride:

FIVE STARS NO QUESTION! This guy is the bollox I needed decent two one in postmodern American fiction did he deliver fuck yes!

Karl didn't even need to buy any books – membership of Study Sherpas© came with access to the eBeW database (every book ever written), a hidden resource of pirated literature, pre-annotated with pertinent, adaptable quotes already highlighted.

He was about to make a start on his second-year BA paper 'Don't Be A Caterpillar: Self-Actualisation in Caribbean Poetry' when Janna called up to the attic to say she had business in town and did he want anything?

This bought him a good hour to investigate the under-stairs cupboard again, but it was getting late and he was too rattled by his earlier disturbance. It seemed likely that Stu would get back while he was in there, and Genevieve was already late home and he wasn't sure if he wanted her to know he was prying. No, the key had to be returned before anyone realised it was gone.

He tiptoed into Stu and Janna's bedroom, carefully sidling through the part-open door rather than opening it further. Janna's work clothes were discarded on the bed. He tried to remember if the key had been upside down or not, decided not and placed it back in the corner of the windowsill. The gnarly foot was still kicking gently in the bramble garden.

It wasn't until the following morning that Karl remembered he still had the Polaroid of Genevieve in his pocket. He didn't want to lose it, but he thought through the situation and decided that there was some advantage if he knew about the photo being stolen and Janna and Stu didn't know he knew.

On Wednesday morning he waited for half an hour after they'd all left for work, judging this long enough for any forgot-my-keys-type returns, and took the opportunity to check the cupboard out properly. Stu and Janna's bedroom was dark and when Karl flicked the light switch he saw that the wardrobe doors were open and several outfits – a salmon-pink shirt, a blue pinstripe suit, a smart grey dress and some boots – were strewn over the bed.

He checked the windowsill. The key was gone. His breathing made a cloud of condensation on the window.

Downstairs Karl slid the Polaroid of his wife halfway under the door of the cupboard and then flicked it the rest of the way in.

# 9

WEDNESDAY WAS KARL'S first night to cook. His tablet announced that he was to make a simple but nourishing cheese and egg tart with wholemeal pastry and a spinach salad with home-made vinaigrette. The ingredients were all in the Smart Fridge and Smart Cupboard. When Genevieve got home from work she found him in the kitchen wearing a blue and white striped apron. He had flour on his forehead.

'Ha ha ha!' she said.

'Thanks,' said Karl.

'You know, pastry is one of those really simple recipes which is almost impossible to get right,' said Genevieve.

Karl flicked a fingerful of raw egg and grated cheese at her and she screamed.

'My work clothes!'

'Oh. Sorry.'

'God.'

She stalked upstairs and Karl listened to the rest of a documentary about peak oil as he kneaded the bowl.

'It's delicious, Karl,' said Stu. 'Genevieve, did Karl cook much before?'

'Pasta and pesto,' said Genevieve. 'Fish fingers.'

'Well, he's a natural, isn't he?'

'Please,' said Karl. Although he was pleasantly surprised by the texture of the pastry – flaky but consistent. Janna poured a greenish liquid into their glasses from an oddly shaped bottle: a tall, wide neck and square base with the periodic table printed on it. Saturday was alcohol night – the rest of the week was dry.

'This is a vitamin drink developed by one of our former protégés,' she said. 'The ones before the ones before you guys. It made the *Journal of Nutritional Science* – one of the first supplements to genuinely enhance your diet. I don't know anything about the technical side, but … She's a millionaire now.'

Karl took a sip of the cold vitamin drink. It tasted a little like Germolene.

'Mm.'

'So do you have protégés staying with you all the time?' said Genevieve. 'It must be exhausting. Are our replacements already lined up for when we leave?'

'No,' said Stu. 'It's the same for all the mentors: six months on, six months off.'

'Like a lighthouse keeper,' said Genevieve.

The tablet prompted them both to keep a journal at 10 p.m. every night. There were no rules on the content, but it had to be at least 500 words and the grammar check could tell whether or not it was basically literate.

'This is going to be a *novel* by the end of the scheme,' Karl complained.

Genevieve looked up from her typing.

'That's the point,' she said. 'The best ones are made available to future protégés. We get access to the online library in week 3. Karl, are you actually reading any of the daily bulletins?'

'The what?'

'Are you paying any attention at all?'

'Sure.'

'I get the feeling your heart's not really in it.'

'I've had a lot of work.'

'I mean *you're* the reason we're here.'

'I'm aware of that.'

'I know you are.'

'Well, then.'

Genevieve laughed.

Karl began transcribing their exchange on his tablet.

Halfway through his first sentence he looked up. When Genevieve paused he said, 'How does this work with our TGU vows?'

'This? Oh, it's not relevant,' said Genevieve. 'This is a private network. It's not the same at all.'

'I don't know if I'm comfortable with it,' said Karl.

'So call your sponsor.'

'We haven't spoken in a year.'

Karl hadn't felt the need to consult his sponsor in a while. As far as he was concerned the Great Unsharing had broken the worst of his internet addiction and he no longer needed to observe its dogmas. The Great Unsharing had been founded three years previously by a child named Alathea Jeffreys. The logo was a graphical silhouette of her face at nine years old on a blue background. Alathea represented the first generation to be 'commodified without consent';

from birth to early childhood everything about her had been documented, stored and shared with complete strangers by her parents, the first wave of social networkers whose internet use had transitioned over a decade from drunken party photos to political posturing to holiday snaps to baby scrapbook. 'Where was our opt-out?' asked Alathea. 'What choice did we have? I was a public domain image when I was still in my mother's womb.' Alathea called for a mass strike from social networks, and then from the internet in general. A degrading, dehumanising place. The Great Unsharing gathered publicity from columnists and commentators and via the very networks from which it encouraged withdrawal. 'I want to share something that happened to me in the coffee room after church last month,' ran a typical editorial at the time. 'I was there with Simon and our newborn. A young man of our acquaintance asked if he could take a photo of my baby. A little unusual, perhaps, but I tend to look for the best in people. I said yes, of course. He held up his smartphone and, flash, that was that, or so I thought. But later I saw him leaning against the wall working avidly on his phone. I approached and saw that he was playing a computer game. He made no effort to hide it from me, so I looked over him at the screen. The sick game involved drop-kicking an animated baby at a rugby goal, or over a rainbow or into the sea, and the program was able to use photographs to alter the appearance of the baby. With horror it dawned on me that he was kicking *my* baby.'

The movement struck a chord with Genevieve and, after discussing it, she and Karl agreed to sign up. Karl often found himself sitting with his smartphone going between five social networks and three separate email accounts, and, if he had no new messages, a simulation of a social network called Humanatee which was entirely computer-generated and passably amusing for its similitude to the real thing, albeit with no repercussions. Achieving nothing, praying for the battery to die so that he could read a book. One night they held hands and deleted their profiles from three networks, twelve years' worth of photos, opinions and comments on other people's opinions. It felt like flushing a toilet. The Great Unsharing encouraged participants to delete their email accounts, too, which they both felt was a bit extreme. Within two years the movement had reduced the user base for social networks by a third.

'We're not trying to be sanctimonious or didactic,' read Alathea's official statement. 'The fact is, most of the time you go online, within about five minutes you've directly engaged with something that makes you genuinely unhappy. You've either given or received indignation. This is a reduction of what you are and what you can be as a human being. Imagine if instead of doing that you asked an elderly neighbour if they needed anything from the shops? Or went for a walk. Or studied Greek. Or had a conversation with someone in your house. Just try it for a week and observe the effects on your mental health.'

The following year it was revealed that Alathea Jeffreys didn't exist; that she was the invention of a middle-aged American academic called Dr Cary Gill and formed part of his post-doctoral Sociology research into authenticity for the University of Bristol. By this point the followers of the Great Unsharing were no longer involved in the forums where the hoax was revealed and so they missed much of the outrage, the debates and the counter-outrage.

# 10

**THURSDAY OF THE** first week. It was 7 p.m. and the moon was already visible as a shadowy crescent. After finishing the very creditable pumpkin and spinach curry his wife had prepared, Karl was sent outside to pick his way through the runner beans in the dark, the collected rainwater seeping through his fuzzy trainers. He could see through the garage's screen door. In oil-stained jeans and a white T-shirt Stu hunched over the bonnet of a bright-green Honda Civic, rubbing its immaculate paintwork with a piece of sandpaper. He looked up when Karl pulled the door open.

'All right, Karl?'

'Hey. Janna said you, um …' He inhaled the smell of turps.

'Yeah, first workout – just let me finish …'

Stu went back to sanding the bonnet.

'This Lime-Green Car my Prison,' said Karl.

'What?'

'Came into my head. Is that for …'

'Rat look,' said Stu. 'Security feature, really. You downgrade a fairly expensive car so it doesn't get vandalised or stolen. Sorry. Just finish this bit.' His sanding sped up for a moment, then he rose and sat down on a stepladder, motioning Karl towards an old paint-spattered wooden stool.

'We'll start with a little cardio,' he said. 'And then get straight into the weights – there's no need to hold back. I've got you a kit.'

He handed Karl a canvas bag. In it he found a pair of white running shoes, some black shorts and a black Aertex shirt, a brand he remembered the more popular kids at school wearing.

'Go up and get ready and I'll join you once I've washed my hands.'

Karl noticed the steps in the corner of the garage. His wet trainers squeaked against the steel and he hauled himself up to a mezzanine bedecked with oily gym apparatus. It looked like the set of a grim science-fiction film.

They were running, side by side, on a double treadmill. Stu was able to keep a conversation going as if they were sitting in a bar. Karl, who only ran when he needed to catch a train, felt a little less able to draw breath, let alone speak.

'People say running clears your mind,' said Stu, 'and you know what the key to that is?'

'N … No.'

'You keep doing it,' said Stu. 'You keep doing it until *all you can think about* is how much you hate running and how much you don't want to be running any more. Suddenly, magic! All the cares of this world have melted away. You just want it to end. You are a non-physical being, a spirit of pure hatred of running.'

'That,' said Karl, clutching the stitch in the side of his stomach, 'is something I can get behind.'

Twenty minutes later he was pouring with sweat, sitting in a weight-lifting machine the like of which he had only ever seen in Hollywood montages.

'We ran two miles,' said Stu. 'Feels good, right?'

'No.'

'Start on level three,' said Stu, taking the push-pin out of 16 and placing it on the second hole. 'First week on three. People always start too high and get demoralised. Do ten.'

Karl pushed the bars, which felt light. He brought the bars back to his sides again and pushed. A little more resistance.

'So what's the story?' said Stu.

'You mean how I got here? Somewhere between fraud and tax evasion and incompetence,' said Karl.

'No, no, I know all that,' said Stu. 'I mean with you and Genevieve. How'd you meet?'

Karl finished his tenth lift.

'Ten more,' said Stu.

'University,' said Karl. 'She was a friend of a friend. I was obsessed with her.'

'Not hard to see why.'

'In fact it totally ruined my three years of university. I didn't even talk to another girl the whole time I was there. Then I didn't see her for a decade. I had, like, three pretty joyless relationships with women who weren't her. And then one day Genevieve just sent me an email asking if I remembered her.'

'How long have you been together?'

'Four years,' said Karl.

'And how's that going?'

'I feel very lucky.'

'Good.'

'Very lucky.'

'You are. She's gorgeous.'

Karl smiled. He liked other men admiring Genevieve.

'Now don't get me wrong,' said Stu, 'you're a good bloke and I'm sure you have your qualities – but there's a fairly standard way someone like you gets a girl like Genevieve.'

'Oh? What's that?'

'You won't take this the wrong way?'

'No, of course not.'

'I tell it as I see it,' said Stu. 'Some people don't like that.'

'Tell away,' said Karl. If Stu said something he didn't like, it would only serve to make him value Stu's opinion less.

'You're a fairly ordinary-looking guy,' said Stu.

'I've always thought so.'

'So is she damaged goods?' said Stu.

'I'm sorry?'

'Come on,' said Stu. 'When she got back in touch with you, after ten years … I'm not asking you to tell me what she survived or the condition she was diagnosed with or whatever. I just wanted to say that I've noticed. You look after her. I couldn't see it at first, but I do now.'

'Right,' said Karl, relieved that Stu had brought the conversation round to a form of compliment again, something easy to accept. 'Well, thanks.'

'You're caring, which is good. What I want to give you,' said Stu, 'is a little more self-esteem. I've been insulting you and you're not even offended. Men keep their self-esteem in the biceps and pectoral muscles. You should feel that you're in an equal relationship with Genevieve. Does that make sense?'

'I guess so,' said Karl.

'I guess so,' said Stu. 'You sound like a Muppet. I don't mean like "*you muppet*", I mean like an actual Muppet, from *The Muppet Show*. Lose the Americanisms. Try to sound like yourself.'

Karl swallowed.

'We'll finish with a hundred press-ups,' said Stu.

'I'm sorry?'

'That sounds more like your real voice. We'll do them together. Come on.'

'I don't think I can do *twenty*,' said Karl.

'You can do a thousand,' said Stu. 'Might take you a week, but there you go. We'll do a hundred, as long as it takes, then you can go and have a shower.'

Karl laughed.

'What's funny?'

He assumed the position. His arms already burned from the weights, but the first five press-ups were relatively easy. After the eleventh, Stu waited, supporting his weight with one hand while Karl completed his twelfth press-up.

'Don't give in at the first sign of resistance,' said Stu. He sounded genuinely cross. 'This is important.'

Slowly Karl lowered himself so that his nose was touching the rubber floor.

'Come on,' said Stu. 'That's it.'

Karl tensed his chest. He felt like he was made of loose Meccano. He forced himself up again.

'Eighty-six to go,' said Stu.

His arms shaking, Karl lowered himself again.

'Eighty-five and a half.'

'This is ridiculous,' stuttered Karl.

'This is ridiculous,' Stu mimicked. 'That's fifteen. Good ... Why aren't you moving? Your wife will be wondering where you are.'

'Twenty-three,' said Stu. 'You said you couldn't do twenty. Karl, I've seen better men than you lose a woman like Genevieve because they stopped working for it. Do you want that to happen?'

While Karl didn't think this was likely, he tried to channel his embarrassment, his rage and his temporary loathing for Stu into his twenty-fourth press-up. It took almost a minute.

'That's fifty-eight,' said Stu.

Karl was shaking all over. His temples felt like they were going to explode and his stomach was like a sack of snooker balls. He tried very hard to lower himself again, but his arms gave out. He collapsed, hitting his nose on the floor, and started to cry.

'I'm sorry,' he said. 'I'm sorry.'

'Hey,' said Stu. 'Hey. Karl, stand up.'

Karl clambered to his feet and Stu took him in his arms. Karl cried hard, took big breaths and cried, his nose streaming with snot on Stu's shoulder. Stu stroked the back of Karl's head.

'Let it all out.'

'I'm sorry,' Karl sobbed.

'Do you know how much the last guy held out for?' said Stu. 'Thirty-one. And that was the best so far. You did great.' He patted him on the back, hard. 'You did fucking great.'

# 11

## 'WHAT HAPPENED TO YOU?'

'I was working out.'

'You look like you've been hit by a car.'

Karl gingerly climbed into bed and put his head on Genevieve's shoulder. She smelled of a medicated facial scrub she used sometimes, a smell he associated with their university halls: bare-brick stairwells, a pasted-up lightning crack in the side of the building.

He only realised he'd been asleep when the room filled with light. Janna and Stu were standing at the end of the bed, holding two envelopes. Karl sniffed, sat up in bed, nudged Genevieve.

'Really sorry to wake you,' whispered Janna.

'We won't make a habit of it,' said Stu.

'Is something wrong?'

'No, no.' Genevieve shuffled out of the bed and stretched. 'Don't apologise. I don't know what ... We never fall asleep this early.'

'You're exhausted,' said Janna. 'Poor things.'

'We'll keep this quick,' said Stu. He held the envelopes out to Karl.

Karl found it hard to move his arms from his sides; it was as if an important pulley system had snapped.

'What are these?'

'We want you both to read a newspaper,' said Stu. He sat on the end of the bed and Janna sat down against the wall.

'We've got you subscriptions,' said Janna. 'To *The Guardian* and *The Telegraph*. Every day.'

'Every *day*?'

'You get up an hour early and you read them both, quickly, cover to cover, then swap. Get into the habit. It's like keeping an allotment.'

'I've tried to read newspapers,' said Karl, rubbing his left eye. 'It doesn't feel like they're for me.'

'And that's the problem,' said Stu. 'You need to be an active participant in society. We got the paper editions because the symbolism is important – you could just read it all on your tablets, but I want you to think about your parents, and how serious they seemed when they were behind newspapers.'

'It's not that we're not interested in what happens in the world,' said Genevieve. 'Really it's just that I'm busy or I *would* read one. At least once a week.'

'But you're apolitical.'

'I'm disillusioned.'

'No,' said Stu. 'The problem you've got is that you don't feel worthy of newspapers. Be honest. A part of you still feels that newspapers are for grown-ups and that you're not grown-ups.'

'Look at this,' said Karl. He had been rifling through *The Guardian* to the property section and had now folded it on Bargain of the Week, a two-bedroom flat for £1.2 million. 'This is supposed to be the newspaper for intelligent poor people,' he said, 'but we're completely unrepresented.

Newspapers are written for the wealthiest fraction of a fraction of society.'

'We spend most of our lives living in a fantasy of the future we think we deserve,' said Janna.

'This is part of the programme,' said Stu. 'This is something you have to trust us on. Try it for the next couple of weeks. You read the papers first thing. We discuss home and international news over breakfast. Deal?'

'If we can talk about X-Men comic books over dinner,' said Karl.

'Okay, second nag,' said Janna. 'Teeth. Has either one of you ever been to a dental hygienist?'

'How does that differ from a dentist?' said Karl.

'It's like the difference between a doctor and a coroner,' said Stu. 'Not even joking.'

'We are *incredibly* backward about teeth in this country,' said Janna. 'It's seen as separate from health. Most of the population, they might as well be walking around with radioactive waste in their mouths. Name any disease: your teeth and your gums can give it to you. Do you floss?'

'No.'

'Genevieve?'

'Once.'

'Why did you stop?'

'I meant once in my life. It was horrible.'

'Okay. We'll start with flossing. There's a complete guide on your tablets with films.'

'I can't believe this is part of The Transition,' said Karl.

'There's very little point in any of this if you're not even taking care of your own mouth,' said Janna.

# 12

**6 A.M. KARL'S** tablet played the theme from Super Mario Bros. 3 and Genevieve's played Rachmaninov's Piano Concerto No. 2, very loud. A fresh copy of *The Guardian* and of *The Telegraph* lay at the top of the ladder.

'You know the servants used to iron the newspaper for the master of the house?' said Karl, rubbing his eyes and dropping *The Telegraph* on top of Genevieve.

'Why?'

'I don't know. Because it was crinkly, I guess. Which do you want to start with?'

'Ugh,' said Genevieve. 'I don't even care about *myself* in the morning, let alone the bloody *world*.'

Soon, though, they were talking about a fire in a National Trust property which had destroyed a gargantuan cache of Pre-Raphaelite paintings; the unusually high temperatures on the Continent; and the cultural tensions between the French- and German-speaking citizens of Switzerland, and were able to continue the conversation over breakfast with Janna and Stu.

'You really need to start with the decline of the Roman Empire to understand the situation,' said Stu, taking a bite of croissant. 'The original population were Helvetic Celts.'

'I'm pretty sure that's a font,' said Janna.

Once he was alone in the house, Karl took to reviewing a retro-look anti-SAD desk lamp with unusual enthusiasm. It was fun having opinions about things. Also, he had been keeping up the press-ups, trying to do ten every hour so that he could hit the ground running in Stu's next work-out. The tension in his chest muscles was a novelty, and when he dropped the paperclip he was fiddling with and leaned out of his chair to pick it up, his stomach didn't feel like a balloon he was trying to fold in half. It hurt, certainly, but it was a new kind of pain, an earned pain. 'This lamp is the Switzerland of desk apparatus,' he wrote.

He checked Study Sherpas© and found that someone called Cynthia Palmer needed an A-level coursework essay on contemporary British fiction. 'Really need an A*' was her only communiqué. A-level essays were a cinch – he could ace them in an hour while talking to someone on the phone. Karl spun the fruit machine in his head, tapped out a title – 'A Comparison of Representations of Masculinity in the work of Martin Amis and Ian McEwan' – and brought up three novels apiece on eBeW.

After three hours he had finished the essay and four reviews and thirty press-ups, in spite of thinking about his Polaroid of Genevieve. He started to consider his position. It meant that Janna and Stu were snooping and, well, so was he. It meant that either Stu or Janna was looking for some kind of an edge. Or fancied his wife. Or had designs on his wife of some kind. Or it was part of The Transition which would later be revealed to him. Or Stu was a bigger perv than he was, and Genevieve was his wife, dammit, and that was *his* photo of her awesome body. Karl stood up and started pacing from his study to the bedroom and back again. That's the problem with self-respect, he thought. You start to feel offended when someone insults you.

He completed eight circuits of the room and the study. He was an inveterate pacer. Genevieve said it was the only reason he wasn't fat. He stopped in the bedroom, looked out of the window and decided to channel his irritation into some more press-ups. He hit the floor, staring straight ahead at the foot of the bed. One … Two … The familiar pulsing in his temples. Three … Four …

Something caught his eye. The word *NOT* was carved in tiny letters into the foot of the bed, next to a rough downward pointing arrow.

'Not?' said Karl, out loud.

He started patting the floor under the bed, feeling under the bed frame. He stuck his head under the bed. He turned on the tablet for light and slid it under with him. not_all_transition.com was carved into one of the wooden slats under the mattress.

Karl put *www.not_all_transition.com* into his tablet, and the screen went white. He hit refresh and the same thing happened. Then it told him that the connection had timed out. The second time it told him that the site was unavailable, and then the screen froze. He made a mental note to check in an internet cafe. There were still internet cafes, presumably.

He restarted the tablet. When it came back on, the screen was prompting him to complete his 500-word journal from last night or lose a merit point. He texted Keston.

— Favour to ask you.

The reply felt almost implausibly instant:

— Anything for my favourite screw-up.
— That was quick. Bored much?
— I'm at work. This is one of eight conversations I'm having, mother. <PICTURE OF OWN JUNK>
— Haha.
— Haaaaaa. So this favour? U want someone killed?
— Any chance you could look into our mentors' previous protégés?
— WHAT?
— Just the names.
— Karl, what do you think I am, a PI from the 50s?
— So no then?
— I could *probably* find out. *Probably*, but for the love of God, why do you want to know?
— Curious.
— Is it all going wrong? Are you not having fun?
— Everything's fine.
— My advice, Special K, is to keep your head down for six months and count yourself very bloody lucky you're not in prison.
— You'll do it, then?
— SIGH. EYEROLL. Don't make me use emoji again, K-dog.

– You're the BEST, Keston. Beston. <heart>

When he was making his 4 p.m. cup of tea, Karl heard a key in the lock and saw an outline of a tall man through the glass. Stu was first back, which was unusual.

'Hey there,' he said and dumped his heavy shoulder bag in the hall with a thud.

'Good day?' said Karl. It flashed into his mind that the bag was full of human limbs. He shook the image off.

'Meh,' said Stu. 'Got another one of those?'

Karl took down a mug.

'What do you actually do at The Transition?' said Karl. 'Apart from looking after us, obviously.'

'God,' said Stu, rubbing his face. 'Don't get me wrong – I love the company, but it's like having three jobs some-times. There are some pretty ordinary things about running a building of that size – the stationery and catering alone have their own finance team, you know? And now we're having some issues with Transition Netherlands … it's exciting, but it's more chaotic than usual. I work in our Relationships department. Dispute resolution. When things break down between mentors and protégés, etc. …'

Stu had taken off his boots and replaced them with some kind of textured rubber socks. He paused to take a swig of tea.

'Ah. Doesn't come up often, you'll be pleased to hear, but, well, we're all human, aren't we? Not everyone's as lucky as me and Janna.'

'Aw.'

'Seriously – you're a peach. You're both peaches. Got a couple "on the run" at the moment. Silly sods. I liaise with

Legal a lot. Strategy meetings. Internal and external reviews. They find a way of making a pretty sweet racket you used to care about into a royal pain in the arse. Like any job, basically.'

'That's the truth,' said Karl.

'We're actually going to be advertising an IT position soon,' said Stu. 'Could use someone with your work ethic.'

'Ha!' said Karl. 'My work ethic.'

'I'm serious,' said Stu. 'I know you worked your arse off trying to pay down those seventeen credit cards. I'm going kiteboarding – could you tell Janna? Next workout on Sunday, okay, big guy?'

# 13

**THEY SLEPT LATE** on Saturday morning and then watched a chef and an actress searing scallops on the corner television.

'Do you like her?' said Genevieve. 'She's your type, isn't she?'

'I like women who look like you,' said Karl.

Genevieve mimed retching.

'No, it's true. Whenever I have a crush on someone there's something oddly familiar about them, and then I realise it's because they remind me of you in some way.'

'So your ideal woman,' said Genevieve, 'is someone who looks like me but isn't actually me.'

'That would be super-hot,' said Karl, stretching.

'It's hurtful. You think you love me, but you don't love all of me.'

'I'm sorry,' said Karl, 'I've lost track of whether this is a serious conversation or not.'

'It's always serious,' said Genevieve.

'What part of you don't I love?'

'You don't love me when you think I'm ill. You think I'm a different person.'

'When you're ill,' said Karl, 'you're annoying and you're mean to me. Afterwards you don't remember anything you said or did. I'm supposed to love that? It's not *you*.'

'But it is part of me.'

'No it's not.'

Genevieve laughed.

'No, look,' said Karl. 'If you broke your leg I would love you, but I wouldn't love the fact that you'd broken your leg. I'd *hate* that you'd broken your leg.'

'So you'd stop loving my leg,' said Genevieve.

'No.'

She looked at her legs. 'Which leg are we talking about, just to be clear?'

'That's beside the … Let's say your right leg.'

'Poor old righty,' said Genevieve, patting her leg. 'Best not get broken if you want to keep your husband.'

Once Stu and Janna were awake Karl slipped downstairs and timidly enquired what the itinerary for the day might be. Janna laughed and said it was whatever they usually did on a Saturday. Except it had to be free. They took a walk in the park.

'This is a great park,' said Genevieve, surprised. 'I can't believe we've never walked around it before.'

Stu's Iro looked especially pointy that evening. He cooked sea bass with kale and charlotte potatoes and, as it was Saturday, they drank a lot of white wine, a Riesling so dry it was almost salty.

'We're going to talk about money,' said Janna. 'This is going to be invasive and disrespectful and I apologise in advance.'

'We're not proud,' said Karl.

'This is a parable from the Transition handbook,' said Stu, holding up a glossy black paperback with a thoroughly cracked spine – the *Mentor's Edition*. He read: '"A stray dog was starving to death outside the butcher's. Over time he learned to do tricks. He walked on his hind legs, he balanced a stone – a little piece of gravel from the front garden next door – on the end of his nose and flipped it in the air, catching it in his mouth. It was impressive. Every now and then, a customer would pat him on the head and tell him he was a good boy. Once, *once*, a kind old woman gave him a piece of her chuck steak. Day in, day out he carried on walking on his hind legs, getting better and better at flipping the stone off his nose. Some people were amused, but a lot of people didn't really care for dogs anyway, especially strays. Meanwhile the other dogs went round the back to the skips at the end of every working day and helped themselves."'

Genevieve added a sugar to her coffee.

Janna and Stu looked at Karl.

'Do we discuss the parable?' said Karl.

'Just let it filter in,' said Janna.

'Keep it in mind,' said Stu.

Janna was staring at Karl. 'This is going to be a little uncomfortable,' she said. 'That's normal. Play along, okay?'

'Okay,' said Karl.

'Do you like your jobs?'

'Sometimes,' said Genevieve.

'No,' said Karl.

'Genevieve,' said Janna. 'What do you bring in a month, net?'

'Fourteen hundred,' said Genevieve.

'Karl?'

'It varies.'

'On average.'

'I usually clear a grand,' said Karl.

'I think you need to be a little more realistic,' said Janna. 'What was your rent?'

'Six fifty a week,' said Genevieve.

'Christ.' Janna sat back. 'Savings?'

'Oh, we're both in *significant* debt,' said Karl.

'There was a problem with a car,' said Genevieve.

'And you want to have children?'

'At some point,' said Karl.

'Sooner rather than later,' said Genevieve.

'The thing I don't understand,' said Janna, 'and forgive me for being direct, but what, exactly, is it in your circumstances that you expect to change? Are you hoping to win the lottery? Sell a screenplay? Write a hit single?'

'We're hoping for a land reform act,' said Genevieve. 'First kill the landlords.'

'Let's be honest,' said Janna. 'Some grim realities. There was an era, some years ago, when teaching could be considered a career. Those days have passed. If you choose to do a job like that you really need a private income.'

Karl could faintly hear Genevieve's teeth tapping out an angry reply, although she wasn't moving her lips.

'Karl, you've at least had a look at what the world's like now and tried to adapt accordingly,' said Stu. 'All the content creation. But really, what you're doing … It's like you're scalping tickets when you could be up on stage.'

'Honestly,' said Janna, 'you both need to sit down and take a good hard look at yourselves, at your skills, at your ample capabilities and the potential they give you to *thrive*, for God's sake. Literally just write a list. You've both made some terrible life decisions—'

'Karl, what was your MA in?' Stu interjected.

'The Metaphysical Poets,' said Karl.

'You've both made some rotten life decisions, but we don't blame you for that at all,' said Janna. 'You've been lied to and misdirected your whole lives.'

'It's not that you were allowed to do whatever you wanted, or even that you were *told* to,' said Stu.

'You weren't given a choice,' said Janna. 'I know what school was like when you were there – basically a big car showroom for unprincipled "universities".' She did scare quotes.

'You were forced, kicking and screaming, to follow your dreams,' said Stu. 'That's our generation's fault.'

'I'm going to make a suggestion,' said Janna. 'You don't need to react to it now. Just let it filter down and maybe write about it in your journals. It's non-compulsory, of course. The suggestion is this: within the first month of The Transition you should both quit your jobs.'

'Ha!' said Genevieve.

'This is …' said Karl.

'Nobody's going to pay you to feel sorry for yourself,' said Stu. 'Unless you're planning to lobby to bring back the Arts Council.'

'Just think about what I said,' said Janna. 'At some point it was instilled in you that money isn't important. Think hard about that. Think about the people who told you that.

Did they live in collectives growing their own beetroots and selling woven baskets? No. They were probably comfortable, well-off professionals who thought they could live vicariously through you.'

'It's the post-structuralists,' said Stu. 'They told you: don't read the classics – study *EastEnders*. But what had *they* read? The classics!'

'Stu, honestly, it's not as if *you've* read the classics,' said Janna.

'What little I read,' said Stu, 'it had better be classic, that's all.'


**'THE BLOODY NERVE,'** said Genevieve. She was straightening her hair and the smell of coconut oil hung in the room. Neither of them had said anything for half an hour.

'Keep smiling,' said Karl.

'You think I should quit teaching?' said Genevieve, letting the straighteners drop to her lap.

'God, of course not,' said Karl. He was almost superstitious about the teaching profession. It had rescued Genevieve, and she, in turn, rescued the kids who spent every break time getting into fights, who couldn't write the letter *e* or the number *8*, whose parents arrived drunk at the gates.

'She's so needy,' said Genevieve. 'She needs everyone to approve of her. That's all this is. She needs *me* to approve of her.'

'Exactly,' said Karl. 'This is more about them than it is about us. We just have to play along for six months and walk away.'

'On the other hand,' said Genevieve, 'I feel so, so sick of teaching, sometimes.'

'We've talked about this,' said Karl. 'Job satisfaction is a bourgeois affectation.'

'The levels, the paperwork, the marks for *six-year-olds*; the fact that they'll do absolutely anything to prevent you from having a real, lasting impact on the most difficult kids. Remember I set up that lunchtime club? They actually *hate* me for doing that. They think I'm trying to be a hero. You know Cathy's leaving?' Genevieve took a bite of an apple she must have picked up downstairs and wandered over to the skylight.

'You *do* have a lasting impact. Everything you do in that school makes a significant improvement to the state of the human race,' said Karl, trying to play it relatively cool. 'How many people can say that? I know *I* can't.'

She crunched her apple again.

'You want some of this? The snake said it was fine. Look, Karl, relax. It's just interesting to be offered a way out, isn't it? Janna would probably go to the school herself and cancel my contract. I'd love to see Upton trying to deal with Janna. She'd crush him.'

Karl stood behind Genevieve, put his hands on her shoulders and then started fiddling with the clasp of her bra.

'Don't. It makes me feel sleepy. You know that.'

'What's wrong with feeling sleepy?'

'I've got marking to do.'

'Just stick a gold star on everything.'

# 14

**THE NEXT NIGHT** it seemed that Genevieve and Janna had put the conversation out of their minds. Karl entered the room with two cups of camomile tea and they were laughing at something in a copy of *Vogue*. When they all had their drinks and Karl had sat down by the cast-iron coffee table, Stu handed Genevieve a gold coin with £100 engraved on it.

'Is this real?'

'Seed money,' he said. 'Representative of it, anyway. Little competition. All the other couples on The Transition have been given one of these tonight – ours tend to win this. The money will be on your tablets and you have to invest it, over the rest of this month. The couple to bring in the most wins an upgrade to their first home: an extra room, an extension – there are various options.'

'Goody. Do we get to keep the money?' said Genevieve.

'The money goes to the charity of your choice,' said Stu.

They were meeting late because Genevieve had had lesson prep to do, which she hadn't finished until almost nine. Now she was wearing pyjamas decorated with a black cat-face motif and sitting cross-legged on the sofa. Girlish. Karl wasn't sure whether he liked it. On the landing, on their way down, he caught her as she jumped off the ladder, an arm under her thighs, and lowered her to the floor. He hugged her and felt her body through the thin material. The sensation of her skin against the material. It felt as if his lungs were filling with tiny glowing asterisks. He didn't know what he thought about her sitting there in front of Stu. It gave him the tense feeling of waiting for results, opening a bank statement. He enjoyed it and flinched from it in equal measure. What was it he liked about men admiring his wife? Did he want them to be jealous? Did he want Stu to feel jealous? No. It wasn't about that at all. It was … He didn't examine the thought any further.

Janna was talking about patrons and investors; words like networking being overused, misunderstood. He liked her voice. It was clipped and anxious when she was 'teaching', self-conscious in a way that made Karl want to take her hand and say, *hey, you're doing really well*, even though he wasn't really listening to her. He stared at the thick grey impasto on the big canvas behind her. It was like the surface of the moon. He thought about how many thousands of pounds the painting must have cost. The lilies needed refreshing. Genevieve giggled again.

She was only giggling to be polite, he supposed, but it sounded genuine. It seemed more real than many of the things she said to Karl, many of the noises: laughs, sighs, hmms. Sometimes she said, 'That's funny' instead of laughing. Occasionally, he was quite sure of this, she disguised a yell of pure rage behind a sneeze. The sneeze was real; it was an opportunistic yell, which might as well have come out then, when she happened to need to sneeze, as ever.

Karl was able to come out of his reverie to say, 'No, none whatsoever,' when Stu assumed that Karl hadn't made any private pension arrangements.

And when he thought about it, Genevieve never used to laugh at anything he said but at something intrinsically funny about him. The first time he met Genevieve (she was a friend of a friend of Keston's) he spent as much of the night as he could staring at her without being creepy, pretending he was looking over her head at someone at another table, or checking the time or trying to catch someone's attention at the bar. He didn't say a word to her until his friends were leaving and he said, 'Well, bye,' and she laughed.

They spoke, once after that, on the flimsy intra-hall telephones, which allowed you to make calls between rooms for free.

'Hello?' said Karl.

Genevieve started laughing.

'Is this Genevieve?'

'Yes, this is Genevieve.'

'Why are you laughing?'

'Because you're funny.'

'Okay,' said Karl. 'I was just calling to see—'

'Karl,' she interrupted, '*I* called *you*.'

'Oh, did you?' said Karl. 'Oh dear.'

# 15

**IT WAS THE FIRST** Monday of half term and Genevieve had an Inset day – IT training – which started late. Lying in bed idly masturbating and thinking about how he might try to convince her to have sex, which was never really on the cards in the morning, Karl was puzzled to hear the pneumatic sound of the espresso machine several times in a row without the accompanying smell of coffee. Espresso machines always sounded like they were about to blow to bits, but there it was again, louder than before, and this meant either that Genevieve was failing to get Janna and Stu's espresso machine to work, or that she was destroying Janna and Stu's espresso machine. The two weren't mutually exclusive. He shimmied down the ladder and ran down both flights of stairs, but when he entered the kitchen she turned around with a smile.

'Try this.' She handed him a little red cup. He took a sip. Swallowed.

'Oh my God, that's disgusting,' he said.

'Hmm,' said Genevieve, her head tilted to one side, disappointed.

The granite worktop was strewn with bits of torn and crumpled paper.

'What's all the …?'

He picked one up. They were empty teabags. Ten … twenty of them.

'Tea espresso,' said Genevieve.

'I think you've invented the worst thing ever.'

'I just thought it would be fun,' said Genevieve.

Karl ran a glass of water, gargled and spat into the sink.

'How long have you been up?'

'Well,' said Genevieve. 'Don't be angry, but I got carried away with the stock market. Our little £100 is now £134. I've been up since three.'

Karl made a face he hoped looked like Munch's *Scream*.

'That's a thirty-four per cent return,' said Genevieve. 'Not bad for one day, right?'

Karl got very upset when Genevieve woke up before six in the morning. It made him worry that she was losing her mind.

'You know I hate it when you don't sleep,' he said.

'I thought you'd be pleased!'

'I'm impressed that you made £34,' said Karl.

'You might have a go at it yourself today,' said Genevieve. 'It's fun! You might at least get involved.'

'I will. Promise me you won't get up early tomorrow morning?'

'Oh, Karl, you're obsessed. I got *carried away*. I'm *sorry*.'

'You don't understand how much it worries me.'

'I'd understand if I was actually getting ill,' said Genevieve. 'This is different.'

'You always say it's different,' said Karl, 'and it's never different. You start off not sleeping, then you start talking too fast, then you take on, like, a hundred different things, then you can't even order a cup of coffee without confusing everyone, and then I become an enemy to you.'

'You sound like a little boy with a burst balloon.'

'You're taking your meds, aren't you?'

Genevieve stiffened as if he had told her there was an intruder in the house.

'Yes, I'm taking them,' she said, quietly.

'Then it makes me wonder if they need adjusting. We could make an appointment to see Dr Blend.'

'Karl,' said Genevieve, 'have you ever read *The Yellow Wallpaper*?'

'Genevieve,' said Karl. 'Have you ever read *Tender is the Night*?'

'There's a growing body of evidence that the whole psycho-pharmacopoeia is just like throwing darts over your shoulder at a dartboard five hundred metres away.'

'Who paid for that research? Chiropractors? Big Yoga?'

'There are alternatives,' said Genevieve. 'And should I choose to explore them, this strikes me as a fairly good time to do it.'

'Living with strangers,' said Karl. 'I don't want you to get ill here. I don't know what I'd do.'

'I have to go to work. Can you stop looking at the floor? I hate it when you're like this.'

'Yeah, yeah,' said Karl. 'Blame it on me. It's me.'

He stared at the carpet. He liked the carpet – it was black and cream and looked like a tile pattern. He ran his eyes around the pattern until Genevieve sighed and left the house, closing the front door just hard enough.

# 16

IN KARL'S FIFTH review of a Space Pen which could write on any surface, even underwater, he chose to focus on the act of writing as being that which separates us from beasts. But what if you could separate yourself from your fellow man, too? he argued. He had heard her on the stairs, but he was surprised when Genevieve opened a can behind his neck. He smelled cider.

'I'm going to go out,' she said. 'Is that okay? Celebrate the holiday.'

'It's Monday,' said Karl.

'Yeah, town will be lousy with teachers.'

'No, I mean it's not Drinking Day.'

'Oh, I checked with Janna,' said Genevieve. 'It's fine. They're not insane, Karl. I said *Is it okay if I go out with some colleagues?* and she said, *Oh, God, of course, you don't need to ask.* Then she gave me twenty quid and said *Have one on me.*'

'Nice of her.'

'You won't worry?'

Karl looked at Genevieve. Her pupils were normal-sized. She sounded like herself. She was wearing a black beaded necklace he had bought her when they were students.

'I'm sorry about this morning,' he said.

'It's fine. You're hyper-vigilant. No worries.'

'No worries,' said Karl. The phrase always made him think of serious academic books with pithy titles: *On Worries*.

Genevieve propped her tablet up on the old steamer trunk. 'Let's see how our hundred quid is doing,' she said.

'Hyper-vigilant?'

'One hundred and fifty-six!' said Genevieve gaily. 'I'm a natural! Buy! Buy! Sell! Sell!'

Karl enjoyed staying in. He loved reading *Retro Gamer* while channel-hopping between sitcom repeats, music videos and panel shows to create the illusion that he was being entertained. Most of all, he loved being free of the responsibility of having a good time. As a pleasant corollary, all of this non-effort was received by Genevieve as benevolence.

He'd watched her get ready, straighten her hair, choose an outfit. When she sat on the bed in her underwear he curled around her hips like a cat.

'You're sure you don't mind?'

'No, go,' he said. 'Have a good time, say hi to the girls from me.'

When she was gone, he made a ready-salted-crisp sandwich, with a pint glass of Ribena, took off his clothes and crawled under the duvet with the remote. In their old flat he would fall asleep with the TV on, wake up just enough to switch it off a few hours later, then wake up again to find his wife next to him, smelling of stale smoke with high notes of alcohol. He'd kiss her.

'You're a nice boy,' she'd murmur. 'You're one of the only ones.'

But that night Karl drifted into a deep sleep then came round to find that it was 6 a.m. and Genevieve still wasn't home. He grabbed for the lamp on his bedside table, tried calling her tablet and it rang from her bedside table. Genevieve never took her tablet with her. Karl put on some jeans and a yellow Belle and Sebastian T-shirt and began to climb down the ladder, blood thumping in his ears.

Genevieve was still in her going-out dress, asleep on the white sofa with a beaded blanket tucked around her.

'Genevieve?' he said, rubbing her shoulder so the beads clacked together. She stirred. 'Genevieve.'

'Oh.' Genevieve opened her eyes. 'What time is it?'

'I was worried.'

'Worried?' she yawned.

'It's six. I thought you were still out.'

'I got home at midnight, silly.' She shuffled into a sitting position and adjusted her dress. 'I stayed up talking to Janna. I must have fallen asleep.'

'What did you talk about?'

'Did I have a good night, do you mean? Don't be weird. Sit down.'

He looked at her.

'Why not come upstairs?'

'I feel a bit sick.'

★ ★ ★

They took turns in the award-winning shower, Karl second. He tightened the towel around his waist, took slightly too much product out of the tub and ran it through his hair.

'Looking good,' said Genevieve.

'I'm a new man.'

He looked at her, wrapped in only a scarf, sprawled on the bed with a *Teach Yourself Italian* book.

'You're beautiful,' he said. 'Even with a hangover you're beautiful.'

'*Vicino … Lontano.* You're blinded by love.'

'You always say that,' said Karl. 'The opposite is true. I don't even *like* you. I just think you're beautiful. It's what keeps us together.'

'*Ho una prenotazione.* You know, I realised something last night,' said Genevieve.

'Mm–hmm?'

'No, be more interested, say: Oh? What did you realise?'

'*What did you realise?*'

Genevieve sat up and closed her book.

'I don't really miss what I thought I missed,' she said. 'What I thought of as freedom … It's not much fun, really. I'd just as soon stay in and learn Italian.'

'Okay,' said Karl. 'I'm glad you got it out of your system.'

'I mean what are we doing, really? Why does drinking feel like a new adventure every time?'

'A lot of things never get dull,' said Karl. 'Breathing, eating, Schubert.'

'Sex,' said Genevieve. 'But with drinking it's never a new adventure. It's always exactly the same old adventure every time.'

'That's narrative,' said Karl. 'Also, it makes you feel terrible afterwards. That's a factor.'

'Do you want to … you know?'

'Of course I do. I always do.'

'I was rude to you yesterday. I know you were just worried about me. But there's really nothing to worry about. I feel great. Actually I feel like … Never mind.'

'You feel like what?' said Karl, starting to unbutton the shirt he was halfway through buttoning. Genevieve threw her book at his chest.

'Ow.'

'Ha ha.'

'Don't throw books at me.'

She lay back and kicked her legs in the air as if pedalling.

'I've been thinking,' she said, 'about Janna's suggestion.'

'What have you been thinking?'

'I'm not sure yet.'

Genevieve rolled off the bed and started putting on a pair of leggings – the ones with a black-and-white street scene print.

'Was that a joke, about sex?' said Karl.

'Oh. No – I just forgot. I'm feeling pretty hungover.'

'Girls hate hangover sex,' said Karl. 'Why is that?'

'Well,' said Genevieve, 'I can't speak for all womankind. Maybe some women like sex when they have a head cold or severe back pain. Do boys like it? Hangover sex?'

'Boys would like nothing more.'

'That's weird.'

'I think because you feel like you're going to die, so you're biologically compelled to continue your lineage.'

'Ooh, biological determinism. Turns me on.'

'It's my theory.'

'Well, you'll have to continue your lineage by yourself.'

'I'm not hungover.'

'Can you pass the book – don't throw it!'

Karl lowered his hand and tossed the book onto the bed so that it landed just out of her reach.

'*Quest'uomo è fastidioso.*'

# 17

**THE TEXT FROM KESTON** arrived later that afternoon while Karl was finishing his twelfth article about an ecological hand-drying system.

- Kelly and Barnaby Reddick; Maria Reynolds and Lottie Friedlander; Jonathan and Alice Jonke. That's as far back as I can trace.
- Cheers.
- CHEERS?! IS THAT IT, K-FED?! IS THAT ALL I GET?!
- I'm grateful. If I wasn't on a government scheme that places strict sanctions on my financial activity I'd buy you dinner.
- Well, you can let me buy *you* dinner, you crummy one-eyed lush.
- One-eyed?
- Don't say you're busy.
- Can't do tonight.
- Boring.

★ ★ ★

With the automated shopping delivery there was very little reason for Karl to leave Stu and Janna's house and he felt the need for some air. Thankfully, the cupboard had failed to materialise a tin of coconut milk, which Genevieve needed for the Thai curry she was preparing, so he had an excuse to go to town. Karl remembered the web address when he passed a shop that appeared to be a cross between a shisha bar, a phone accessory store and an internet cafe. He paid the clerk £4.50 for thirty minutes. not_all_transition.com took him straight to a promotional page for a band. He snorted. So it was a band, the band of a former protégé. Bands were so silly. There were black-and-white photos of three easy-on-the-eye youngish people in a forest, doing fake-earnest expressions or captured in an unguarded moment of horsing around, or posing in trees. There were links to discography and merchandise, and a description:

not_all_transition is a three-piece post-rock instrumental outfit featuring Alice Jonke, Barnaby Reddick and Sebastian Francis, emerging from the ashes of PAY ATTENTION in Brighton. Their debut album TAKE WHATEVER MONEY YOU CAN GET YOUR HANDS ON AND GET OUT RIGHT NOW was released on Honey Badger in the UK and Metaxas in the US. Their sophomore effort, YOU ARE BEING LIED TO, was self-released and the band are currently seeking new management. BEFORE YOU DO ANYTHING ELSE, CHECK OUT THE T-SHIRTS!

Karl clicked on a diagonal link to merchandising. There were three black T-shirts, one with NOT ALL TRANSITION in white sans-serif letters, one with a little Jack Russell looking back over its shoulder and a third dense with small text. Karl clicked this one for a close-up. The T-shirt text comprised a couple of lengthy quotations from Gramsci, and Karl was about to give up when it resolved into a series of zeros and ones and the following in the same font:

> These are instructions on how to hack the rudimentary stock-exchange program on your tablet and redirect the funds to the following account which can be used online.

A string of digits appeared which Karl recognised as complete credit card details. This was followed by a series of numbered systems instructions which Karl saw to be fairly straightforward. He took a photograph of the screen on his tablet. The text continued:

> Any system of profit depends on winners and losers. You need to get hold of their book, *The Trapeze*. By T. Piven. You need to read this book if you want to understand what they're about. Our advice is to run, right now, and don't look back. We've given you every opportunity to do this in the next quarter of an hour, so don't say we didn't warn you. If you need convincing maybe you could try breaking a few of the rules and see how long you last. If you want to know more why not catch us on our tour?

Karl clicked on the TOUR DATES tab, but the last date was almost two years ago at a venue called 52 Pritchatts Road. He looked it up on the map. Other side of town. He received a message from Genevieve wondering where the coconut milk was.

**AFTER DINNER GENEVIEVE** went upstairs to mark. Karl left her to it for half an hour. He prepared notes for the Henry James dissertation. When he went to check on her he found her sitting in the middle of the bed reading a crumpled photocopy.

'This would have been Dad's birthday,' she said.

'Oh,' said Karl. 'You never mentioned before.'

'Didn't I?'

'Do you want to do something?'

'Like what?' said Genevieve. 'Get blind drunk? This is the only thing I have of his. He used to write these sarcastic round robins.' She handed Karl the sheet.

Salutations and a happy new year! It's been some time since I penned one of these newsletters and I apologise for keeping you all in the dark. Unfortunately my drinking has been 'out of control' (my youngest's words; from the mouths of babes, etc.) and it's not always easy to gather the stray events and misadventures into a coherent story. But what a year it's been for our family! Matilda remains quite mad and claims not to know who I am during visiting hours, which is fairly galling after thirteen years of marriage. Genevieve and Nina continue to defy medical science by refusing to be cured of their anxiety and eating disorders – I forget who has which and suspect they occasionally swap just to try their old man's patience. We lost a lot of very valuable possessions in the floods and the ground floor remains toxic, but sadly we still have each other. Listen to me – I'm like the little Buddhist who wouldn't accept that life is suffering! Work is fairly abysmal so I've been developing a new raindance. We plan to take our annual holiday to Brigadoon as soon as the monsoons cease. Wishing you and yours a life of peaceful repentance.

'Wow.'

'He sent them to literally everyone,' said Genevieve. 'It was the only thing that made him happy.'

Karl took Genevieve's hand.

'Oh, I'm not sad,' she said.

'I know,' he said. 'I'm just taking your hand. It makes me feel useful.'

She leaned into him.

# 18

**KARL DRANK HIS** cup of tea in the blue light of his tablet screen. It was early Wednesday morning and Genevieve was still in bed. Thanks to her, their stock profile had risen to £202. Karl had already hacked the program, but stopped short of siphoning off the money. He had no reason to believe it would work, besides which playing the stock market was making her happy. If he was going to light that fire he needed to be sure it would actually smoke out something useful. He searched for information on the names Keston had sent him. In spite of those which appeared on not_all_transition's website and the fact that someone had clearly scratched the address into the bed, all three of the couples had pretty coherent success stories which seemed to check out, as far as Karl could tell by triangulating his stories with interviews, network profiles and client reviews. Alice Jonke ran Graceful Apology, a public relations firm 'specialising in total disasters'; Maria ran a private music college and Barnaby Reddick was a dealer in Chinese woodwork, with some items dating back to the twelfth century BC. Karl whistled. He searched for Jonathan Jonke, Alice's husband, but could find no mention of him attached to Graceful Apology or any other start-up venture. Lottie Friedlander, Maria's partner, turned up nothing, and neither did Kelly Reddick. Silent partners, perhaps, or looking after the kids. He could find out nothing pertinent about the four Sebastian Francises he tracked down. Maybe it was all just a scam to steal the stock money from Transition participants. Maybe not_all_transition was engraved into *all* of the protégés' beds. An elaborate test.

He heard Genevieve moving around in the bedroom. He heard her brushing her teeth for several minutes. They had their appointment with the dental hygienist later on. It felt odd, sharing the house with her during the day – the shape and atmosphere it took on once Stu and Janna had left for work had been his private domain for days now – but it also made him feel he was an expert in something Genevieve was new to. This made him oddly tentative, like when he found out G hadn't watched anything by Tarkovsky; he was so anxious not to sound condescending that he made his favourite director sound dull, and Genevieve had never watched the DVDs he got her.

But while he was studying the tech spec of a new kind of desk fan, she appeared behind him, put her hands over his eyes and said, 'So what have you discovered while you've been here all by yourself?'

After going through the records by solo artists they had heard of but never listened to, Genevieve said that the grey painting was a bit A-level and that she needed some coffee. On the way to the kitchen she pulled the handle of the understairs cupboard.

'It's the only thing that's locked,' said Karl. 'I saw lights between the floorboards.'

'What do you think's down there? Sex dungeon?'

Karl shrugged. 'Wouldn't that be kind of depressing?'

'Are you joking? It would be amazing!'

'I think the dullest thing about anyone is their sex dungeon,' said Karl. Then he added, 'You know, I nearly got in there last week.'

'What?' said Genevieve. 'How?'

She pretended to be horrified that Karl had been in their hosts' bedroom, but was soon in there herself, sitting on the chrome trapeze and swinging as high as she could without kicking the ceiling.

'Please be careful,' said Karl.

Then she went through Janna's wardrobe and chest of drawers.

'Oh my God, look at all the Agent Provocateur stuff,' said Genevieve, stretching a translucent lilac thong with red ribbons at the sides. 'Do you know what this costs? There must be like ten thousand pounds' worth of underwear in the chest of drawers alone.' She held a black swimsuit with three zips slashed into each side up to her chest.

'Shall I borrow it?'

'It's quite Barbarella,' said Karl.

'*Barbarellllla* …' sang Genevieve, turning.

A small, heavy key fell out of the swimsuit and landed on Karl's foot.

'Wait,' said Genevieve. Karl had turned the key in the understairs cupboard lock. 'I just feel seedy now. I wish we hadn't gone through her stuff.'

'Oh come *on*,' said Karl.

'It's clearly private. They trust us enough to leave us in

their home. I think we should put the key back and go and visit your dad.'

'Well, we can do that afterwards as penance,' said Karl. His ten reviews of the WarpGate3000 personal air-conditioner could wait. He turned the handle, but Genevieve grabbed his hand.

'I feel like a creep.'

'You're not curious?'

'I went through her underwear,' said Genevieve. 'She's someone I like and admire and I went through her underwear. Do you remember that guy at uni who was coming in people's shampoo?'

'Robbie?' said Karl. 'That was never proven.'

'I can't believe you're still defending him. Tash *caught* him. He was *arrested*. Anyway, I'm disgusted with myself.'

Karl thought of the photo of Genevieve. Maybe it was still on the floor of the cupboard, or maybe up on the shelf again. Either way, it was possible that she'd see it, which would be weird because she didn't know that he had taken a picture of her sleeping naked or that he'd kept it, or that it had been stolen. Besides which, he knew where the key was now so he could always check it out himself once Genevieve was teaching again. The most advantageous move here was for his wife to believe that he was honourable, and sensitive to her opinion. He turned the key clockwise, fake-sighed and handed it back to her. Genevieve nodded once and bounded up the stairs.

★ ★ ★

**KARL'S FATHER,** a retired Religious Studies teacher, had suffered a pulmonary embolism two years ago and walked with a frame. With help from Tara, Karl's eldest sister, he sold the family home and he moved to a chalet in a little cul-de-sac managed by a semi-private care firm. Frontier town, John called it. *Some day all this will be culs-de-sac.* Tara was pushing for round-the-clock care and maintained he showed the early signs of dementia, but she was a worrier. He seemed okay to Karl. When he put this to her she thought he was after money, which was only partly true. Divided between the four of us it would buy us each a used mid-range hatchback, she told him. Do you want one? You can have ours.

Tara had no idea about Karl's problems or The Transition and neither did his father. Why worry him? He had just sent him an email with Janna and Stu's address, and said they were living in a shared house.

John opened the door to his maisonette and said, *Oh,* when he saw Karl and Genevieve standing on the door-step, as if puzzled by sudden weather or an unusual wild animal on his tiny patch of lawn.

There was a framed print in John's kitchenette, a painting which depicted the vast grey side of a mountain, replete with little Day-glo coloured blobs: climbers. Karl stood staring at the print he remembered from childhood – he used to find it unsettling and couldn't remember why. Genevieve sat with his father, who took a noisy slurp of tea. He had been silent a while.

'John?' she said.

'Vishnu tells him to jump into the pool,' said Karl's father, 'and …'

He was silent for five seconds then he slammed his hand on the table, causing the tea to lap over the sides of the brightly coloured cups.

'You send a messenger,' he said. 'He gets lost so you send another one to find him, and then –' he shrugged – 'messenger party. What were we talking about?'

'The Bhagavad Gita,' said Genevieve. 'The story of Narada.'

'That's it. Narada jumps into the pool,' said Mr Temperley. 'When he comes out the other side he's … a princess, the daughter of a king. Years pass. He lives a long and tragic life. Marries for love. I don't … I don't … She marries and her husband dies horribly …'

'There's a disagreement which turns into a war between her husband and her father, the king,' said Genevieve.

'That's it.'

'Her son is killed in the war, along with her husband. She takes their bodies and she throws herself onto the funeral pyre with them and as she enters the flames …'

'She, or rather he, steps back out of the water. Narada.'

'And he's crying.'

'Of course he's crying.'

'And Vishnu, who's been waiting by the pool for only a matter of seconds while Narada's lived through a whole saga, says, who is this son you weep for? Something like that.'

'Who is this son for whom you weep?'

Karl pulled the lid off the biscuit tin and it clattered on the breakfast bar. He took out a malted milk biscuit, the familiar two-cow scene. It felt soft, so he put it back and closed the tin again. He could never concentrate when he was with his father. He felt like he was wearing earplugs.

'Vishnu tells him that what he just experienced, a whole lifetime as a princess, was only the very surface,' said John. 'The gods themselves don't know how deep it goes. And then I suppose Narada just walks away and has to get on with *his* life. Which must have felt sort of dull and sad at first.'

'Have you ever had a dream,' said Genevieve, 'that you missed when you woke up?'

'All the time,' said John. 'Karl?'

'I dream about the old house,' said Karl. 'Every night. Sometimes it's happy. Sometimes I'm being chased. Sometimes I'm looking for something and I feel like I wake up just as I'm about to find it.'

'You're looking for your childhood,' said John.

'Oh, he's still very childish,' said Genevieve and poured John another cup of tea from the patchwork teapot.


## 'BETTER?' SAID KARL.

They were in the dentist's waiting room sitting in front of a fish tank full of clownfish as brightly coloured as toy cars.

'No,' said Genevieve. 'I feel we've reduced ourselves somehow.'

'Nah,' said Karl.

Karl was up first. The dental hygienist was an intense little man with a long, monastic beard. Karl lay back in the chair, which tilted him and stretched his spine.

'Have you ever seen the backs of your teeth?' the hygienist asked him after a preliminary inspection.

'No.'

'I'm going to take a picture,' said the dental hygienist. 'I'll have it sent to your tablet. It looks like an ancient ruin back there. You look at it every day and you floss, do you hear me?'

'Uh-huh.'

'Do you want me to tell you about the role of oral bacteria in heart disease?'

During a period of protracted scraping, the dental hygienist told Karl a story. Or maybe it was a joke – Karl wasn't sure.

'Two dental hygienists go into a dental hygienist's,' he said. 'The first one says, *My dental hygienist told me I'm brushing too hard*. The second one says, *My dental hygienist says I need to floss more*. The dental hygienist says to them, *Why are you telling me this?* and they say to him, *Because we want a second opinion*. The dental hygienist calls his old mentor and says, *You have to help me*, and his mentor, a senior dental hygienist, says, *What?* And the dental hygienist says, *I have two dental hygienists in my office asking for a second opinion*. And his mentor says, *They need to floss more. They're brushing too hard.*'

Karl gargled and spat.

'I don't really know what to take from that,' said Karl.

'What you need to take from that,' said the dental hygienist, 'is that you're brushing too hard and you need to floss more.'

Lying in a white fluffy towel gown, Karl tried to read his *Telegraph*, but Genevieve was too animated. She kept putting down her *Teach Yourself Italian* and pacing around the little room.

'We've wasted most of the week,' she said. 'I mean, I know you have work, but we should really do something with our time together, don't you think?'

'Yes, of course,' said Karl. 'I can work harder next week.'

'There are so many things you can do for free,' said Genevieve. 'I haven't even been to the museum since they refitted it. And we should have lunch tomorrow. We can afford to have lunch, surely?'

'I have a £50 note under the mattress,' said Karl. 'For a rainy day.'

Genevieve jumped onto the bed on her knees, waded over to Karl and kissed him on the lips.

# 19

**KARL WATCHED HIS** wife smoke. It still felt odd, even after four years, calling her his wife. She screwed the cigarette butt into the lemon tree's fibreglass pot and lit another. He liked to watch her. There was a tremor in her hand as she brought the fresh cigarette to her lips. Her fingernails were painted gold. She only painted her nails when she was exercised about something; the pear-drop tang of wet nail varnish caught in his throat and made him brace himself for impact. The little bottle was still open on the black granite breakfast bar, next to a cup of instant coffee giving off steam like a stage-prop cauldron. It was a Chanel nail varnish called Gold Fiction. He screwed the brush and lid back on. Genevieve smoked as if it fuelled her. She looked over her shoulder and noticed him staring at her from the kitchen window. Her lips curled and she blew smoke towards the house. Even though it was too late to pretend he hadn't seen her notice him, Karl stepped behind the vast Smart Fridge, duck-egg blue like a Cadillac in a poster, and pretended he was putting something on the noticeboard. Then he stepped back into the middle of the kitchen and held up his hand: *hi* or *stop*. Genevieve mouthed something.

# 20

**THE VELUX BLIND** glowed like a cinema screen at the end of a film. Karl could hear the first sparse chirrups of the dawn chorus, along with what his wife maintained was someone crying in the attic next door. He rolled over and tried to put his arms around Genevieve, but she was stiff and tense. She was so still that he shoved her and she said, 'What?' in a voice disconcertingly alert.

'Turn around,' said Karl. Genevieve sighed and rolled over. Her mouth was slightly open and her eyes were dull, although her eyebrows were raised.

'How long have you been awake?'

'I don't know. A while.'

It was as if her pilot light had gone out.

'What's wrong?'

'Nothing's wrong.'

'I love you.'

'I love you too.'

'You sound wrong.'

'I don't know what you mean.'

'You look wrong.'

Genevieve rolled over again and edged away from him.

'Babe, what is it?' he said. 'Why won't you tell me?'

'I won't tell you,' said Genevieve, in a monotone, 'because there's nothing to tell. Stop digging.'

'This again,' said Karl. 'You're all over the place. Did you take your medication last night?'

'Oh God, Karl,' said Genevieve. 'Yes I did. I'm sorry I'm such a burden on you.'


**THE SECOND TIME** he ever met Genevieve she was smoking alone on a balcony outside a crowded hall party. The dress code was classic cinema, but Karl's household had just come as assistant directors and cameramen, which was how they dealt with every fancy-dress party. Genevieve was dressed as Gene Tierney in *Laura*. She told him that she loved smoking because it was self-destructive, and that the self-destructive part of people was sort of beautiful, she thought.

'Thanatos,' said nineteen-year-old Karl, who had just had a seminar on Freudian literary theory. 'The death drive.'

'Ah,' said Genevieve, narrowing her eyes. 'You're one of those men who likes to *tell* me things.'

'Oh no, I didn't mean it like that,' said Karl. 'I just wanted to sound knowledgeable.'

She drew on her cigarette. Karl took a bite of his burger and a lot of sauce fell out of it and over his bleached jeans.

'I put in too much sauce,' he said. 'I can never decide, so I just put in every sauce.'

'You're funny,' said Genevieve, coughing. 'I haven't met anyone funny since I've been here.'

'I'm the least funny person I know,' said Karl.

The email she sent him ten years later ended: *Something is wrong with me and nobody will look after me. This probably isn't even your email address any more. You probably don't even remember me. Oh well.* Karl's hands were shaking so badly that he had to retype every sentence at least twice. Of course he remembered her. He had thought of little else since he'd met her, he wrote.

**EVEN NOW HE FOUND** arranging a date a little too close to organised fun. Once he'd encouraged Genevieve to get out of the house, they tried to go to the museum, but it was closed on Thursdays.

'Where for lunch then?' said Karl. He hated the way he sounded when Genevieve was unhappy. The jolly pastor addressing his listless congregation.

'I don't know,' said Genevieve.

She was staring at a traffic light. When it changed to green she said, 'Where would you like to go?'

'This is for you,' said Karl. 'What do you want to eat?'

'I'm not really that hungry. Why is it for me?'

'It's your treat.'

'Why are you putting pressure on me?'

'Oh God, throw me a life ring, Genevieve,' said Karl.

'Ha.'

'I want you to have a good time, that's all.'

'You always want something from me. Why can't *you* have a good time?'

He sneered theatrically. 'You'd like that, wouldn't you?'

Genevieve didn't laugh.

'Shall we go to the new tapas place?'

'Whatever you want.'

'Or there's the gastropub, which we know is good.'

'Just. Make. A. Decision,' said Genevieve.

'Right,' said Karl. 'We're going to McDonald's.'

They took a window seat next to the children's section which had plastic toadstools for chairs. The rest of the restaurant appeared to have been refitted by somebody Scandinavian.

'They've really spruced this place up,' said Karl. 'Is that national? They're trying to look classy.'

'It's profoundly sad,' said Genevieve.

Karl slurped his strawberry milkshake and chucked a handful of fries into his mouth. On the pavement two pigeons tussled over half a seeded bun.

'Why are we here?'

'Because we're going to ride this out,' said Karl. 'I'm trying to create the most imperfect moment so you don't feel any pressure to be happy.' He took a large bite of his Big Mac and wiped his mouth on his sleeve. 'I'm not expecting it to work,' he continued. 'I mean, I'm not expecting it to make you happy. That would be self-defeating.'

A child was crying and Karl couldn't hear anyone trying to console it or do anything about it. He hated that.

'You're funny,' said his wife.

# 21

ON FRIDAY GENEVIEVE said that she needed to go for a walk by herself. Two hours later she came back wearing a floor-length wax jacket with a billowing hood. It smelled like a carpet showroom and looked several sizes too big for her. She kept it on, sat on the edge of their bed and kicked her legs. Karl looked up from his screen.

'What are you *wearing*?' he said.

'It's a coat. It rained. I was cold.'

'Where did you get it?'

'Charity shop. You don't like it?'

'You look like the widow of a farmer who killed himself because of his wife's coat,' said Karl. Genevieve didn't say anything, so he said, 'Sorry. I'm being a dick. I just … I love your taste in clothes. I love how you dress. And it doesn't look like something you'd normally choose. But you should wear whatever makes you happy.'

'Why do you love me?' said Genevieve.

'Genevieve.'

'Seriously. What are you doing with me?'

'The week I met you,' said Karl, 'I couldn't eat. After I met you, I couldn't think about anything else. The way you talked to people … You were like the first genuine person I'd ever met.'

'That's just silly,' said Genevieve. 'You fancied me.'

'I was enthralled. Still am.'

She furrowed her brow. 'I don't feel like there's anything *to* me.'

'It's the coat,' said Karl, sitting next to her and taking her hand. 'It's cursed.'

'I feel like …'

'What?'

'I … I don't want to say it.'

'What don't you want to say?'

'I …' She took a deep breath.

'You can tell me. It doesn't matter what it is.'

'No,' said Genevieve. 'It's best if some things stay thoughts. I don't really feel anything at all right now.'

'This'll pass,' said Karl. 'It doesn't feel like it, but it will.'

'And if it doesn't?'

'Well,' said Karl. 'I suppose we won't know if it's going to pass until it passes.'

In the afternoon Karl reviewed blackout curtains while Genevieve lay in bed playing the stock market and taking breaks to read her Italian guide. The coat was hanging over the cupboard door and Karl planned to secretly dispose of it the next time Genevieve was at work. She barely spoke other than to say thank you, in Italian, for two cups of tea at an interval of one and a half hours. Eventually she fell asleep.

Karl got a new assignment from Study Sherpas©: a third-year student on a literature and psychoanalysis module. Karl knew his departments and this one was notoriously batshit. In the past he'd done well taking books from his childhood out of context, so he decided to go with that again and typed:

Beatrix Potter's *The Tale of Two Bad Mice*: Baudrillard vs Deleuze's Simulacrum.

*The Tale of Two Bad Mice* concerned a mouse married couple, Tom Thumb and his wife Hunca Munca, infiltrating a doll's house and trying to eat the beautiful food laid out on the table. When the food turned out to be fake plaster models, the mice went on a rampage, smashing everything and trying to burn it in the doll's-house fire, which was also fake. He paused in his first paragraph to check a date.

Karl also had a message from a randomly generated account: 'Hello. You are receiving this message because you expressed an interest in our band. If you wish to stop receiving these updates please unsubscribe. What did you think of our demo tape? We are eager to generate user feedback. not_all_transition have released their first EP in two years: T. Piven's *The Trapeze*, described by the *NME* as "necessary".'

Karl remembered the name of the book from the website, so between jobs he decided to look up T. Piven's *The Trapeze*. He checked eBeW, but could find no record of the book's existence, let alone a full scan. He conducted an image search and found copies of the front cover, but they were oddly various. The first was a small, cheap and battered-looking hardback which appeared to have a spelling mistake: THE TRAPEEZE T. PIVEN in foil on one line. He swept past it. The second cover looked like a Penguin

Modern Classic from the seventies, a Giorgio de Chirico-style print of an isolated figure in the high window of a grey obelisk, dental-green border with sans-serif title and author at the top. The next looked like a children's book: a simple, winsome illustration of an acrobat in a harlequin outfit hanging by one foot from a trapeze in motion. *T. Piven's The Trapeze* was superimposed in cursive. The fourth was drawn in the photo-realist style of a pulp detective novel, angry capitals and an empty metal trapeze in a spotlight. Then Karl swiped forwards and yelped. The image was a photograph of a rabbit's head, skinless, red musculature and pink eyes protruding. He picked up the tablet again and swiped forward, but that was the last image.

T. Piven's *The Trapeze* is a notorious hoax in the occult book world. It was rumoured to have existed as an anonymous text alongside a popular exegesis of the Quadriga, the specific covine-type of the Crooked Path. There is no record of the text's existence, but numerous books have been written by forgers based on what little is known of the skeleton plot. It is said to be an account of obedience, control, of binding another to yourself, taking the metaphor of the trapeze artist as its central motif, and the unshakeable trust involved. A novel, a manual, an incantation, it takes the form of a *Bildungsroman* in which Bilyana, a young Bulgarian woman, is on the run from

The text ended there. Karl checked the source for the page and saw that there was a regular deletion, every fifteen minutes in fact, from a user named 'Tpivaen41'. Karl stayed on the page to see if he could catch any text before it was deleted, but got bored and went back to his Bad Mice essay.

Saturday passed in much the same way. Karl finished the third-year student's paper and concluded that the cradle, intentionally a fake for the doll's house, but reappropriated by the mice as an actual cradle for their baby mice to sleep in, was the only significant item the mice are able to carry over the threshold of fantasy/reality, likening it to an amulet in a fantasy story which keeps its power even after the user wakes up. He quoted some Žižek. Genevieve said several sentences in Italian and Karl said 'Wow.'

Everything, in fact, was fine until the evening meal.

Retrieving the salad tongs Genevieve had let fall from the bowl as she passed it, Janna said, 'Clumsy.'

Genevieve raised her eyebrows and said she was sorry.

'I was looking,' said Janna, 'for my passport earlier. I have to go to Germany overnight tomorrow. Have you seen it?'

'No,' said Genevieve.

'Someone keeps tidying things away,' said Janna.

'I had a housemate who did that,' said Genevieve. 'She'd gather up everyone's things in every room – wallets, important letters, essays, shoes, phones, car keys – and she'd shove them in a box or a drawer or something, and then she'd just literally *strew* her own stuff all over the house.'

Genevieve's expansive hand gesture sent her glass of red wine across the table where most of it splashed over Janna's expensive-looking cream off-the-shoulder jumper and the rest spilled over the end of the table into her lap.

'Oh God, I'm so sorry,' said Genevieve.

'It's all right,' said Stu, scraping his chair back. 'I'm getting towels.'

'I'm so sorry.'

'It doesn't matter.' Janna walked to the kitchen, pulling off her jumper. Karl stared at her back, the thin black straps of her bra. They heard her say, 'Don't do that,' to Stu.

Genevieve was sitting low in her chair, childlike.

'It was an accident,' said Karl, quietly, concerned at how annoyed Janna seemed to be. 'Don't worry.'

Janna came back into the dining room buttoning a black shirt. Stu followed with a dishcloth, mopped up the wine from the table and Janna's chair before they both sat down again.

'Where were we?' said Stu.

'Genevieve, darling, don't look so upset,' said Janna. 'It's a fucking jumper.'

'I'm just so sorry,' said Genevieve. 'I don't know what's wrong with me.'

Janna picked up her full glass of iced water and casually threw the contents at Genevieve's chest.

'Whoa,' said Stu.

'Well, now we're even,' said Janna.

Karl watched Genevieve's chest rise and fall as her expression of shock resolved into a smile.

'You bitch,' she said, beaming at Janna.

'Come on,' Janna took her hand. 'I've got a hundred outfits you'd look beautiful in.'

# 22

**WEEK THREE INVOLVED** a focus on relationships. Janna gave her standard speech about trying to get something positive out of the experience, even if they felt like resisting it, even if it felt demeaning. Dedicating your life to someone else was about as big a commitment as you could make in your mortal tenure and, like anything else, it was beneficial to … It's fine, they told her.

Karl was to spend evenings with Janna, and Genevieve with Stu. The moment this was announced, Stu took Genevieve out of the house, leaving Karl with a glass of vitamin juice and Janna, who had put on a pair of spectacles and produced a pen and paper and a digital recorder.

'What's this?' said Karl.

'Call it marriage counselling,' said Janna. 'I'm going to ask you a series of questions.'

'Right.'

'You've been faithful to each other?' Janna made eye contact with Karl and held her fountain pen to her lips.

'Yes.'

'You're certain?'

'I'm certain I have. I can't speak for Genevieve. I believe she has.'

'I have a feeling you wouldn't mind. If she hadn't.'

'What makes you say that?'

'I have a feeling you'd actually quite like it. Being cuckolded.'

'Stop.' Karl hit the pause button and Janna laughed.

'I'm sorry, I'm sorry. Oh, your face!'

'What? I'm smiling.'

'You look completely terrified! That was wrong of me. I'm incorrigible. I'm sorry. Do you want to stop?'

'No, no, of course not.'

'God, you're so obliging. It's a wonder you're not more successful.'

'You make a pretty odd marriage counsellor.'

'You're supposed to react like this. I'm supposed to provoke you, that's the purpose of the exercise. When a priest is going for ordination they pick his faith apart and he has to rebuild it. Same with how we see our relationships.'

'This is part of The Transition?'

'You have to face issues you've been burying. Your teeth, your marriage, everything. But you hit the stop button whenever I go too far – that's good.'

'I'm okay to carry on now.'

Janna pressed record again.

'She flirts. She really flirts. You're okay with that?'

'I don't see it that way. I don't see it as flirting.'

'You mean you don't mind?'

'There's nothing to mind. If you call it flirting I'm sure I do it too.'

'No you don't.'

'I don't?'

'Flirting would involve a modicum of guile. You're very transparent.'

'Am I?'

'Where do you draw the line?'

Janna leaned forward and kissed him on the lips, quickly but so softly that it felt pleasing and right, like joining two pieces of sky in a jigsaw puzzle.

'There?'

'Why did you …'

'Will you tell her I kissed you?'

Karl thought about it.

'No.'

'Because you liked it?'

'I think there are some things you don't need to tell someone.'

'So you'll keep it a secret.'

'I just won't tell her.'

'A sin of omission.'

'Oh, come on.'

'It was a tiny little kiss. You'd greet your mother that way.'

'Which is exactly why I won't tell her. It's insignificant.'

'When she asks what we did together.'

'Is Stu doing the same thing to her?'

'You'll have to ask Genevieve. Maybe she'll think it's insignificant too.'

'So what did you do with the chief?'

'We went to the cinema,' said Genevieve, dropping her shoulder bag in the corner of the bedroom.

'Oh. What did you see?'

'I don't even know what it was called. *Blunt Force Genital Trauma*, I think.' She unzipped her boots and kicked them off. 'There were scenes where the antagonist swung the protagonist around and around and then let go and he slammed into a wall and some of the brickwork fell down.'

'I don't really understand why he took you to the cinema.'

'He could see I was low. He said we'd go to the cinema and pretend we'd done the session. Which was sweet of him, I thought.'

'Hmm.'

'What did Janna do to you?'

'Some messed-up marriage counsellor role-play thing.'

'Ha *ha*! She said she'd do that.'

'She kissed me.'

'What?'

'I wasn't going to tell you.'

'That bitch,' said Genevieve. 'I'm going to seduce her husband.'

'You're funnier when you're depressed,' said Karl.

'How did she kiss you?'

'Sit still.'

Karl leaned in and kissed Genevieve sharply on the lips.

'Like that?' Genevieve had her eyes closed. She sounded almost disappointed.

'Mm.'

'Well, that's not so bad, I suppose,' she said.

'I think she only did it as a test — to see if I'd tell you,' said Karl.

'We'll pretend,' said Genevieve, 'that you didn't. Why don't you call her bluff? Encourage her. Act like you've fallen for her.'

**'THE THING ABOUT LYING,'** said Janna, the next evening, 'is that it's habit-forming. I used to lie to Stu a lot, even though I didn't need to. If I bought some shoes I'd tell him they were in the sale and I'd halve the price. He wasn't even asking me; I'd *volunteer* the information and I'd lie about it.'

'I do things like that all the time,' said Karl. He rubbed his hands together, one of which was doused in sandal-wood oil, and began working on Janna's back.

'*Full* of knots,' he said, as soon as he reached her neck. It was something you had to say. You say whisky is smooth, you say someone's back is full of knots.

'But then one day – don't hold back, Karl, I need it – one day I found the invoice for this lining he'd bought. It was for one of his silly cars – this black fur lining for the inside, all over it, the ceiling, the door trim, shaggy black hair, so it feels like you're driving around in some kind of cocoon. Disgusting. Guess how much the shitty fur lining was?'

'God, I don't know. A hundred?'

'Another zero. It looked like troll hair. You know his dream is to introduce Rat Look to the yachty crowd. Can you imagine? A Rat Look yacht? For all I know he's prob-ably got one docked somewhere. Why did you and Genevieve get married?'

'We … loved each other,' said Karl.

'But why marriage? I don't understand why anyone would get married nowadays. Is she religious?'

Karl worked his thumbs hard into Janna's shoulder blades.

'There's something to be said for making it really, really difficult to leave someone, isn't there?' he said.

'Higher up. That's romantic.'

'I love you so much that if, one day, I desperately want to leave you, I won't be able to do it without a humiliating legal battle,' said Karl. 'But yes, she is religious. She never talks about it.'

Janna was small and angular and it felt wrong using any kind of force. While they weren't so different in build there was something more robust about Genevieve's back – her spine was less visible. He took a course a year ago because she liked it so much and he wanted to make sure he didn't mess up her back by kneading and punching it without any education. It was an anniversary present.

'It just feels like such a throwback,' said Janna. 'Ooh, more of those, please.'

'Twists? I'm sorry if my generation let you down,' he said. 'I've been thinking about what you said, about using my time here. I'm going to look into coding.'

'Oh, Karl, that's brilliant,' said Janna. 'A little lower. There. Really try to hurt me. That's such good news – I mean it.'

'I told her you kissed me.'

'Ohhhh, there again. Again. What did she say?'

'She was fine with it.'

'Would she be fine with this?'

'A massage? Sure.'

126

Janna rolled over.

'And now?'

'So?'

'You first.'

'Tenpin bowling.'

'Bullshit.'

'For real,' said Genevieve. 'He massacred me, got like seven strikes. We had burgers. It was a sixties-themed place.'

'Wow.'

'It was fun.'

'It sounds like a date.'

'And you?'

'She was upset. Stressed.'

'Aw. Poor Janna.'

'She asked me if I ever got high. Stu has some really good weed.'

'And?'

'I offered to give her a massage.'

'Karl Temperley, you ladykiller.'

'Hmm. We took all the cushions off the leather sofas and she lay on them.'

'Well, I bet she loves you now. You too tired to do me?'

'What? No, of course not – I'll get the oil.'

'Nah,' said Genevieve. 'Actually I'm not in the mood. Let's just go to sleep.'

**HE DIDN'T TELL** Genevieve about Janna rolling over and that he had said now I think probably yes, yes she would have a problem. And he didn't tell her that Janna laughed and rolled onto her stomach again and said don't stop, I was teasing, it's not a big deal, right? It's nothing you couldn't see in the average museum or art gallery. He didn't tell her that he worked on Janna's back for another fifteen minutes and neither of them said anything. He didn't tell her that actually he was about to go through to the kitchen and wash his hands when Janna, still face down and naked to the waist, said, 'Karl?'

'Yes?'

'Can I ask you to do something weird?'

'What?'

'Write on me. On my back.'

Karl stood with his hands up and the oil slowly running down to his wrists. After a while he said, 'I don't have a pen.'

'There's one in my bag. There. Not the fountain pen. The biro. It has to be a biro.'

Karl didn't move.

'I know it's weird,' said Janna. 'It would help me relax.'

'I'm not judging,' Karl shrugged. He wiped his hands on his jeans and started rifling through Janna's handbag. Her BlackBerry, purse, packet of Polo mints, fountain pen. Biro. 'What do you want me to write?'

'Just ...' said Janna. 'Just start at my neck. Write whatever you like. Write a poem.'

Karl touched the nib of the biro very gently to the nape of Janna's neck and felt her tense.

*Dear Stu,*

He pressed lightly on Janna's back and had to go back to redo several letters.

'Just write normally,' said Janna, 'like you would on paper.'

*This is ridiculous.*

Karl pressed harder. Janna relaxed under the pen.

*Is this some kind of test? Of what? If you're swingers or something you can just come right out and say it.*

He wrote.

*If you're just trying to see if we'll stay faithful to one another I think that's more than a little unethical. Ultimately the exceptional contour of Janna's back and the pleasing feeling of skin under the pen nib cannot save this from being an awkward and unwelcome experience. Overall I give this part of The Transition one star out of five.*
    *Yrs,*
    *Karl*

'Okay?' said Karl. 'Janna?'
Janna was half asleep and murmured, 'Don't stop.'
'I'm out of back,' said Karl.

★   ★   ★

**HE DIDN'T TELL** Genevieve any of that, and yet after an hour with the lights out he could hear her making a strange sound in her sleep, a snuffling breath which he realised, when he put his hand on her back, was a gentle sobbing.

'Karl,' she said.

'What? Genevieve? What's wrong?'

'Don't. Don't turn the light on. Just hold me.'

'What is it? … Genevieve?'

'What if I hadn't always been faithful to you?'

'What do you mean?'

'What do you mean what do I mean? Just tell me.'

'Are you telling me you've slept with someone else?'

'What if something happened. Once. Or twice. When I was ill.'

'Oh,' said Karl. 'I wouldn't really think of that as you being unfaithful.'

'Because you don't believe it's really me, when I'm ill?'

'No.'

'You think I'm possessed by a demon?'

'No.'

'It's still me, Karl.'

'You don't even remember the conversations we have. It doesn't feel like you at all.'

'Okay.'

'Okay?'

'Yes.'

'Good,' said Karl, smiling. And he felt, as her shoulders relaxed against him and her breathing evened out into sleep, that it was very easy to be a good man.

# 23

**'OH WOW, £478,'** said Karl. 'You're doing really well.'

'There are still some undervalued companies in the Eurozone,' said Genevieve, and went back to her lesson plan.

'Guys?'

'Janna?' Genevieve looked up again.

'Guys?'

Karl rolled onto the floor and leaned over the entrance to the attic. Janna was hanging off the ladder, holding up a piece of ivory card. Her face was unnervingly close to his.

'Hi Janna.'

'We're having a party,' said Janna. 'We'd be really happy if you could both make it.'

'On a school night?'

'Has to be, I'm afraid. Stars are aligned.'

Karl took the invitation and Janna said, 'Good, then,' and vanished down the stairs.

*A Gathering*
*chez Janna and Stu*
*Sushi and Sashimi*

Genevieve whipped it out of his hands.

'Should we bring something?' she said. 'I mean *get* something? What's the etiquette? Oh my God, are we going to meet their friends?'

'You've cheered up,' he said.

Genevieve smiled.

'It's lifted,' she said.

'A little suddenly.'

Genevieve mouthed *fuck off*.

Karl gathered a few quotations for the Henry James thesis. He wondered if the theme of ellipsis might be best explored with an elliptical essay, maybe even one which excised commentary altogether in favour of a series of curated quotations. He checked the institution. No. Too cute. Then he got distracted by another well-paid A-level commission on Anti-War Sentiment in the Great War Poets, which he estimated would take him forty minutes and in fact took thirty.


After work Genevieve offered to help Janna prepare the sushi while Stu and Karl moved the furniture around. Janna said that's so sweet and touched Genevieve's face. Now they were eating some samples of temaki.

'This is really good,' said Karl. 'Are you formally trained?'

'It's a hobby,' said Janna. 'I worked in Japan for three years.'

'It was a holiday from me, really,' said Stu.

'That's more true than you know,' said Janna.

'So is this going to be other couples from The Transition?' said Genevieve. 'Other mentors?'

'Oh God, no,' said Janna. 'It's important to have some semblance of a life outside work. Just some friends.'

She sent Karl out to buy tonic water, which the Smart Fridge always forgot. At the front door she stopped him, gave him a £10 note and two little white pills.

'What's this?'

'Will you do it with me?' said Janna.

'What is it?'

'I can't function socially without it. It makes everyone seem a little warmer, that's all. I've done them a thousand times before – they're weak-as.'

'Weak ass?'

'Weak-as; as weak as …'

'As what?'

'It's a saying, dummy,' said Janna. 'Weak as fuck, I assume.'

'Or a kitten, maybe,' said Karl. '"Hard as", I've heard before. Hard as nails. As fuck.'

Janna held a pill up to the misty sun and popped it. 'I'd just feel better if I knew you were doing it too.'

'What about Stu?'

'He's not really into pills,' said Janna. 'Actually he thinks they make me really annoying. So don't mention it to him, okay?'

'Ha ha,' said Karl, tossing both pills into his mouth. 'Understood.' Janna patted him on the shoulder and, Karl couldn't be sure, either winked or twitched.


**THE HOUSE MADE SENSE** at night with the side lights low: you felt at home wherever you stood, as if it was your own private area. There must have been thirty guests, disorientatingly various – he had just squeezed past a giant old man with a green velvet bow tie talking to a young blonde woman with dreadlocks and a hula hoop, only to come face to face with a vaguely Eastern European-looking boy in a leather jacket.

'Sorry.'

'No matter.'

Karl wasn't sure if any of them knew about The Transition or who he and Genevieve were to Janna and Stu. He rather hoped not. The music was a quiet but obtrusive form of free jazz: chairs scraping, drum kits resolving into a beat then falling down the stairs, angry-goose saxophone. If Karl concentrated for too long he felt like it was undoing something in his head. Something he wanted to keep tied up. In the living room he needed to sit down, but there wasn't any space. He looked into the grey abstract and felt something at his side. A very young woman with long white hair was ladling punch into his crystal glass from a bowl on an occasional table.

'Thank you.'

He took a sip and detected the petroleum taste of rum, lime juice, triple sec, maybe. It was far too sweet.

'Did you make this? It's good.'

He looked at her. Her eyes were set far apart, which made her look even younger, but she couldn't have been more than a teenager and her hair clearly wasn't dyed – it had the uneven texture of real hair, like the long, kinked white hairs Karl used to pull out in the mirror until they became too numerous to do anything about. He remembered stories of people's hair turning white after some kind of trauma, but he wasn't sure if that really happened.

'I'm just decanting.'

'Well, thanks anyway. I'm Karl.'

'Samphire.'

'Like the seaweed?'

She smiled.

The woman next to Samphire grabbed her arm. She wore a similar dark lace dress, although her long hair was shiny and black. When she turned, Karl saw that she was old enough to be—

'Mum. You're drunk already?' said Samphire. Samphire's mother had her eyes half closed. 'This is Karl. He knows his seaweed. Karl, this is my mother, Lorna.'

'How do you know Janna and Stu?' said Karl.

'You have a good voice,' said Lorna. Hers was a little dry. She could even have been Samphire's grand-mother.

'Thank you.'

'You can tell a lot by timbre. You're … *concerned*. You're thoughtful. Careful. Too careful. Afraid to tell anyone who you are or what you think. You'd be a terrible liar.'

'Lorna,' said Samphire. 'Don't. The voice reading. It's creepy.' She turned to Karl. 'We've known them since for ever – Mum was Janna's violin teacher about a century ago.'

'I didn't know Janna played the violin,' said Karl.

'Ah,' said the old woman. 'Say her name again.'

'Janna.'

'You *like* her, don't you? But I expect you have crushes on a lot of women. A voice like yours falls in love almost instantly.'

135

'I don't know,' said Karl, smiling.

'You're an embarrassment,' said Samphire, and let go of her mother's hand – Karl realised she had been holding it up until now – and made a kind of rat-like face at her. Then she smiled in resignation at Karl. 'It was nice to meet you.' He watched her leave the room, her white hair down to her waist, and almost reached after her.

'Likewise.'

'There's a particularly interesting flaw,' said Lorna. 'In your voice, I mean. Everyone's got one. You're very angry. It's laid low. Almost out of my range. But, well, that's not exactly a revelation, is it? You're a man.'

'I'm sorry,' said Karl. 'I'm a little high. I don't see myself as angry.'

'Do you see yourself as a man? You should be especially watchful,' said Lorna. The music stopped and there was a pause as the track changed. 'The same life, looked back on, can be heaven or hell,' said Lorna, quietly, leaning towards him. She smelled of damp forest. 'The same memory can be heaven or hell.' A lilting, melodic piano started. 'I know I can trust you with my daughter, even after the way you stared at her just now.'

Karl felt a pulse in his head, as if it was putting up a force field.

'You don't act on very much, do you?' said Lorna. 'Your impulses – they might as well be dreams. That's a virtue.' She handed him a little pink card. 'Community Chest,' she said. 'It's her number.'

Karl tucked it into his pocket.

'I can tell she likes you, and I want her to talk to more men like you,' said Lorna.

'Angry men who don't tell anybody what they really think?' said Karl.

'Men who use their gross insecurity for good rather than evil,' said Lorna. 'Besides, she's seventeen. She's been talking about studying English at university – maybe you can put her off?'

'Did I mention I studied English?'

'No. Why?'

'You guessed. It's that obvious?'

'Everything you say is in quote marks,' said Lorna.

'Why did you name your daughter after a seaweed?'

'"Said Karl, irritably changing the subject". It may do you well to act on your misgivings once in a while,' said Lorna. 'Some thoughts belong in the attic, some belong in the basement.'

'What belongs in the basement?'

'You, perhaps,' said Lorna.

He hadn't seen Janna or Stu all night – they must have been circulating on a different rhythm. On the other side of the living room Genevieve was sitting on the floor next to a young vicar. His black tunic made him look High Church. Genevieve looked wonderful, he decided, wearing her long brown dress with one leg folded underneath her, leaning on the couch. How was it possible to look so natural? His breathing, as he looked at her, felt somewhere between pleasure and pain – like before you cry. Trying to feel that he was entitled to do so, he walked across the room and sat next to Genevieve.

'Check it out,' said Genevieve. 'Dude doesn't believe in the bodily resurrection of Christ.'

'Oh God, Genevieve, straight to big talk,' said Karl.

'It's fine,' said the vicar, smiling. 'Usually people just ask me if I'm in fancy dress.'

'Hmm, in a sense I suppose that's what I'm asking too,' muttered Genevieve.

'It's maybe just a matter of language,' said the vicar. 'What might sound sacrilegious to the laity is actually a necessity for any kind of theological discourse.'

'But you, yourself, you agree with whatshisname?'

'Grabes. Minor scholar. His point is that it really doesn't matter. That this is where symbolism and fact converge. The Church is the body.'

'What I don't understand,' she said, accepting a cigarette and letting him light it, 'is you believe in a telepathic Jew who was born to a virgin and can forgive your sins. Why not accept the whole caboodle?'

'You don't say "caboodle",' said Karl. 'Since when did you say "caboodle"?'

'If you believe in the quality of omniscience – if you can hold something like that in your head … I mean, presumably you believe in God, right?'

'Well, that's another question,' said the vicar.

'I think you're both in need of a drink,' said Karl.


The kitchen was crowded. The heavy, bearded man with the bow tie was playing bartender.

'You are?' said Karl.

'Gregory,' said Gregory. 'Where's the fucking gin gone?'

Behind a group of skinny men in lumberjack shirts who were playing some kind of ironic drinking game, Karl noticed Samphire and her mother by the oven. He realised

**138**

they were remonstrating with one another, hissing. Samphire glanced in his direction. When she noticed he'd noticed she smiled at him, and then they both looked away. His head ached. He picked up three glasses of neat vodka.

'Hey,' said Gregory. 'Those aren't done. Hey!'

When Karl got back to the living room the vicar was alone and swigging from a bottle of champagne.

'Here you go,' said Karl. 'Your health.'

They drank their vodka. The vicar coughed and then he drank Genevieve's too.

'Your wife,' he said to Karl. 'She's very lovely.'

'Where did she go?' said Karl.

'Sturdy fellow with a — what's the word? Spiked hair. Took her by the arm and steered her out of the room.'

'Stu,' said Karl. 'Wait a minute, you don't know Stu?'

'Stu?'

'You're a friend of Janna's?'

'Who's Janna?'

'This is their house,' said Karl.

'Oh, right,' said the vicar. 'Sorry, I thought it was yours. No, I'm just here with a friend. Henry?'

'I don't know him.'

'We were at Magdalen together. I'm not sure how he knows … Stu.'

'I'm going to look for Genevieve,' said Karl.

'Tell her hi from me,' said the vicar. 'Lovely girl.'

★   ★   ★

139

There were people sprawled on rugs under the cherry tree in the garden. Some of them were eating cherries – the tree was exceptionally fruitful. Karl picked one up off the ground and brushed off the dirt. He spat the stone at the house.

'Have you seen Stu? Or Janna?'

A couple, who were wearing matching cherry-red hot pants and lime-green vests, just giggled at him. The boy went back to stroking a black-and-white cat which kept rolling onto its back and trying to grab his hand.

'Easy,' he said to it.

'I'm looking for Janna or Stu,' said Karl.

'They're around,' said the girl. 'Relax. Grab a kitty. I'm Alice.'

'Alice Jonke?' said Karl. She was the woman from the woodland photo of not_all_transition.

'How do you know my name?'

'I'm a fan of your band.'

'What are you talking about?' said Alice.

'I recognised you,' said Karl. 'You were in not_all_transition. Sorry if I've got you confused with someone else.'

'Oh,' said Alice. 'Oh, I forgot that even happened. It was totally abandoned. Years ago.' She frowned at him. 'There's no band. It was just a photo shoot – a mock-up.'

'I found the site.'

'You're on The Transition?'

'Yeah,' said Karl. 'I'm living here.'

'It's great, right? I'm one of Stu and Janna's. What, five years ago now? Feels longer. I still love this house. Now I'm in PR.'

'Public's always going to need … relations, right?'

'Well, that's what we tell them,' said Alice. 'Plus I moonlight as an admissions officer for The Transition, but that's pretty much voluntary.'

'So you were in the band back when you were on the scheme?'

'There's no band,' said Alice. 'My boyfriend, well, he was my boyfriend then, he was trying to get a music photography business off the ground. We were pretending. Then Stu was like, oh, I can use these. I'm surprised it still exists. It was a … what's that term … A false-flag operation.'

'For what?' said Karl. 'What do you mean a false-flag operation?'

'You know,' said Alice. The cat hopped off her lap and went to investigate the back of the garden. 'Like a deliberate own goal. When your side plots against itself to frame its enemies.'

'The Transition's enemies?'

'There was some negative publicity at the time. A handful of disgruntled protégés. Maybe they had rubbish mentors, I don't know. Just conspiracy nonsense. They were making it out to be a secret society. Usual mixture of inferiority complex and good old-fashioned paranoia. But they were starting to get some media attention. So Stu had the idea that we could set up a fake resistance movement, make it just the right side of believable, then go public if necessary. God, how embarrassing it's still online. Tell Stu I'll kill him. Do you know where he is, actually?'

'No.'

'Well, it's nice to meet the new generation,' said Alice. She held out her hand and he helped her to her feet.

★ ★ ★

Upstairs he found Samphire sitting outside the bathroom with a glass of something greyish. She had put her long white hair in a ponytail which lay over her shoulder.

'I can't find Janna,' he said.

'Are you okay? You look really weird.'

Karl sat down next to her on the carpeted step.

'I'm sorry about Mum. She thinks the voice thing makes her interesting. I literally wanted to die.'

'You know ancient monks had this embroidered thing called a *paraman*?' he said. 'They wore it under their habit. One of the things on it is a big skull. To remind you of death. Although because of the embroidery pattern they looked sort of like an 8-bit computer game. Like Space Invaders or something. That's probably all it would remind me of. If you play computer games you say *I'm dead* all the time. But I think it actually makes you *less* aware of your own mortality.'

'O-kay,' said Samphire.

'Your hair,' said Karl. 'I think it's wonderful. It would be my *paraman*.' He sneezed, twice, and coated his hand with phlegm. 'Yuck. Sorry.'

'That's her, at the door,' said Samphire. 'Your Janna.'

Karl craned his neck around the banister and saw a woman dressed in a long, blue dress – it looked shiny under the halogens, with a dusty coating; it almost looked rubber. She walked down the hallway. In the second it took her to leave his view she looked up and didn't quite meet his gaze. She looked as if she'd been crying.

'Janna?'

He ran down the stairs, but the corridor contained two men in dinner jackets, wrestling. He thought he saw the door to the understairs cupboard move slightly, although it was closed and he couldn't be sure. He strode over the wrestlers.

'Janna?'

The understairs cupboard was locked.

'Did someone just go in there?' he asked them.

'That's a pin,' said the man on top.


**HE LAY IN BED** alone and half awake. It was 4 a.m., but the smell of cigarettes and the dogshit smell of hydroponic weed and the mixed voices still drifted up to the attic. People supposedly took drugs to escape, but Karl always found they had the opposite effect on him; he would obsess over grudges he thought he had forgiven and forgotten. He saw himself in a snow globe, standing in front of a plastic log cabin. He checked the window. It was a solid plastic log cabin. The ground was covered in phosphorescent pieces. Each one, he realised, was a well-worn memory, but when he tried to pick one up it disintegrated into filmy pieces. All he could do was wait for someone outside to shake the snow globe. Man is the plaything of his memory – who said that? He felt a lurching sensation. He remembered a night one year into their marriage. They had gone to visit his father for a long weekend. Some cooking, some wine, keep him company. Karl's sister was there too, taking some time off from the kids. It'll be fun, she assured them. We'll make it fun. You know how much Dad loves Genevieve.

In the event Genevieve talked rapidly and mostly about things and situations that held no relevance to her audience – friends she hadn't mentioned for years, people not even Karl knew, let alone his sister and father – and what started out as tedious but tolerable, after half a day and most of a night became as trying as a constant burglar alarm nobody was doing anything to shut down. Eventually, after preparing salmon and new potatoes against a constant monologue of secondary-school grievances, Karl's older sister had said, Genevieve, sweetie, could you give it a rest? And Genevieve, disturbingly brisk, had said yes, fine, of course; she was feeling a little tense, that was all, and sometimes that made her talk too much, but if Tara could just be *honest* with her when she was talking too much, if she could just *tell* Genevieve instead of insinuating things, that would be great and Genevieve would know she was talking too much. Yes, Karl's sister said, calm but testy, yes, and that's exactly what I'm doing. Is it? Genevieve had wondered aloud. Tara had laughed. Genevieve had said right and dropped the empty teacup she was holding so that it cracked on the tiles.

They left soon after that and Karl was scowling at the middle lane of the motorway, barely responding to Genevieve, when she said,

'I'm *very* disappointed in you.'

'What?' said Karl.

'You let that supercilious bitch say whatever she wants to me.'

'By supercilious bitch I assume you mean my sister,' said Karl.

'You don't like it when I swear, do you?' said Genevieve.

'God, Genevieve,' said Karl. 'I don't care.'

'I wonder,' said Genevieve, 'what it would be like to be married to someone who ever took my side on anything.'

Karl turned the windscreen wipers up from intermittent. *Don't fan the flames,* he said to himself. *You see yourself as a patient and compassionate person. You're not, but that's by the by. You see yourself that way, so try to behave like it.*

'I don't understand.'

'What do you mean you don't understand?'

'I mean I don't understand what you're saying to me or why you're saying it.'

'Oh,' said Genevieve, putting her left hand to her temple as if Karl had monumentally missed the point. 'You're picking on my *words.*'

'I'm not trying to pick on your words.'

'Everything is falling apart and you're picking on my words.'

'I'm sorry that you see it that way.'

'That's not an apology. You're sorry that I'm *wrong,* you mean.'

'I'm sorry that I'm coming across that way. It's not how I want to come across. Can we start again?'

'You see me as some kind of *text* to interpret.'

'Words are what we *talk* with!' said Karl.

'Don't shout at me.'

'I mean what else have we *got*? Jesus, Genevieve, you're like a forest of brambles.'

'Uh-huh, and you're the prince. Fuck you, Karl.'

'It's like somebody cross-bred brambles with a hydra.'

'What's a hydra, Karl? What's a fucking hydra?'

'What's a hydra? You *taught* me what a hydra was,' said Karl. 'I hadn't read *The Odyssey,* you were like, *You haven't read* The Odyssey*? What's wrong with you?* I mean, do you remember a single conversation we've ever had?'

'You really don't like it when I swear, do you? You swear at me all the time, but you don't like it when I do it back.'

'I'm sorry for swearing,' said Karl. Then he felt cross and said, 'Who *are* you? Where is Genevieve?'

'I'm sorry?' She sounded like a politician on the radio.

'Why are you talking to me like this?' said Karl. 'What have I done? I'm not on your side? *You* create these situations: *you*, and then you don't even have the grace to forgive the slights you imagine everyone gives you.'

'I can't believe this is happening to us,' said Genevieve. 'To *us*. I never thought we'd end up like … We're going for counselling. As soon as you've parked the car we're going for counselling.'

'Stop talking,' said Karl. 'Stop talking, stop talking, stop talking.'

'Everything you say it's like you're *hitting* me,' said Genevieve. 'You'd like to hit me, wouldn't you? That's what's underneath all this. Ooh, you're a nice boy, you'd never even countenance hitting a woman, but that's the most dangerous kind of a man: my mother told me that. Nasty, weak little … Do you remember once you raised your hand to me? Concentrate on the *road*!'

Karl swerved back into his lane.

'No,' said Karl. '*No*, I do *not* remember that, Genevieve, because it never fucking happened. You're gaslighting me.'

Genevieve screamed at him.

'You are so *awful* to me, Genevieve.'

'Pull over. Pull over pull over pull over.'

'I can't pull over: we're on the fucking *motorway*.'

A sign informed them that the next service station contained more amenities than the average shopping centre, and that it was seventeen miles away. They drove without speaking.

After five minutes Genevieve looked at him incredulously and said, 'Why are *you* crying?'

Karl shook his head and gripped the steering wheel.

'Do you want this to stop?' said Genevieve, after a while.

'Yes,' he said, softly, 'yes, I want it to stop.'

This was how it went. You felt you'd achieved some kind of catharsis, the point at which an argument should be over.

'I'm going to start telling my aunt about the things you say to me,' said Genevieve, tearfully. 'She never liked you.'

Karl parked wonkily in the bay. Genevieve was out of the car before he could pull the handbrake. He opened the door to yell, 'Where are you *going*?' and watched her disappear through the automatic door.

In the service station Karl leaned against the wall between the Noddy car and the 50p massage chair. A little girl climbed into the Noddy car and said, fix it, Mummy, fix it. Her mother sighed, and went through her bag for change. Karl smiled at her. Amidst the throng of families and couples heading to the coffee, chicken and pizza franchises a separate stream of women emerged from the toilets, exchanging wide-eyed glances. *For God's sake.* Karl swallowed a sudden absence of saliva and marched towards the Ladies, holding the door for a smart, white-haired woman who wore an expression of detached amusement, before walking through himself.

'I'm sorry,' he said, before the concerned murmurs began. 'I'm sorry.'

He could hear Genevieve weeping hysterically between bouts of deep breathing.

'She's with me. I'm really sorry.'

The toilets were so busy and the noise of constant flushing and the taps running and the banks of hand-dryers so dominant that it was impossible to explain himself to the occupants before they got replaced by the next wave: tutting, some laughter, ironic screams. Karl had to accept that as long as he was in the toilets he was to be treated with distrust and incredulity. Only one woman, younger than him, her hair dyed pink, who had washed her hands and dried them, stayed long enough to talk and Karl did his best to ignore her.

'What's going on?' she said.

Genevieve wailed from the cubicle.

'She's not well.'

'She doesn't sound sick,' said the woman. 'She sounds terrified.'

Karl knocked on the fourth grey stall door. Genevieve didn't react or break her keening.

'Genevieve, it's me, I'm sorry. Please come out.'

He knocked again. Then he kicked the door.

'What is he doing?' said someone who had just entered the room.

'Don't do that,' said the young woman with pink hair. 'Jesus.'

'What the actual fuck?'

Women gathered around him.

'I'm really sorry about this,' said Karl.

The door must have been half broken already because with the third kick the lock came loose and the door swung inwards. Genevieve was sitting on the lid of the toilet, using a paper sanitary disposal bag to breathe into. Even this irritated Karl. *Breathing into a paper bag. Like a cartoon character.* Genevieve took the bag away from her mouth and looked at him in disbelief.

'Leave me *alone!*' she shrieked.

'I think you need to get out,' the woman with pink hair said to him. She turned to Genevieve. 'Do you want me to call the police. Or security? I can call security.'

'This isn't what it looks like,' said Karl.

'I don't know what it looks like,' said the woman, 'but I think you should leave.'

She entered the cubicle and put her hand on Genevieve's shoulder.

'Fuck's sake,' said Karl.

'Please,' said Genevieve. 'Just get him out of here.'

'Oh, my God, baby,' said Karl. 'Why are you doing this? This is about nothing. It's literally about nothing.'

'*Please,*' said Genevieve, looking at the woman, who took Karl's arm and squeezed it hard.

'Come on.'

'I'll see you outside, then,' said Karl, aware that his voice sounded spiteful.

'Just *go,*' said Genevieve.


It took ten slow minutes for Genevieve to emerge, arm in arm with a tall, businesslike woman who had the air of having seen this before.

'This him?'

Genevieve nodded and sniffled.

'You're with her?'

'Yes,' said Karl and was about to try to explain something, *anything*, to the woman who had successfully extracted Genevieve from the cubicle, but before he could form a sentence she just said, 'All righty then,' and walked away. *All righty then.*

Karl tried to take Genevieve's hand but she snatched it away and walked with her hands behind her back.

'Can we just …' said Karl. But the moment they were through the automatic doors Genevieve bolted again.

'Genevieve!'

She ran across the car park, away from their car, past the Travelodge and towards the entrance to the motorway. It was sheeting with rain. Karl gave chase, but Genevieve seemed to have developed an extraordinary speed and his breathing soon became ragged. He could taste blood.

'Lord Jesus Christ,' said Karl, between breaths, 'Son of God, have mercy on me, a sinner. Lord Jesus Christ, Son of God, have mercy on me, a sinner.' As a teenager Karl was so obsessed with Salinger's *Franny and Zooey* he had sought out a copy of *The Way of a Pilgrim*, the book Franny is obsessed with in the novel. He found it a bit mawkish. 'Lord Jesus Christ, Son of God, have mercy on me, a sinner,' he said.

He chased Genevieve around the landscaped hillock where drivers let their dogs shit. She hadn't looked back once. She was heading towards the roundabout. He was still a little way behind her and before he rounded the corner he heard a screech of brakes and a long, incredulous blare. He ran, he spat rain, wiped rain out of his eyes. 'Lord Jesus Christ, Son of God, have mercy on me, a sinner.'

Genevieve was darting left and right in the hard shoulder as if she meant to cross six lanes of motorway.

'Genevieve!'

The memory of a hundred miserable PE lessons returned to him: being taught to play rugby in the suburban drizzle, gooseflesh and knee-length maroon socks, the excremental smell of the clay; a small, hairless child against boys who seemed, improbably, to have already gone through puberty. He sprinted from the exit ramp, flew at Genevieve, grabbed her around the waist and slammed his head into her arse: a perfect tackle into the scrubby earth past the cat's eyes. A 16-wheeler rumbled by. They rolled over, Genevieve on top of him, her head tucked into his neck. They hadn't even hugged one another in weeks and Karl realised, with dismay, that he had an erection. *What is* wrong *with you?* He hoped she couldn't tell. He could feel her body convulsing with sobs, which subsided against the background of furious traffic, rain-slick wheels, chanting engines. He was about to say something, but stopped. He put his hand in her soaked hair.

She was asleep.

'I love you,' he said.

Lying on his bed, Karl couldn't be sure if he'd really said *I love you* at the time or if he'd just picked her up and staggered back to the dented little Punto in silence. He loved her, he was sure of that, and he thought he was long over the silly incident in the service station. But sometimes it returned and made him so cross he would clear his throat with a kind of anguished growl, or, if he was alone, punch the wall. On those occasions it seemed that it had just happened, or that it was in the process of happening, or that it was bound to happen again, and that it was more exasperating than he could reasonably be expected to cope with.

# 24

**THE NEXT MORNING** Genevieve looked very pale and, after responding to a couple of questions with a low wince, she ran to the en suite to throw up. While she straightened her hair he blew his nose with a loud, gnu-like honk and asked if he could call in sick for her. She told him she was used to it.

'*Today we're going to be learning about volume!*' she said into the mirror, beaming like a children's TV presenter.

'As in sound or space?'

Genevieve didn't answer him. She was putting in her grandmother's amber earrings.

'Well, if you're sure,' said Karl. 'So what the hell happened last night? I haven't seen you since the vicar.'

'The what?'

'He said you left with Stu.'

'Oh God, his friend's a rum dealer or something. He had a suitcase full of rare and terrible rums. Guy's a rep for The Transition from Holland. He offered me a job. He was pissed, but he meant it. I said I was studying Italian and he said in that case he could get me a job in Italy. And I said, I'd have to check with my husband and he just looked at the floor and shook his head and went *boh, boh, boh, boh, boh.*'

'You could have called me.'

'You were flirting with a schoolgirl.'

'I was not.'

'I thought I'd leave you to it.'

'You barely spoke to me the whole night.'

'Sorry.'

'And Janna? Was she in on the rum tasting?'

'I don't think I saw Janna at all.'

'Me neither. I figured you were having a private party without me. Pax?'

Genevieve curled her little finger around his.

'Pax.'

'Were you in the basement?'

'Was I where?'

'Did they take you to the basement?'

'Oh yeah,' said Genevieve. 'There was an altar, which was actually just three big Cuban guys kneeling in a row, and they sacrificed me on it. We were in the garage, Karl.'

A crisp new *Guardian* and *Telegraph* lay at the mouth of the attic. Karl tucked them behind the wardrobe. He saw his wife out – she flinched when he went to kiss her goodbye and accepted a kiss on the cheek. Karl put his head in the living room expecting chaos but the place was immaculate, as if the party had never happened. Only several standing crates of sparkling clean glasses in the kitchen served as proof.

He felt like hot chocolate – something to line his stomach. Karl poured milk into Genevieve's bird-print mug and decanted it into a small pan. He noticed something, as the gas caught: tucked hastily between a bottle of olive oil and a tin of paprika he saw the laminated bible-thick volume of *The Transition: Mentor's Edition*. He opened it up in the middle. A block of prose, numbered 178:

The writer is on her deathbed. Her best friend since childhood is at her side. They used to jump into the lake together, holding hands. She asks her, her voice failing, she asks her, Do you have all of my writings? All of them, says her friend. Do you have all of the poems? she asks. Yes, says her friend. We have all of your poems. Do you have all of the short stories and essays? she asks. Yes, we have all of your short stories and essays. We have them tied in bundles in two tea chests. And the works in progress? she asks. Yes. We have all the works in progress and your letters and your journals, says her friend. Burn it, she says. Burn it all. You don't mean that, her friend says. And the writer grabs her by the wrist, using every ounce of energy she has left, digging her nails between the tendons so that her friend cries out and looks right into her eyes, which are wide and crazy, like she's horrified by what she's looking at, and she says, her last words, she says, Burn it all. After the funeral her friend drags the two tea chests down to the furnace one by one. She places the first bundle – a sequence of poems and drafts about Leda and the Swan – in the grate and it catches fire. She nudges it with the poker, but it smoulders and barely moves. There's a lot of smoke. She coughs. She looks at the two tea chests. She realises this is going to take a while.

Karl listened to the usually inaudible station clock snicker through a few seconds. The milk was beginning to steam. He scattered a spoonful of drinking chocolate into the pan and watched it film out onto the too cool surface. He turned to another page. Another block of prose, numbered 293:

It was my fiftieth birthday and I drank a bottle of beer with the chancellor. He had two bottles of beer in his desk. Warm, but it tasted heavenly. I commented on this and he reminded me that it was the first thing to pass my lips in forty-eight hours. We were that focused. Your body is so grateful, he said, it's giving you a gift in return.

I took the Bentley back to the suburbs.

At home I found my six-year-old son holding a funeral for his favourite teddy bear. He was weeping and would not be comforted. The little bear was lying, face up, on a cardboard altar. My son had placed a strip of towelling over his eyes.

'What are you talking about?' my wife said, and her voice suggested that she was approaching the end of her tether. 'He isn't dead. Mr Waffles isn't dead.'

My son was inconsolable. He died, he insisted. Mr Waffles got ill and died.

'This isn't right,' I said. 'Why do you think Mr Waffles is dead?'

Just look at him, my son maintained.

We buried the bear.

He turned to the last page – it seemed like a good place to check. He didn't know how long it would be before Janna or Stu came into the kitchen, and he had a talismanic obsession with final pages. At school he would near a book's conclusion, whether it was pulp science fiction or *The Return of the Native* with one hand firmly clamped over the ultimate paragraph, in case his eye lit on a single word which might rob the entire story of its point, spoil the answer to the riddle of why he was reading it. When he shared this with Genevieve she admitted to him that she always started a book by reading its final page, that she still did, but wasn't sure why. He flipped through the back pages and found a table of small-print figures and percentage charts, adjacent to an advert for a property developer called Tern and Doughty: Creating a New World One Street at a Time.

Karl flicked through the *Mentor's Edition*. As far as he could tell it was nothing but inscrutable prose poems, numbered 0 to 400. He opened an early one. 11:

The Popular Teacher. As with addiction programmes, you must presuppose a level of cynicism. Your protégés will feel superior to the programme, will resent most direct advice. The truth of the matter is that they blame anyone but themselves for their shortcomings and they are not ready for the humility of self-knowledge. Working with this attitude is a delicate business, and they must feel that you are on their side, working the programme even though you all know it to be foolish. As well as the authority, you must be the jester who makes the hypocrisy and capriciousness of courtly life palatable; the popular teacher who mocks the education system but gets everyone straight As in their exams. Stress the end results, ridicule the means, insisting on them with a world-weary …

Eleven was an odd number, just like the others, but it was also a prime number. Karl knew the prime numbers up to a hundred from a foundation course in mathematics he had taken when he first had aspirations to learn to code. He flicked through to 67:

The Salvage Yard. It may well be that one of your protégés outshines the other from the outset, and it is always worth bearing in mind that the vast majority of couples have come to you through the malpractice of one, not both. You will have to use your judgement here; assess the relationship with a clear eye. Is it toxic? Are there elements of Epistemological Abuse? Test, gently at first, their commitment to one another. In extreme cases …

'Karl?' Janna's voice from the hallway. He hadn't heard the door. He held his breath and pushed *The Transition: Mentor's Edition* back towards the spice rack. His breath still held, he sprinkled more drinking chocolate into the milk, which was starting to simmer.

'Hi, Janna.'

'I wanted to apologise.'

'You? For what?'

'For the party. For leaving you alone like that.'

'It's nothing. I had fun,' said Karl. 'You have some fun friends.'

'I had a bit of a turn. The pills. I hope you were okay.'

'I was fine.'

'I haven't told Stu,' she said. 'About the massage or the writing or anything.'

'I hadn't thought about it. Are you okay? You sound ...'

'Are you scared of him?'

'He hasn't given me any reason to be.'

'But you're relieved I'm not going to tell him?'

'I suppose I must be a bit scared of him,' said Karl.

'It's important to me,' said Janna, 'that you like me.'

'Of course I like you.'

She hugged him. He put his hands on the small of her back and they stood that way until Karl smelled the milk burning.

# 25

**THE NEXT MORNING** buzzed with Stu's weed strimmer before Genevieve's alarm went off. Karl had to meet his accountant at lunchtime and offered to walk her to work, even though the extra hours in bed after Genevieve left at seven were among his profoundest sensory pleasures.

'Well, aren't you sweet?' she said. 'Are you going to wear your weddings and funerals suit?'

'It's just Keston,' said Karl, pulling a twenty-year-old Pavement T-shirt over his head. 'I don't need to impress him.'

'But you're going to his office.'

'It's Keston.'

Genevieve often said that Keston was an idiot, but she said it as if she was talking about a lovable older brother of whom she ultimately approved.

'Do you remember,' she said, as they left Janna and Stu's road, 'when we had pasta at his flat that time and there was a number on his wooden spoon?'

'No. What number?'

'Twelve. He asked me to stir the sauce and there was a number drawn on the spoon in felt tip.'

'Why do you remember this? What does that mean?'

'Oh, Karl,' said Genevieve, barging him with her hip so that he stepped off the pavement. 'Master's in Metaphysical Poetry and he has all the observational prowess of a syllabub. It means he swiped his wooden spoon from a pub – a table marker. He's a man who won't spend ninety-nine pence on a kitchen utensil if he doesn't have to. That's the kind of person you want as your accountant.'

He said goodbye to Genevieve by the postbox before St Matthew's Primary and took out his tablet. He entered the postcode for Tern and Doughty as he remembered it from the advert in the back of the manual, but the map didn't recognise it. Did he mean an alternative postcode with an L instead of a Y? He supposed so. It was 6.4 miles away. Karl followed his map, holding his tablet before him, a pulsing blue dot on a grid which resolved into a real-time film of the road he was walking along. He could press a button to discover his personal relationship with the road (*he had walked down this road zero times before*) and another to overlay the film with recreations of the same street in its past incarnations. In the centre of town the tablet took him through a cut-away called Abattoir Lane, abutted by tall redbrick halls. He passed an expensive patisserie and a hand-made greeting-card shop. The road had sloped stone gutters on either side to collect blood. How we used to do everything in plain sight. He held the tablet in front of his face and witnessed a busy scene of vintage trucks loaded with the bleating and the lowing. He imagined a tablet that could also recreate the cries of agony and the stench of effluence, our reasons for outsourcing clearly more than sanitary and economic.

At one point he got stuck on an overpass near the train station which narrowed to a point, the railings meeting in a V hanging high above the library. It took him ten minutes to find the steps to the road below. He stopped for a sausage roll, which managed to be both clammy and dry and altogether so unappetising that he threw it away and stopped somewhere else for a different sausage roll, which was passable. He walked down a road of pet shops, guitar shops and bookies and then crossed a main road and a bridge by several blocks of flats. Then his pulsing blue dot was on top of the static red dot and the tablet said, 'You have reached your destination.' He looked up. There was a long-abandoned pub with nicotine-coloured ceramic tiles and muddy green windows, many staved in, some boarded up. Next to the closed pub the city petered out into a flat grey dust bowl, the foundations of former factories and warehouses beneath the entrance to the motorway. It felt like a fitting location for a civil war, but for the vast, ugly wild flowers, sprouting from the cracks, taller than him and top-heavy, swaying obscenely in the breeze like they belonged there and he didn't – the place hadn't been disturbed in a long time. Short of the slip road he saw a familiar light blue sign with a white outline of a house and the legend, *Tern and Doughty: Everyone Deserves a Home*.

The tarmac road, which started and finished abruptly and was yet to connect to the main drag, was shiny and black as a new laptop. A track of dusty boot prints had adhered to its surface, and Karl almost felt like polishing them off with the bottom of his T-shirt. The estate was made up of a corral of twenty small white houses. The windows were covered in a blue plastic film, some half-peeled. The buildings looked incongruously bright and clean and Lego-like in the scrubby landscape, as if they had been constructed by a giant child. They were detached, but very close together – almost touching. Karl went to the nearest, number 4. He peered through one of the half-peeled windows. The house was still a shell – no interior walls, thick hanging wires and tubes on the inside. They made Karl think of Le Corbusier's Futuristic houses – machines for living in, as small and efficient as possible. They really weren't any bigger than the converted conservatory he had rented with Genevieve for three years.

'Bastards,' he said out loud.

Karl's tablet ran out of charge while he was taking a picture of the Tern and Doughty estate. It was the first time the tablet's battery had gone flat – an impressive feature. It died just as number 4 was coming into focus and before he could press to take the photo. Never mind. It wasn't like he was an investigative journalist. He put the dead tablet in his inside pocket. Without his map he got lost trying to find his way back to the centre of the city. He had to hail a taxi from outside one of the tower blocks. It dropped him by the reassuringly old-fashioned frontage of Keston's company's office. Edson Hinks. Bevelled glass and racing-green joists.

He had shared a room with Keston in their first year of university. He called him as soon as the Inland Revenue let him know he was being investigated, and although it was the first time they'd spoken in five years, Keston was as familiar as if they were trying to pool enough loose change for eight cans of beer. He said that they would sort him out. Keston had lost most of his hair in what he described as a tragic hair-losing accident.

There was nobody at reception, but his office door was open and Karl could see him flipping through a green loose-leaf binder.

'Hey Brosecco,' said Keston, without looking up. 'Getting any?'

'Brosecco?'

'I'm trying it out.' He put the folder down. 'Urban slang meets mid-range sparkling wine.'

Keston was wearing a tight–fitting grey suit. His tie was like a thin strip of high–end gift wrap. Karl sat down opposite the dark wooden desk and put his left foot up on his right knee, then he frowned. It was a little office with smart blue wallpaper and mahogany trimmings. It smelled like cigars, but the speakers of Edson's PC were playing something by the Lightning Seeds – the same album Keston played over and over again while he was revising for his accountancy exams or writing assignments when they shared a room.

'Such a terrible band,' Karl said. 'Actually, seeing as you asked, Genevieve and I haven't had sex since I was charged with tax fraud.'

'Whoa,' said Keston. 'Really didn't need to share that. What, as, like, punishment?'

'I don't think so,' said Karl. 'Not consciously, anyway.'

'That's a long time, Little Bro Peep.'

'It is a long time, isn't it?' said Karl.

'Kind of thing can trigger an early midlife crisis,' said Keston. 'You want?' He put down two tumblers and poured a measure of whisky into both.

'No thanks,' said Karl.

'Oh, go on,' said Keston, nudging the glass towards Karl. 'Still, you're a lucky boy, aren't you? I remember you pining after her the whole three years. Moping around the library. Reading your wrist-cutting poetry. But you *did* it, didn't you? You finally got in her pants. Do you know how many people actually get what they want?'

'One in … four?'

'That's cancer. Now, this won't take long. Couple of forms to sign – just moving some fictional money around. Good news is you're out of the shitstorm you were in last time I saw you. There's an issue with your wife's PAYE, but I'm trying to get to the bottom of that. This is still unknown territory.'

'Hang on,' said Karl. 'Hell's wrong with Genevieve's PAYE?'

Keston rifled through a green sugar-paper file. 'Your net salaries are being paid straight into a holding pen and, at the end of the programme, you retain forty-six per cent of it plus interest, which becomes your deposit on your dream home.'

'About that dream home,' said Karl.

'Only there's a complication because between the arrears, the instalments on the fine, your tax return from last year and the consolidated debt from your entire adult life so far, someone's got their wires crossed. I thought it would be easier this way, but it isn't. It's not your problem, it's mine. Like I said, unknown territory.'

'About the dream home.'

'Yes?'

'I want to know what my options are.'

'You move in when you get to the end of The Transition. The Transition is a good product, Karl.'

'What if I ... What if Genevieve and I don't want to? What if we don't like the house or the area or whatever?'

'Well, I'm told that the move is an integral part of the process. I'm also told your dream home will be built to the highest spec available at the price in a desirable up-and-coming area.'

'What if we want to back out of the process?'

'That means it might get a Waitrose one day. I'm sorry,' said Keston. 'I'm up to my elbows in mud and raw sewage digging your escape tunnel with a spoon and I *think* I just heard a little voice behind me saying he wants to shuffle all the way back into his prison cell.'

'Hypothetically.'

'Karl,' said Keston, 'K-Temp, you don't ... I'm not even going to look up the terms and conditions. There's no way out of this at all. Any of it. It's a broadhead contract.'

'What's a broadhead contract?'

'You know those arrows which are designed to cause more damage when you pull them out than they did going in?'

'Eww.'

'Yeah. Like a cat's dick. So unless you want to go to prison.' Keston shrugged. 'Actually I'm not even sure if that's an option any more. It's this or the chair. You don't like the house, you can sell it.'

'Seriously, Keston, nobody would want it. It's on the side of a motorway.'

'Is this why you asked me to look into your mentors' last protégés? They're all doing fine. You'll be on the property ladder, is the point. And how would you have any idea about the house? It's five months until you get the keys.'

'I heard about the contractor. I paid a visit to one of the sites.'

'Then you'll have seen families picnicking, children chasing balls into fields – your children, they could be.'

'It's still under construction,' said Karl. 'It looks like a doll-size Bauhaus penal colony.'

'They've had a variety of contractors in the last few years … Not everyone moves into new builds. Some take jobs with The Transition itself. Some even become mentors.'

'Keston, are you involved in The Transition?'

'What?'

'You wouldn't lie to me, to my face, if I asked you a direct question, would you?'

'I don't know,' said Keston. 'Ask me something directly.'

Karl took a tiny sip of his whisky. He didn't like whisky. He made eye contact with Keston, who tilted his head to one side.

'How do you even know about The Transition? Do you work for them?'

Keston pursed his lips and rocked back on his chair.

'Okay, you merciless son of a bitch,' he said. 'I don't work for The Transition. I get a small commission for everyone I successfully nominate for the scheme. Happy?'

'I'm glad to oblige. Do you recommend broadband providers too?'

'Gah,' said Keston. 'They told me in accountant school: never take on one of your friends.'

'I'm not angry,' said Karl.

'I wouldn't do it if I didn't believe in it. It gets results, K-bee. Five months from now you'll be living in your own home, even if it's a little on the modest side, and you'll be doing something you care about. I've seen twelve people in your position go through it in the last five years.'

'I got a warning. Someone told me to get out of the scheme.'

'A warning from whom?'

'A website.'

'A website. Careful, K-Pax,' said Keston. 'You'll unravel the whole establishment.'

'It was fairly damning.'

'If you want my advice,' said Keston, 'don't get involved with any conspiracy nuts or Stalinists or anyone who wants to bring down Western civilisation. I love Western civilisation. It's brilliant.'

'A few weeks ago Stu said there was a couple on the run he had to deal with. Why do people run away if it's such a good scheme?'

Keston blew a raspberry. 'Do you want me to look into that for you?' he said. 'I can find out who they are and what the deal is. Would that make you feel better?'

'Maybe.'

'Fine,' said Keston. 'I'll let you know. Now get back to your loveless marriage.'

# 26

**WHEN KARL GOT IN** he could hear a creaking, pummelling sound coming from the first floor. He didn't call. He took off his coat very quietly. From the staircase he could tell that it was coming from Janna and Stu's bedroom and he paused by their door before climbing the ladder up to his quarters. Their bedroom door was old and still had a keyhole from the era when everyone had locks everywhere. The thudding and creaking had an irregular rhythm, sometimes resolving into a rapid drumming whose pattern soon changed. Karl held his breath, got down on his knees, closed one eye and pressed his cheek to the cold metal of the lock mechanism. His vision was bordered black, but he could see clean across the bedroom to the trapeze, which was winched a little higher than when Genevieve had swung on it.

Janna was dressed in a blue two-piece Lycra running outfit. She sat on the trapeze with both legs dangling from one side of the bar, leaning against the rope like someone lying in a hammock in an American novel. Then she flipped downwards as suddenly as an illustration in a pop-up book and hung from one leg, her hands together pointing to the floor. She worked up a swing and grabbed the bar with both hands, spun fully around twice and brought herself down so that she was supported on the bar by her stomach, as if swimming in mid-air, then she jumped, wrapped one leg around both ropes, twisted as if unravelling and landed on her feet facing away from him.

Karl almost burst into applause. He was shaking. Any transgression, he had noticed, gave him a pronounced tremor. Then Janna peeled off her top and rolled down her leggings and stretched. Karl stared at her through the keyhole, and told himself that now would be a good time to move quickly and quietly down the stairs, but he didn't. He watched her tie a pink towel under her shoulders.

'You can come in if you like,' she said, as if to no one in particular.

Karl stopped breathing momentarily.

'Honestly,' she said, untying her hair. 'I don't mind. I think it's sweet.'

Karl stood up, his face burning. He turned the door-knob with a noisy click, pulled the door open, but didn't enter the room.

'Look at you,' said Janna, smiling. 'Don't be so embarrassed.'

'I'm …' Karl felt like a little boy. 'I'm really sorry for spying on you.'

'You were just curious,' said Janna. She tightened the towel under her shoulders. 'It's a trapeze.'

'I know,' said Karl. 'I thought it only swung back and forth.'

'It's Intelligent Cable,' said Janna. 'Can be hard as a crow-bar or bendy as a bit of string. You just twist the end. Developed –' she grinned – 'by one of The Transition's protégés. Do you want a go?'

'Oh, no thanks,' said Karl. 'I think I'd need to be in better shape.'

'Well, you'll get there,' said Janna. 'I'm going to have a shower. I'm afraid there's no keyhole in the bathroom.'

'I don't … do that,' said Karl.

'You don't need to hide who you are. Or what you are,' said Janna. She touched him on the arm.

'It's not what I am.'

'You think I'm going to judge you?'

'I would,' said Karl. 'It's a disgusting thing to do.'

'You look like you're going to cry. Honestly, Karl, you're fretting. You had some formative sexual experience you probably don't even remember and it's given you a minor predilection which, if I can help you satisfy, then I'm glad. We all have our tastes.' Karl felt dizzy and sat on the corner of her bed. 'I think I'm starting to understand you,' said Janna, sitting next to him. 'I think you feel ashamed all the time. I think you go around in a … cloud of shame.'

He heard the front door and jumped from the bed.

'I have to get upstairs,' he said. His voice sounded strange to him, as if it was someone else choosing the words and he only had to voice them. 'I have to …'

Janna was smiling at him sadly as he crossed the room.

'You don't need to be afraid,' she said.


It was Karl's night to cook. He began hollowing out the peppers.

Genevieve cleared the table and Janna read a parable from the *Mentor's Edition*.

'"The princess was famous for her melancholy – and the king had pledged her hand in marriage to the first man who could make her smile, thus had a competition begun among the" – so on and so forth,' she said, turning the page. '"Bring me a wave from the ocean,' said the princess. So the suitor gathered a team of thirty soldiers and had the blacksmith forge a pewter trough two miles long. He marched the soldiers down to the shore and bid them lower the trough when a suitably ferocious wave broke. Once the wave was caught, the suitor marched his men back to the palatial arboretum and summoned the princess – who arrived in time to see the contingent of soldiers pour several hundred gallons of seawater over her marble floor. 'A wave from the ocean!' announced the suitor. But in spite of encouragement, the wave remained quite still. 'You see yourself,' said the princess, 'that this is not a wave at all. It is a puddle.'"'

'Who wants brandy?' said Stu.

'Meee!' said Genevieve.

'It's not Saturday,' said Karl. 'What's with all the booze?'

Stu fetched oversized glasses and poured a generous measure for everyone. Karl took a sip. It tasted slightly less like soap than Keston's whisky.

'What?' he said. 'Is it my birthday and I've forgotten?'

They were all looking at him, smiling.

'What's going on?' said Karl, inching up the sofa as if ready to make a run for it.

'I have an announcement to make,' said Genevieve.

She was wearing the Gold Fiction nail varnish. Karl thought he could feel his heart beating at the base of his tongue.

'Yes?'

'I've handed in my notice,' said Genevieve. 'I'm leaving in a month, at the end of the Spring term. I'm joining the Transition head office – it's just an entry-level position in Marketing, but the pay's better than … and they need someone who can give presentations and …'

'And she's very presentable,' said Janna.

Karl swallowed and found that his mouth was too dry.

'Is this true?' he said.

Genevieve laughed.

'"Is this true?"' she said. 'Yes, baby. I want to try it. I've not been happy with teaching for years, you know that.'

'I didn't … know that,' said Karl.

'We should let you two talk,' said Janna. 'Come on, Stu.'

'It's a brave decision,' Stu called back over his shoulder as Janna ushered him through the door.

'Genevieve, what the hell are you doing?'

'I did what you said,' said Genevieve. 'I thought about it and I thought: Yes.'

'Since when have you been unhappy with your job?'

'Do you have any idea how miserable I feel every Sunday? Or like the whole last week of a holiday? I can't enjoy a single day, a single hour, because I'm dreading it starting again.'

'That's why they pay you.'

'I handed in my notice and it was like a pain I didn't even realise I had, just –' she spread her fingers – 'Paf. I don't even need to work out my notice; The Transition pays them off and brings in a temp. It's like changing a phone contract.'

'You love working with children.'

'Have I ever said I love working with children?'

Karl looked at his shoes. The twilight of the living room meant that the glow-in-the-dark stripe had started to intensify. He got up and turned on the standard lamp.

'I thought you said you did,' he said quietly.

'I don't *dislike* children,' said Genevieve. 'Karl, this is a shock for you, isn't it? You're more shocked by it than I thought you'd be. I'm sorry for announcing it like that.'

'It's not that.'

'It isn't such a big deal. It's a new job. Doesn't change anything.'

'Are you really sure this is sensible?' said Karl. 'I mean, really? You seem kind of wired.'

'Don't start on me. I'm excited, that's all. I'm happy.' She scowled at the floor.

'I didn't mean to assume … Look, this is fine,' said Karl. 'I'm shocked, but I'm kind of impressed too. You took something in your life you weren't happy with and you changed it. Very few people …'

She leapt to her feet and put her arms around him.

'I love you.' She rested her head on his shoulder. 'You don't think I'm crazy?'

He held her tight.

'Karl?' Her voice was muffled.

'Yes?'

'Are you making a frightened face over my shoulder like they do on TV?'

'No,' he said.

'Are you sure?'

'I'm smiling beatifically.'

# 27

'ALL RIGHT, KARL?' said Stu. 'Can't sleep?' His Mohican was still up, but wilting slightly in the steam of the kettle.

'It doesn't take much,' said Karl.

'I'm making some valerian tea,' said Stu. 'Want some?'

'Nothing works,' said Karl. 'When I was a student we studied feminist literary theory and I didn't sleep for a week because I was worried I might be a misogynist.' He picked himself up and shuffled onto the breakfast bar, the black granite cold through his pyjamas.

'*Are* you a misogynist?' said Stu.

'I don't think so,' said Karl. 'But for a whole week I just lay there at night thinking *what if I am and I don't even know it?*'

'Well, if you're that worried about it …' said Stu.

'I'm not any more,' said Karl. 'But I don't think worrying about it proves anything.'

'You're right there,' said Stu. 'Worrying doesn't solve anything.'

'That's not … I'm concerned about Genevieve,' said Karl. 'Sometimes she makes big, drastic decisions when she's feeling a certain way, then regrets them when it passes.'

'She's a woman,' said Stu.

'That's not it,' said Karl.

'There's a danger, isn't there,' said Stu, 'that once some-one has a certain label you just ascribe all of their faults and qualities to that one label?'

'Well,' said Karl, 'hypothetically, I suppose, yes.'

'*He reacted that way because he's depressed, she did that because she's diabetic.*'

'Yeah,' said Karl. 'That's not what I'm doing.'

'Sometimes I think men are rather afraid of women,' said Stu. 'Maybe it's not that you're a misogynist, maybe you just fear the passion, the spontaneity, the strength, if you like, of women.'

'I don't really worry that I'm a misogynist any more,' said Karl.

'What I think,' said Stu, 'and by all means tell me to piss off, but what I think is you need to let go a little. You're so watchful. It's like you try to edit what she says. Maybe this *is* a mistake, but you need to let Genevieve find that out for herself.'


**SITTING UP UNCOMFORTABLY** against the headboard, Karl took a sip of his tea, but it tasted like a wicker chair. He watched Genevieve sleep. Then he turned on the televi-sion. Classic Cinema had a film noir season. He thought about their wedding anniversary last year. Genevieve was tired from work and they decided to make it low-key. They cooked and then went to a pop-up cinema in an old warehouse which was screening *Double Indemnity*, which Karl raved about and told her was the best film noir ever, the characters are life-insurance salesmen for goodness' sake – it's amazing. But something felt flat that evening –

Karl overcooked the pasta, the wine didn't taste right, Genevieve was restless throughout the film, wriggling in her uncomfortable chair, and Karl felt bad for recommending it. And then came the final scene where Barton Keyes finds Walter Neff on the office floor and they have a heart-to-heart. Neff asks his boss why he never married and Barton reminisces about a woman he was engaged to years ago. He loved her. She loved him. He was so happy. But then he started investigating her – he couldn't help himself. Neff acts like this is an occupational hazard, something they've all been tempted to do. What did he find? It was bad, Barton says to Neff. He's discovered that his fiancée dyes her hair, and that she has a manic depressive in the family. On her mother's side.

*Oh my God, on her mother's side*, thought Karl, feeling the room go swimmy, *a manic depressive on her mother's side, not even in her immediate family.* What to do? Stand up, take her hand and walk out in protest, climbing through the rest of the audience? Would that make things worse, or would it be a romantic gesture? Was it better to pretend he hadn't noticed? Too long had passed by then anyway.

Genevieve didn't say anything, and neither did he. You didn't call it manic depression any more, of course. You were supposed to believe that mental health was destigmatised, but it seemed to Karl that privately most people sided with Barton: a fear, dread and shame which no amount of social-media campaigning could ameliorate. So frightened of the shadow of a rumour of a condition that Genevieve directly suffered from. When the film was over they watched the credits in silence. What he *wanted* to say was that the point of the speech was really that Barton had

**177**

ruined, or drastically reduced, his life by his … The point was that the joke was on Barton, that he'd become obsessed with the techniques and suspicions of his profession, techniques which were never supposed to be used in your personal life, that … But Karl wasn't even convincing himself – he felt heavy and sad. He'd had no recollection of the scene at all, so clearly it didn't matter to him when he first saw *Double Indemnity*, but now it felt as if he'd directly insulted Genevieve. God knows what *she* was thinking right then, sitting with her legs crossed on the tin seat, nursing the last mouthful of wine in her plastic cup. Maybe it didn't even bother her.

Of course it bothered her. Because it was a reminder. Because it didn't matter that you weren't supposed to think that any more. Because a little gesture of tolerance felt insignificant when compared to centuries of asylums and straitjackets and write-offs, a vast heap of discarded human beings.

At 3:36 Karl still couldn't sleep so he collated a few more Henry James quotes. The trouble was, illustrating elliptical technique seemed to involve quite a lot of explaining what was going on around the ellipsis, which was time-consuming and dull. He felt hungry. Fridge light was his second-favourite light after sunsets. Their old flat had never quite felt like home because the shared kitchen had a fridge with a broken light. Karl even researched the make online – a now liquidated company – and ordered a new bulb from a Korean electrical overstock for £22, but when he changed it, it still didn't work and he swore so loudly the neighbours' dog started barking.

Janna and Stu's fridge was lit with artful sensitivity; a museum curiosity cabinet, an independent bookshop. He liked it particularly, as now, when the rest of the kitchen was dark. He put three pieces of cold tortellini and two cherry tomatoes on top of a big slice of ham, rolled it into a tube and was about to take a bite.

'It's late,' said Janna.

Karl banged his head on the egg rack. He put his snack on the third shelf and withdrew from the fridge, brushing imaginary crumbs from his top.

'Don't let me stop you.' She was wearing one of Stu's shirts.

'No, I, uh,' said Karl. 'You surprised me.'

'Sorry. I like familiar rooms in the dark. Do you remember being a child and how you could feel so afraid in your own house?'

'Oh yeah,' said Karl.

'Sometimes I think that's the only thing you can still access, of childhood – that fear. The rest is gone.'

'Are you still working?' said Karl.

'Always. Tea?'

'No. I just wanted some water.'

He turned the tap and let it run cold.

'I know you're worried. I know you probably think it's a bad idea,' said Janna.

'I want you to tell me you'll look after her,' said Karl.

'Oh, Karl,' said Janna. 'Of course I will.'

Karl took a sip of water.

Janna gave him a hug, but then tugged his hair in mock exasperation. He was surprised and spilled some of his glass of water on their bare feet.

'Don't stand in her way,' she whispered into his ear, then held him at arm's length. She was smiling, broadly. 'Okay?'

'Okay,' said Karl.

'And for God's sake go to bed – it's nearly four.'

# 28

**KARL WAS LOOKING** for the *Mentor's Edition*, but it seemed that Janna or Stu had moved it. It wasn't by the hob or in the little lacquer cupboard in the dining room, and it wasn't in Janna or Stu's bedroom or in the medicine cabinet. When he stepped into the living room he noticed that the light between the black floorboards was on again. He got down on his knees and tried to look through, but only dazzled his right eye. He stood up and stamped his foot. The light between the floorboards flickered and went off. Then it pulsed three times. Then, before he could stamp again, the light between the floorboards intensified, peaked, and slowly faded out, like a very short avant-garde play.

'Hello there?' said Karl.

He went to the back door and opened it in time to see a man in a hi-vis jacket ascending a small concrete staircase, which Karl had never noticed before, to the side of the garden wall.

'Hi,' he said.

'Oh, morning,' said the man. 'Mr Carson?'

'I'm his tenant,' said Karl.

'Oh, okay. Well, tell him it's all sorted.'

'What's that?'

'Fixed-wire testing,' said the man, flashing a grubby laminated card. 'And the new sockets. Quite a job, actually. But it's all centrally connected now, so he can control it from the hub.'

'I'll let him know.'

'Cheers, then.'

'Wait,' said Karl. 'Can I ask you what's down there?'

'Beg your pardon?'

'Is it some kind of … chapel or something?' said Karl.

The electrician regarded Karl with such amusement that he imagined him relating the unremarkable story to a friend later.

'A chapel?' he said.

'Just out of interest,' said Karl.

'Not sure, mate. You'd have to ask your landlord.'

In the en suite he ran the tap until it went hot and then turned it the other way to splash cold water in his eyes. He opened the medicine cabinet. It contained razor heads, ibuprofen, three tubes of ointment curled up like metal leaves. There was no sign of Genevieve's pills, which came in gold and silver blister packs which looked like buttons on a movie spaceship's console. He found the look of them comforting. He looked in her bedside cabinet, under some photos of her lying in a field with her girlfriends, which he looked at and sighed, a compact copy of *Vogue* and some hair slides. He looked in her shoulder bag, which was decorated with a pixelated flower design, as if photographed too closely. In the side compartment he found a squashed cardboard box containing four sheets of metallic blister packs, all completely intact.

**THE NEXT MORNING** Karl sat up on the bed with his tablet propped on his knees, worrying about Genevieve. He hadn't managed to talk to her about finding her pills; it was one of the better-marked minefields in their marriage. He should have been writing his journal, but instead he was playing a short film which had arrived as an attachment from Keston.

   – More former protégé stuff.

There was a photograph of Sebastian Francis outside an antiquarian bookshop and a video clip which resolved into a three-piece band playing in a cramped basement venue. Over the chatty audience they were playing a slow, rhythmic instrumental on three notes, the bass guitar so loud it rattled and buzzed. He recognised the bassist as Alice Jonke, who had told him there was no band.

   – Shit, isn't it?

Keston added.

He could hear a tap running hard in the bathroom. He had already shouted Genevieve? Is that you? and felt relieved by her cheerful Yes.

'Post,' called Janna, slapping *The Guardian*, *The Telegraph* and an envelope addressed to Karl on their floor. The envelope was square, blue, the address handwritten in an elegant cursive. A large first-class stamp depicted a steam train.

'It's not your birthday, is it?'

Karl took it back to the bed to tear it open. Inside, the birthday card depicted a stripy number 1 and a friendly elephant balancing on a ball. Karl opened it up and found a black credit card, thin but un-bendable, plain but for a white H in the centre. When he looked closer, he saw at the top right of the H a tiny white T in a circle, like a mysterious chemical symbol. The same hand had written in the card '52 Pritchatts Road – New Tour Dates Added Tonight Only! 8pm! Side door. Alice x'

'Karl?'

Something ominous in how Genevieve said his name, like she'd been building up to it. Her hair was wet and she was wearing blue eyeshadow.

'Hi, babe.'

She sat on the corner of the bed and started rubbing the palm of her left hand with the thumb of her right.

'I want to talk to you about something.'

Karl's breathing shortened.

'What's up?'

She opened her bedside cabinet and took out a book, which she handed to him. Slim, matte finish, like a volume of poetry. It had a green glowing outline of a brain on the cover surrounded by a circular chart divided into degrees and a second circle with notches in it. The title *Calibration: A New Perspective on Mental Difference* was embossed over the top.

Karl breathed air through his nose.

'I know you don't like talking about this, Karl,' said

Genevieve. 'It's a holistic approach – dietary, lifestyle, circadian. It's about negative oscillations of thought.'

'It sounds like The Transition,' said Karl.

'It's even about what you read and what you watch. It's about what you let in. To your body and your mind. It's about identifying and eliminating stressors. And it's about accepting a certain level of up and down. But being in a safe enough space to allow that. That's why it's called Calibration. It's about recalibrating.'

'Hmm.'

'And it involves coming off all medication. No interference.'

'Oh *God*,' said Karl. 'Why are you listening to them? Why trust them? We don't know them.'

'You immediately assume it's them.'

'Who else?'

'Why do you go straight to thinking someone must have put the idea in my head? It was my idea, Karl! Silly, ditzy Genevieve, manipulated into rash decisions because she doesn't know any better. *I* talked to them. I told them I want to explore an alternative to medication and they told me about Calibration. You're scowling.'

'It's called non-verbal communication.'

'You think I'm the only person who doesn't get a say in what's best for me. And no one's ever made you take anything stronger than a paracetamol, Karl. Can you imagine what it feels like? Having to take a pill that messes with your *thoughts*, with your senses? With your whole sense of *self*?'

'I can imagine. I do imagine.'

'Oh, you sound so *bored*. The trouble, Karl, is that you

believe *anyone* over me. The CPN who's never met either of us before, the GP who's being paid by a drug company to trial a new antipsychotic. Someone who'd sell your soul for a free fountain pen. Why?'

'I just thought this was something we'd been through before. You need the medication. We need the medication. Things go badly wrong without it.'

'You don't love me.' Genevieve was close to tears.

'See, you already sound emotional.'

'Of course I'm fucking emotional! I'm sick of being drugged. I'm sick of feeling like my head's wrapped in a duvet. Of not really being interested in anything. I desperately want to try something new and if it doesn't work, well, fine, I'll go back on. Look, I didn't want to … I'm really sorry about this … The thing is, I'm fine so far, Karl. I haven't been taking anything for over a week now and I'm fine.'

'Right,' he said, trying to sound surprised. 'That's good, I guess.'

'I wanted to tell you.'

'No, I … Hey.'

She was crying now.

'I was worried you wouldn't agree to it, so I just started coming off. And the thing is I'm fine.'

Karl didn't want to look at Genevieve and he didn't want her to see his face. What did he know? Maybe the medication Genevieve took did nothing other than make *him* feel better. He embraced her and they fell back on the bed.

'Whoa,' she said.

'It's okay,' he said. 'It's okay. I'm sorry.'

**HE STOLE ONE** of her cigarettes while she was downstairs talking to Janna and leaned halfway out of the skylight watching the flicked ash bounce between balls of moss. In his head he was standing by the side of the blue Fiat on a long housing estate, staring at the body of the child he'd hit at, say, 36 mph. He had already called 999. The father was running across the road. *Please. Oh, please no.* She came from nowhere. Is that the first thing you do? Claim it wasn't your fault? Maybe the only adequate response to having just killed someone's child was to drop to your knees and wail. No, that wasn't your place. To sit down. To take your head in your hands and rock back and forth silently. Better. But that might look as if you were trying to avoid making eye contact with the father or, worse, trying to pretend nothing was real and the accident hadn't even happened. But then was this really the time for eye contact? You'd have to time it so that the father was cradling the child in his arms, howling at a volume you'd never heard the human voice reach before, and then gently, respectfully, lower yourself to the ground, take your head in your hands and rock back and forth. Let the police cars and ambulances find you like that.

Karl was so satisfied with this conclusion he all but stopped thinking about an unmedicated Genevieve taking a job with The Transition and losing herself altogether. He thought about the notary's worst-case scenario, a military term rather than legal, he remembered: Genevieve might become very unstable and damage her relationship with new work colleagues and with Janna and Stu. This wasn't pleasant, but it was hardly catastrophic. If in a position to do so, Genevieve could take decisions which damaged the business or the reputation of The Transition. This wasn't of great concern to Karl. In fact, all he really had to deal with was the fallout as it affected Genevieve, if she broke with reality, with her very character, if she was never the same again. Therefore if it wasn't possible to influence her, and Karl felt fairly confident it wasn't, he had to let her take the job and monitor the situation very closely. Like some kind of Victorian patriarch.

Later, after finishing a 3,000-word undergraduate essay on terrorism and anarchism in Conrad's *The Secret Agent* for a student named Harry, Karl lay on the white sofa with the television on, picturing himself getting up. He had spent an hour on the rowing machine and half an hour doing weights. He worked out alone now, three times a week. He had become self-regulating, as Stu put it. Karl pictured himself getting up, walking over to the plug sockets and turning off the television. Instead he stared, his brain flatlining, while a woman called Saskia turned a charm bracelet around and around on her wrist and tried to say something interesting about each of its charms; *bit like the Monopoly dog, this one*, she said. Slight Essex glow to her accent, although she was using her telephone voice. He lifted up his shirt and scratched his belly button. He didn't realise Stu was in the room until he cleared his throat, which startled him.

'Fuck,' said Karl. 'Sorry.'

'You're watching an infomercial.'

'It's a shopping channel,' said Karl, half anticipating some act of violence and trying not to show it. 'I'm in love with the host,' he added.

'I need to talk to you,' said Stu.

Karl sat up and straightened his clothes. Stu obliged Karl's expectation by switching off the TV.

'I need to issue you a formal warning,' said Stu.

Karl felt the palms of his hands go sweaty. His stomach knotted. This had to be about the massage. Stu had read Janna's back the night he had written on it. Stu was going to kick the shit out of him.

'What? Why?' said Karl.

Stu sighed. 'This is very early in the process, I understand that,' he said. 'Which is why we need to nip it in the bud.'

'What have I done?' said Karl.

'Good. Good that you're taking this seriously. Karl, this may feel like micro-management, but you haven't been writing your 500-word journal entries,' said Stu.

'Oh, *that*,' said Karl. 'I'll catch up. I can do it tonight.'

'You're coasting. You're not taking your situation seriously. It's affecting Genevieve and it's affecting me and Janna. Let me ask you something: if you were in the prison you narrowly avoided, what would you do when they called for lights out?'

'I'd turn out my light.'

'So show us the same courtesy,' said Stu. 'Follow the instructions you're set. Even if it seems stupid. You have to work the programme.'

'Like the twelve steps. It doesn't seem stupid, Stu. I get the principle.'

'I've seen people, very rarely, but I've seen it, go through the whole Transition thinking they were the exception, thinking the rules applied to everyone else.'

'What happened to them?' said Karl.

'They were given an opportunity to turn things around, a scheme which asks so little and gives so much in return. We're a charity, Karl. We pay our staff but we're a non-profit organisation. We have patrons and benefactors, and our former candidates make a donation in the form of a percentage of profits from the businesses we help them set up.'

'So you're like a massive conglomerate?'

'All of the money goes back into The Transition. The point is they were given, these people, they were given this golden opportunity to turn their lives around and they couldn't do it. Why? Because part of them wanted to sabotage their own shot at happiness and success – I can see you flinching at those words, Karl, and I don't care – I won't let it happen to one of my protégés. Even if I have to be a dick about it. I say this because I care about you, Karl. You're a good guy and I want to help you. You see that, don't you?'

'I'll write the journal entries.'

'I still have to issue you the warning – it's your first of three.'

'What happens after three?'

'You're not going to find out.'


**'ARE YOU OKAY?'** said Genevieve. She was lying with her head on his chest and they were watching a repeat of a topical panel show in bed, drinking lager from the can.

'Am I okay?' said Karl. 'That's not how it works. You never ask me if I'm okay. I ask *you* over and over again until it pisses you off.'

'But now I'm asking you.'

'I'm fine,' said Karl. 'Is there something wrong with how I'm watching TV?'

'Things feel different.'

'I'm fine.'

'Can we watch something else?' said Genevieve. 'I find people trying to be spontaneously funny about things that happened five years ago unbearably sad.'

At seven Karl said he needed to meet Keston for a pint. Need to, eh? said Genevieve. It was Keston's request, Karl told her. Instead he followed his tablet map to 52 Pritchatts Road, a tall grubby tower block made of egg-box-shaped units. Karl walked around the building to the service alley. He found a green metal door with an electric card reader and a sign reading HERMITAGE. Karl put the black card in and the door slid open.

'Yes!' said Alice Jonke. 'Woo! You made it.'

'Hi,' said Karl.

The room was small but clean. It had no window, but was lit softly by standard lamps. It contained an armchair, a desk and an exercise mat. Alice Jonke was sitting in the lotus position on the exercise mat. There was a strong citrus smell and a silent waterfall flowing over the far wall.

'I didn't know if you'd bother,' she said.

'I wanted to know why you lied about the band.'

'Oh, so you know I lied,' said Alice. 'Well, that saves me having to tell you I lied. I couldn't talk about it at Stu and Janna's house.'

'What is this place? Is it your flat?'

'I wish!' said Alice. 'Hermitage have a series of one-room sanctuaries throughout the city and people can rent them for £50 per thirty minutes. It's not for sex. It's a place to catch a break, do some work, meditate – a little niche in the middle of the busiest, most stressful parts of town. It's a Transition business, so I get free use when they're not booked – one of the perks.'

'It's nice. Why did you call me here?'

'I felt bad,' said Alice. 'I told you there was no band. There was a band. And we were serious about turning against The Transition. We got into a lot of trouble. My ex-husband was kicked off.'

'Okay,' said Karl. 'But you finished the programme, set up your own business and now you volunteer for The Transition in your spare time. What happened to Jonathan?'

'Oh, we'd practically broken up before we started The Transition. He was kind of an idiot. Honestly, I look back and I can see how oppressive he was – he was against *everything*. He hated my parents because – I don't even know why – he saw them as materialistic or something. Just because they have a hot tub. I mean, Jesus, Karl. He was holding me back – Janna was right about that. One night he came home late, drunk, and he'd kissed someone in a bar and he was tearful and apologetic and I just thought, *I don't even care*. But this isn't about me.'

'Did Janna and Stu help you with the divorce?'

'Help? I suppose they would have done if I'd asked. I mean they helped sort out the legal stuff, so you could see it that way. And at the time Stu was very good at talking me through what I saw as a compromise.' She took out a smartphone and read from the screen. '"Is it a puzzle that systems contain their own rebellion? What are pistons doing if not struggling like lobsters on their way to the pot? A good system not only contains its own rebellion; a good system harnesses that rebellion and uses it to produce over eighty per cent of its energy."'

'What's that from?'

'Me,' said Alice. 'I wrote it. Pretty good, right? I think I should be a cultural critic.'

'I don't know whether you're warning me or encouraging me or what,' said Karl.

'Well, there's a way out, if you want it,' said Alice. 'But my suggestion is you just play the system for all it's worth, then come and find me once you get a job and we can work on changing the organisation from within.'

'Right,' said Karl.

'Meantime, if there's anything I can do, you let me know.' She gave him a card with her number and Alice Jonke, The Transition, Admissions. 'Or if you, you know, have anything for me.'

'I *don't* know,' said Karl.

'Probably best,' said Alice. 'Well, aloha, Karl.'

# 29

**IT WAS THE DAY** before the general meeting at the Transition HQ. Keston sent him a message.

– Your couple on the lam. Ed and Jess Anderton. Missing eight days. He was caught in possession of cocaine, enough for intent to supply; that's why they're on The Transition. Interestingly, nobody has a clue why they took off. Their journals are nondescript, their mentors had no clue anything was wrong. Just ran away.

Karl felt too addled to work. What he felt like doing was testing the parameters.

He followed the instructions from his photograph of not_all_transition's T-shirt. He broke the trading program and siphoned half of the stock money – which was sitting at £642 – into the sham account detailed on the shirt. He used the account to buy a bitcoin which he could cash in a nearby e-cigarette shop. He would tell Genevieve he had made an unwise investment and apologise for ruining their chances in the competition. Then he stopped. What was he doing? Why was he trying to get away with it? He brought up the photo again and converted the rest of the money into another bitcoin, leaving their stock profile at £1.62.

After cashing the bitcoins, he went to a Mexican-themed bar and bought a margarita, which he drank while reading his *Collected Robert Southwell*. Then he bought three more margaritas and found that his appreciation of Southwell's poems deepened. At the casino he put £200 on 0 and lost it. Then he went to a restaurant and ordered a bottle of red from the fourth page of the wine list for £106. It tasted like medicine and bark chips. Finally he went to a basement bar called Montgomery's, running a Louisiana theme night. Here he drank Sazeracs until he was sick in the toilets noisily enough to get thrown out. It was 3 a.m.

In the taxi home he was sick again and, as per its laminated notice, fined £60 for 'defiling' – 'Defiling!' he said, as he handed over the money – the cab. He swayed on the front doorstep looking for his keys. The door opened.

'Come on,' said Stu, taking Karl's arm and putting a hand on his back, firm as a policeman. 'I'll help you up the stairs.'

Genevieve said that she wouldn't talk to him until he was sober, but Karl felt too nauseated to sleep. Every time he drank a glass of water he brought it up; it sluiced around his system and found some new residue of poison so that Karl had to hunch over the toilet like some sweaty pink toad, hacking up what had to be every last drop before returning to bed, downing another glass and feeling the room gently start to rotate around him again. This went on until the cold misty sunrise appeared in the Velux window.

'I'm very sorry,' he said to Genevieve, returning from his labours for the fourth time.

'There is a time,' said the form of Genevieve, facing away from him, 'to be sorry. This isn't it. Why did you do it?'

'Something weird is going on,' said Karl. 'This isn't what it seems to be.'

'Or is it exactly what it seems to be?'

'This is what they want. They're trying to sabotage things between us.'

'You see, from my point of view,' said Genevieve, 'it looks like *you're* the one trying to sabotage things between us. I'm trying very hard to see things from your perspective.' She was still facing the wall and talking in measured, quiet sentences. Karl stood playing with the cord of his pyjama trousers. 'The stock thing,' she said. 'When I take something seriously and you destroy it, it makes me feel like a child. Do you understand how humiliating that is?'

Karl felt heavy. 'I'm sorry.'

'I'm not upset about the money. I'm not upset about the prize. I mean really, do you think that's what … I'm trying to explain to you … When … I'm so used to being wrong. I'm so used to telling you something and you explaining to me that I'm deluded. That hurts me.'

'I hear you,' said Karl. 'I hear you, I hear you.'

'I'm so used to being *managed* by you: "Genevieve, you're depressed; Genevieve, you're hysterical".'

Karl wasn't sure he'd ever said exactly that, but had just enough nous to keep his mouth shut.

'And then you do something like this and you wreck something I was trying to do and you're throwing up all night and I'm like, *who is this man to tell me what to do?* That's what I've been lying here thinking to myself while I listen to you puking.'

'I hate that word.'

'*Why am I listening to this man?*'

'That's fair.'

'And I think maybe because you're so down on yourself all the time, I confuse that with self-knowledge. I confuse self-deprecation with self-awareness.'

'Now you sound like a …'

'Like a what? You know what *you* sound like? An Englishman.'

Karl shrugged this off.

'I've been doing some investigating,' said Karl. 'I haven't found out very much yet, but I got the instructions to take the money … I got it from … I have reason to believe that not everyone makes it through The Transition.'

'Gah!' said Genevieve. 'I don't doubt that it's possible to fail The Transition. Why shouldn't it be? It's possible to fail anything.'

'Genevieve?'

'What?'

'Do you forgive me?'

'Have you finished being sick? Can we try to get an hour or so's sleep before the taxi?'

# 30

**GENEVIEVE WASN'T IN BED** when his alarm woke him up. He could hear voices downstairs and hurried to get dressed.

'Right, Karl, Alka-Seltzer, bacon sandwich,' said Janna when he entered the kitchen. 'Don't have any coffee yet – it'll just dehydrate you more.'

Karl took an unsteady seat at the granite breakfast bar. It struck him as an unnecessarily dense surface: you could shatter something by putting it down too hard. His hand shook as he drained the hissing glass.

'I'll come straight to the point,' said Stu, who was loading the dishwasher – it appeared that they had had something of a feast in his absence last night. 'We'll conflate the whole misadventure into one warning, okay? The hacked program, the stolen money and the drinking spree. Believe it or not, you're not the first protégé to act out in the first month, and you'll not be the last.'

'We know we've been asking a lot of you in these first weeks and in a way you did well to last as long as you did.'

'It's good you've got it out of your system,' said Stu. 'You're on two warnings, so a good time to turn around, no?'

'If you're okay to move on,' said Janna.

Karl took a bite of his bacon sandwich. The hot chilli sauce felt like a welcome sensation in his fuzzy mouth. He swallowed.

'I don't know what to say,' he said. 'I apologise for my behaviour.'

The sun kept emerging from behind clouds the size of buses to dazzle him through the rear passenger window. There was the occasional desultory shower of rain, scattered as if shaken off. Karl blew his nose and the effort made him gag. Being conveyed in the auto-drive 4x4 with a human chaperone felt different to being driven by a human being, and this morning it wasn't a difference he enjoyed. The swift, flawless, maximum efficiency of the computer made him feel like a cartridge in a printer; its precise navigation of roundabouts and sharp bends felt like spinning around and around in an office chair. Neither of them spoke to the driver when he let them out and he smiled distantly as if, Karl reckoned, he wanted them to know he had seen this before.

The Transition's quadrant of towers were displaying ancient grey stonework – the turrets of a castle. Then the stones melted into smooth, uninterrupted chrome, then back again.

'Look, there's your painting,' said Genevieve. Karl looked at the floor-to-ceiling pinball table. The mezzanine was bustling with young couples, just as it had been a month ago, but this time there were groups chatting and enjoying their free coffees and pastries. Few stood apart.

'Oh, hey,' a shaven-headed man said to Genevieve. He was wearing a shirt decorated with multicoloured dots which, on closer inspection, turned out to be skulls. His accent was somewhere between Irish and American. 'Nick. I remember you guys from the first meeting.'

'Hi Nick.'

'Hey,' said Karl.

'I was the small-batch bespoke pot dealer.'

'Oh yeah!' said Genevieve, delighted. 'My husband was a credit-card skimmer. How's it going?'

'How's The Transition? I'm still trying to get my head around it. We're living in this goddamn mansion with a couple of art-dealer queens. Even their waste-disposal unit is beautiful. They have a horse. A horse! We've been learning to ride.' He rolled up his sleeve and showed them a long, zipper-like graze on his forearm. 'And still my partner wants out. I keep telling him it's only five more months.'

'That's actually kind of a relief to hear,' said Genevieve.

'I keep telling him to shut up and ride the fucking horse.' He laughed. 'Some people, you know? If it's not *their* horse …'

'We've been through a few ups and downs,' said Genevieve.

The lights dimmed and the group took their seats. Stu appeared at the lectern. 'We've given you a longer morning session to share your experiences so far,' he said. 'There'll be time to do that over lunch as well – make sure you talk to as many people as possible. Try to find at least *one* couple who've had a harder time than you, okay?'

Laughter. The winners of the stock-trading contest were announced: Jinal and Ollie, who had made £644. They announced that they were donating it to a nursing home and received the promise of an extra floor on their first home. Genevieve didn't react. Karl felt sick.

The day's four lectures and breakaway circles had a focus on social enterprise, on using your skills for the public good. 'Remember the mirror,' said Stu. 'Reach out to the world, it reaches back to you.'

Karl couldn't concentrate on the talks, the street-gang infiltrations, the recording studios and food banks. Even the scheme closest to his own nature, a voluntary novel- and poetry-reading service for the infirm or bedbound, failed to spark his attention. He was so hungover that it only made him feel ashamed of the cold certainty that he would never actually get involved in it.

'I'm just going to the bathroom,' he said.

'Oh, let me know what the Gents is like,' said Genevieve. 'The Ladies is like a luxury yacht.'

Karl walked down the corridor towards what looked like a glass balcony then he doubled back on himself, took a left and approached the lift. The door opened automatically on the seamless black interior. The woman with the earpiece and the pixie cut stood in the centre smiling like a newsreader.

'Oh, hey,' she said. 'I think we've still got another couple of hours to go – did you need anything? We can send someone.'

'I'm sorry,' said Karl. 'I took a wrong turn.'

He walked back towards the balcony. Over the edge he could see all the way down to the ground floor, which was dominated by a pool of clear water filled with red and gold koi carp. Then the image faded out and the ground floor appeared to be a giant net over a starscape.

'*Karl?*'

'Karl Temperley?'

Karl looked up to see a young couple he recognised immediately as old acquaintances … University … A slight woman and a burly short-haired man. The names didn't come to him right away so he grinned at them.

'Look,' said the man. 'He doesn't remember us.'

'Pavel and Sumita,' said Karl, triumphantly.

'Yay! What on earth are you doing here?' said Sumita.

'I haven't seen you in …' Karl tried to count, 'years.'

'The last time we saw you,' said Pavel, 'you'd just jumped backwards into a hedge and broken two of your ribs.'

'Oh yeah,' said Karl.

'I'm a GP now,' said Sumita. 'Pavel's in data.'

'Really? Same here,' said Karl.

'Is that right?' said Pavel. 'Who are you with?'

'Freelance,' said Karl.

'Oh,' said Pavel, frowning. 'And what brought you here?'

'To The Transition?' said Sumita.

'I messed up my taxes,' said Karl. He paused. 'You don't need to tell me if you don't want to.'

'Oh, I tell everyone,' said Sumita. 'As much as I'm able to, anyway. I was falsely accused of malpractice – I can't tell you the details but it was effectively an insurance scam orchestrated by a hyper-litigious patient.'

'Who's lucky I haven't been able to track him down,' said Pavel.

'Sweetie, don't even joke, don't even say things like that,' said Sumita. 'After a while you get tired of fighting, you realise it's just making you sick, making you less of a person, fighting it. And it was pretty clear from the outset that the case wasn't going to go my way. So a suspension and enrolment on The Transition …'

'Where we end up with somewhere to live,' said Pavel.

'Seemed like the best course of action. Also The Transition has some really advanced private medical facilities, and our mentor said there could be a job there. So who are you staying with? Who are your mentors?'

'Stu, actually,' said Karl. 'The guy who's been running the talks.'

'God, that's amazing. Ours are book dealers,' said Sumita. 'Their house is like some kind of library in a horror film.'

'She spends all her time looking for a secret door,' said Pavel.

'No, it's great,' said Sumita. 'They've got all these messed-up occult and religious books, weird hoaxes and shit. I mean I guess that's what people are interested in, right? You've heard the rumours about *The Trapeze*?'

'I've … heard of the book,' said Karl.

'See?' said Pavel. 'They're toying with us.'

'He thinks they're toying with us,' said Sumita.

'Everything is a test,' said Pavel. 'Every conversation you have is a test. You think it's a coincidence people are spreading rumours about a forbidden book? It's a test.'

Sumita went through her bag and brought out a small red leather-bound book. She handed it to Karl. THE TRAPEZE was embossed in gold on the front and spine. It looked as old and weathered as a prayer book.

'This is supposed to be the novel The Transition is based on,' said Sumita. 'I don't think I was supposed to find it; it was with a bunch of old concordances. There's a story about the basic principles of The Transition all being in there. But we've both read it and I don't think I understood a word.'

'It's just a novel,' said Pavel. 'I couldn't see any relevance.'

'You were always reading,' said Sumita. 'Why don't you keep it and tell me what it means next month?'

'I ... Okay,' said Karl. 'Thanks.'

'Where have you been?' said Genevieve. The floor was sparsely populated and Genevieve was sitting alone with a cardboard cup of coffee, doing something on her tablet. 'I feel like the last girl to be picked up after school.'

'Sorry,' said Karl. 'Do you remember Pavel and Sumita?'

'Who?'

'They were in our halls.'

'Can we just go?' said Genevieve.

# 31

**KARL ACCEPTED ANOTHER** Alka-Seltzer from Janna and excused himself before dinner. He got to his room as quickly as possible, fell back onto his bed and then took out Sumita's small hardback copy of *The Trapeze*. The first ten pages were blank, and Karl began to get cross, but then *The Trapeze* began without title or heading. 'Bilyana Cvetkova could feel the cobbles through the worn soles of her …' Karl dropped the book on his face and woke with a start. He took a deep breath and tried to pick up where he'd left off, but he was on page 47 and couldn't remember anything from the past 46. He leafed back to page 1. 'Bilyana Cvetkova could feel the …' He felt as if he was breathing out a part of himself, as if a part of his soul could leave through his nose and gather in a corner of the room, looking down on his sleeping form, his wife next to him, turning over.

'Hey,' said Genevieve. 'Hey, you're snoring.'

Karl's eyes felt as heavy and oversized as 8-balls.

'What time is it? Where are we?'

'Ha ha,' said Genevieve. 'It is the year 2448 and science fiction has been made illegal. The end.'

'What's going on?'

'You're in bed with your beloved wife, Karly. And you're keeping her awake.'

Karl swallowed. He had an earthy taste in his mouth.

'Where's my book?'

'What book?'

'How long have I been asleep?'

Karl got out of bed and took an awkward step, nearly stubbing his toe on the metal girder again.

'You were asleep when I got in,' said Genevieve. 'Which is good: you need to rest off the hangover.'

Karl walked around the room. He looked under the bed. Nothing.

'I was reading something.'

'Come back to bed. Look for it in the morning.'

Karl picked up his pillow and threw back the duvet.

'Hey,' said Genevieve, dragging the duvet back up again.

'It's gone,' said Karl.


**HE NEVER FELT** more euphoric than in the dying embers of a hangover, the next day when the body realises that it's not going to be like this for ever. Karl was troubled by the evident snatching of *The Trapeze*, but didn't want Janna or Stu to think he suspected them, so he read the newspapers cover to cover to show goodwill. A small news-in-brief story in *The Guardian* caught his attention: A young couple, Edward and Jessica Anderton, had been apprehended outside Glasgow. They had been charged with dealing class A restricted substances and were in hiding. They represented a new class of white-collar drug dealers. It said the police had been searching for them for a week, ever since they broke the conditions of their bail and that their resistance would be taken into account in their sentencing. Karl checked the names against Keston's text. He remembered Stu saying, 'Silly sods.' At the time he had assumed it referred to their running away from a good deal rather than into a worse punishment.

Everyone was being nice to him to make it clear that it was a new month, a new start. He had a lot of information to process and some leads to chase up, but in the meantime maybe he *would* try to get involved in the voluntary reading service after all. While Genevieve was outside helping Stu with the allotment, Karl prepared the roast with Janna.

'Janna,' he said, sweeping the potato peelings into the bin. 'What's in the basement?'

'What?'

'Am I allowed to ask you about it?'

'Why not?'

'What is it?'

'It's a basement, Karl.'

'What do you use it for?'

'Storage, mostly. Why do you ask?'

'Can I see it?'

'No. Well. If you want to, I suppose. Remind me later and I'll try to remember what I've done with the key.'

On Monday a letter arrived addressed to Mr Karl Temperley. It was handwritten. Karl couldn't remember the last time he'd seen that much handwriting.

*So, uh, hey. I couldn't help but notice someone had used the account. Hope you don't mind me following the paper trail. It's a risk writing to you like this, but worth taking. If you want to meet up, I'll be at The Trocadero, Tiverton Road, Tuesday at 8pm. The following is not a newspaper clipping because the article was spiked. The Transition has friends in all the right places. Should have appeared in the Weekender two years ago.*

A paragraph had been copied out, longhand.

*'Sebastian Francis was one of the founder members of The Transition: "Back then, we took on four couples a year. We expanded, and so did our targets. Within five years we had become three-quarters self-funding, exceeding the government quota, employing over two hundred people spread over eight departments, many of them former protégés. Now it's triple that including regional offices with plans to expand overseas within the next three years." But Francis checked out when most would have been consolidating their position. "I left when I could see it was becoming a social eugenics programme, selecting and discarding its protégés, a six-month job interview when it was supposed to be a generational mission. An almost cult-like structure. A rescue programme which, in a word, requires its own rescue programme."'*

*— text from a redacted profile of Sebastian Francis.*

# 32

**THE TROCADERO WAS** a small industrial bar made of scaffolding inside a hollowed-out shop. It was busy for a Tuesday evening and Karl made his way around the room, craning his neck looking for someone who might be Sebastian Francis. The clientele was too young. On the first floor he was horrified to find Janna sitting at a corner table with two cups of coffee. He tried to pretend he hadn't seen her and turned around. She stood.

'Karl,' Janna called. 'Don't be worried. Sit down. Talk to me.'

Karl sighed and did as he was told.

'I'm supposed to be meeting—'

'Sebastian Francis, I know,' said Janna.

'You read my letter?'

'I recognised the hand. I'm sorry for the invasion of privacy.'

Karl shrugged.

'Don't be surly. Karl, if you knew … It isn't the first time this has happened, okay?'

'The first time what's happened?'

'The first time he's tried to get back at us through our protégés.'

'Is it true that he founded The Transition?' said Karl.

'Sebastian Francis is a predatory sex offender who was charged with eighteen counts of indecent assault and was only released from prison two years ago,' said Janna. 'I'm ashamed to say that yes, he was one of the founder members of The Transition, and it pains me to this day that we didn't realise he was using it to pick off and seduce vulnerable young women until someone was brave enough to report him. That's why he doesn't work for The Transition any more. He's also extremely paranoid and totally deluded about his responsibility for his own situation. Which is typical of sex offenders. That's why the article was spiked. The journalist did a little research. Stu and I severed all contact, naturally. We were sad. He was a friend. We misjudged him.'

'Right,' said Karl.

'I don't know why you'd want to get involved with that kind of person, but if you do, here's his number. Unfortunately I still have reason to contact him occasionally. You're completely free to call him if you want to.'

'The thing is,' said Karl, 'this is just your story.'

'And do you have any compelling reason to suspect I might be lying?' said Janna.

'If Sebastian wrote me the letter asking me to meet him, why isn't he here?' said Karl.

'Ooh,' said Janna. 'The master detective. Shall we get a drink while we're here? They do a mean Old-Fashioned. They have the right cherries, you know?'

'Did you write the letter yourself to see if I'd turn up?' said Karl.

'No,' said Janna. 'But either way, you *did*, so maybe I shouldn't trust *you*.'

Karl folded the receipt with Sebastian Francis's phone number into his pocket.

'It's just rather neat,' said Karl. 'It's the easiest way of discrediting someone.'

'It wasn't big news,' said Janna. 'We kept it relatively quiet in the interests of protecting his victims and protecting The Transition, which it could have completely destroyed, you understand. There are records of the case, though. What are you worried about, anyway, Karl? You don't think you're good enough? You think Genevieve's our favourite?'

'I think you could have me killed if you wanted to,' said Karl.

Janna laughed.

'You're being ridiculous. I think, I honestly think you should talk to one of our counsellors, Karl. It's all included. It would normally be pretty expensive. Do you want me to set that up?'

'I think you could harvest and sell my organs,' said Karl. 'If you wanted to. Or if there was someone better than me who needed a heart.'

Janna smiled and shook her head.

'Tin Man over here,' she said. 'It's funny though, isn't it? You've seen the sites. Anyone could have anyone killed for a few thousand pounds. It's a wonder it doesn't happen more often. Shall we change the subject? The counselling service. It's won awards. Based on a Swedish school of cognitive therapy.'

'There's nothing wrong with me.'

'I'm getting a *little* bored,' said Janna. 'We've been nothing but kind, patient and generous, maybe too generous.'

'Maybe showing me your breasts—'

'I misread. I crossed a line. *Mea culpa*,' said Janna. 'I thought maybe you were ready for that, but I was wrong. Listen, you've got the offer of high-quality counselling and the rest of The Transition to go through. I've given you the sex offender's number. It's time to choose sides.'

All his life he had been plagued by impulses to do something inappropriate or despicable for no reason: grab his dissertation supervisor by the ears and give him a big Bugs Bunny kiss, drop the precious vase … These thoughts arose from nowhere that he could account for and, at their worst, caused him to lose sleep. When he read Goethe's statement about every man secretly believing himself to be an undiscovered genius or an undiscovered maniac, he wept with relief. He lived in fear that the thoughts might show in his eyes. Usually though, when he had reason to be offended, his mind was a clear disc of hurt, not a thought of any action, violent or otherwise. But something had changed.

'I think there's something wrong which The Transition isn't going to fix,' said Karl. 'Giving a few dropouts a chance to become DJs or sculptors or whatever, trying to convince us to engage with the system which cut us off in the first place, thinking you can make us into stakeholders again when it's just broken. It's just fucked. Me and Genevieve lived for three years in a taped-up conservatory, Janna. Maybe I don't even want to be on the tiny winning side so I can start bleeding my contemporaries dry, so I can rent out my airing cupboard to a couple of young professionals.'

Janna was smiling.

'Maybe,' she said. 'Maybe there is something wrong. Something wrong with *you* which The Transition can't fix.

Your parents could take some responsibility there. They could have given you more of a sense of enterprise and self-reliance instead of coddling you into believing that the world owes you a living. They could have set you up with the basics in life, but then I suppose they were the sort of people to have five kids without thinking about it.'

Karl picked up his cup and, with a single flick of the wrist, threw the rest of his coffee into Janna's face.

# 33

**KARL LOOKED AT** his grubby velvet trainers, trying to avoid making eye contact with Genevieve. She was sitting opposite him, in between Janna and Stu. Janna wore a black cashmere jumper and her blouse, covered in coffee stains, was laid out on the occasional table.

'This is the situation,' said Stu, twisting the point of one of his hair spikes. 'Karl, you've committed three infractions. The last of which was tantamount to assault.'

'It was lukewarm,' said Karl.

'Tantamount,' said Stu. 'We're willing to see it as a symbolic act of violence.'

'I won't be pressing charges,' said Janna.

'Against one of your mentors,' said Stu.

Karl thought of Janna's face, the coffee running down her neck, some onto the table, how she breathed in and stopped, almost smiling at him, and maintained eye contact until he handed her a napkin and quietly said that he was very sorry.

'It was rather embarrassing,' said Janna, sweetly.

'He's an idiot,' said Genevieve.

'We'd like you to think about your *anger*,' said Stu. 'But there'll be a chance to look into that later on. For now we need to follow temporary disciplinary procedure.'

'Which is what?'

'The B-stream,' said Stu. 'You're suspended from seminars and lectures at the Transition headquarters.'

'Oh right,' said Karl, hoping he sounded disappointed.

'You're suspended from the programme; all Transition-related activity, including the social and domestic situation.'

'I have to live somewhere else?' said Karl. 'I'm being banished?'

'You'll temporarily reside in the basement,' said Stu.

'I've packed your bag,' said Genevieve.

'We'll leave you two alone for a moment,' said Janna. 'I'll just get the key.'

'G,' said Karl, once Stu had followed Janna out of the room. 'How can you possibly be in favour of this?'

Genevieve leaned forward and rested her chin on her hands. 'I've had enough,' she said. 'If you need to go through a disciplinary procedure to realise how ridiculously you've been behaving, so be it.'

'They're breaking us up; they're playing mind games. It's deliberate.'

'Maybe I could believe that,' said Genevieve, 'but *every single thing that's gone wrong* has been your fault, your decision.'

'They're gaslighting.'

'They're what?'

'It's from a ... you change the ... I can't remember. They're messing with our heads.'

'Oh, come *on*.'

'You're letting them separate us.'

'Karl,' said Genevieve. 'This isn't a break-up. I'm *seriously* pissed off with you and I think you're a fucking idiot, but this isn't a break-up.'

'But it literally *is* a break-up,' Karl complained. 'We're being broken up.'

'What, you think we won't even *see* each other? Don't be silly. You'll be in the basement.'

'I think you'll do whatever they tell you.'

'I think it's time you let me make a decision and see how it goes,' said Genevieve. 'I'll take my new job with The Transition, which I *want*. You can bide your time underground reviewing travel toothbrushes and then before half a year is up we'll have a place of our own to live. We can get your chip removed and then have children.'

'I don't have a chip.'

'Karl.'

'Okay, I do have a chip,' said Karl. 'Two years ago. I wanted to tell you. You were on a lot of meds – it would have been catastrophic if you got pregnant.'

'You didn't even talk to me about it.' Genevieve looked more amused than sad. 'I had to find out from Janna. And before you start accusing her of plotting against you, it just came up in conversation – you know they have access to our medical files, right? Our health is a key part of the programme. And she mentioned that Stu had a chip, too, and I was like *too*? And she was horrified because she naturally assumed that you might have discussed it with me. You think you're not like other men, but the only real difference is you're more passive.'

'That's nasty. G, the houses are terrible, they're tiny – there's no room to have kids,' he said. 'I tracked down one of the estates. It's by a motorway. They look like they're made of Lego bricks.'

Stu leaned into the room. 'If you're ready, Karl?'

# 34

**THE DOOR TO** the understairs cupboard was wide open and a bare light bulb illuminated the plaster walls, the little shelf with its torch and jar of screws where he had first found the picture of Genevieve. In the floor a trapdoor had been opened and a thin spiral staircase with metal steps led down to the basement. Karl balefully followed behind Stu, his feet rapping the steps, the metal creaking under their combined weight. Stu hit a light switch and dropped Karl's vast camping rucksack in the corner.

The basement was two rooms knocked together, covered in large yellow tiles. A 'wet room', bigger than the bedroom or living space, had been partitioned and consisted of a toilet, a sink and a wall-mounted changing-room shower head over a plughole in the same yellow tiles as the rest of the complex. Next door a small single bed was dressed in a floral cotton spread. A brown plastic school chair and Formica desk. It reminded Karl of shaky footage of a CIA torture chamber, only one that had been given a bit of a clean, a new coat of paint, and reassigned to paperwork. A mildewed set of French windows gave out onto a wet grey stairwell leading up to street level. Each room was lit by a single-bar fluorescent tube, speckled with dead bugs: the glowing effulgence Karl had seen between the black floorboards a few weeks ago. Karl hated strip lighting, and Genevieve used to say it was because he was part fly. Your eyes are hypersensitive to the flickering because you're part fly. You know flies have compound eyes so to them strip lights appear to be pulsing steadily, like a beacon? Of course you do. The yellow tiles felt cold through his socks. One of them was shattered, and Karl had the bizarre thought of a previous tenant saying, *Hey guys, look at my new bowling ball! Oops!*

'It's not meant to be pleasant,' said Stu.

'I've rented worse.'

'Honestly,' said Stu, 'no one wants this less than I do.'

'Fairly confident I can match you.'

'No,' said Stu, 'believe me. Janna and I get audited every five years for how well our protégés have done. It's the only performance review that really matters if you want to get anywhere in The Transition. And they take underperformance very seriously.'

'They'd fire you?'

'Well … I've known them to change contracts, remove you from mentorship altogether, which is the only reason you're doing the job, you know?'

'Right.'

'So we can agree that we all want you out of the basement as soon as possible. Your wife does, Janna does, I do. And you?'

'This feels like false imprisonment,' said Karl. 'Is this technically false imprisonment? I'm fairly sure I used to know someone who became a lawyer.'

Stu went through his jacket pocket and produced a squat leaden key on a twisted loop of garden wire. He handed it to Karl and nodded at the French windows.

'You're free to come and go as you please. What you won't have access to is …' He pointed at the ceiling.

'Women, wine and song,' said Karl.

'You get one hour with Genevieve every other day.'

'Seriously?'

'She'll come down and visit you.'

'Bringing provisions?'

Stu gave him a white plastic credit card with a T on the front and a magnetic strip on the back. The card was grimy and the plastic coating peeled at the edges. It was as if everything had been meticulously crudded up by an art director.

'Twenty quid a week on that,' said Stu. 'You need to budget.'

'Bud … *jet?*'

'Part of your task here,' said Stu. 'By setting foot in these lodgings you're temporarily forfeiting your place on the A-stream of The Transition with immediate effect. That means you no longer attend meetings and seminars and you're not involved in the tasks associated with progression through the levels.'

'Great,' said Karl, brightly. 'Okay. What else?'

'What else do you want to do?'

'While I'm down here? Prayer and contemplation?'

'We're not affiliated to any major religion,' said Stu, 'but if it gets you through the day.'

'So nothing, then?'

'It depends.'

'I prepare simple meals and I get to see my wife for an hour every two days,' said Karl. 'It feels a little easy. And boring.'

Stu shrugged. 'What does anyone do with their time?'

'And if I want to get out of the basement?'

'There's the door.' Stu indicated the French windows. It was getting dark outside.

'No, I mean …'

'Go on,' Stu smiled.

'If I want to get back onto The Transition.'

Stu clapped him on the shoulders and beamed. 'That's it, Karl. That's good. I had to wait for you to ask – it's the first step. *Shows a sincere desire to make amends and improve their situation.* Didn't know if you'd make it today.'

Stu scraped the school chair across the tiles and sat down. He motioned for Karl to sit on the bed.

'I held out for three nights,' said Stu, slowly. 'That's right,' he held up his hand, 'I was put on the B-stream nine years ago. We're not so different, Karl. We're not joiners. We have a healthy suspicion of authority and institutions. I recognise a kindred spirit.'

'I didn't even know you'd been on The Transition.'

'Oh, almost all of the mentors came through the programme themselves,' said Stu. 'Some of us kicking and screaming. So let's talk process, okay? We'll have you back on The Transition within a month or two. You have some time to get your bearings—'

'Done.'

'– then you enrol on one of several available work placements. I was apprenticed to a blacksmith, if you can believe that.'

'There are still blacksmiths?'

'Placements vary in length from five to eight weeks, so I'll make some calls and give you your options in a couple of days. Alongside the practical element, you have a 10,000-word essay to write. Title hasn't changed since I was on it: "Why I Hate The Transition".'

'Ten thousand words?'

'It's not just a punishment,' said Stu. 'We're actually very interested in what our rebel element has to say. The dissertations have been responsible for −' he checked his phone − 'no less than seventy-one alterations to Transition policy in the last decade. We're not looking for a mass of secondary citations − just an honest appraisal of why you felt the need to commit your infractions; what, specifically, about The Transition you find objectionable. Once the practical element and the critical element are complete you submit your report and it gets assessed. And then you're back upstairs. Okay? Proud of you, Karl.'

He stood up, offered his hand, which Karl squeezed as hard as he could.

'Last thing.' Stu took Karl's tablet out of the front pocket of the rucksack and made some adjustments to its settings. 'You're not allowed online or to use any of the devices or privileges − they're all part of the A-stream.'

'Wow,' said Karl. 'That sucks.'

'No phone calls,' said Stu. 'But you can send three messages a day − basically if you need to contact me or Janna in an emergency, so don't waste them.' He handed Karl the tablet. 'Don't get lonely. Your wife will be down in two days.'

# 35

**KARL WOKE UP** with cold feet and put on two pairs of socks. He had used drawing pins to attach a towel to the basement's only window, but the top right pin had fallen out during the night and the dog-ear of window filled the room with the grey light of a chilled-food aisle. He had been reading at 10 p.m. when the lights suddenly went out. At the time he assumed it was a power cut, but in the chill of the morning he remembered meeting the electrician some weeks ago, and his comment about the central control for lights and electricity. Prison rules. A tomcat had sprayed the stairwell and the smell was so strong it filtered through the door. Cat pee: the espresso of pee.

When he was dressed, Karl left via the French windows, which didn't close right, and walked to the high street. He bought a doughnut and got £10 cashback then caught a bus to the library, its itchy-jumper seats rubbing his back. In the library he tried to read a literary periodical, but couldn't concentrate. At the counter he found that he couldn't take out any books because he didn't have proof of address.

Karl walked through the abandoned warehouses behind the library. One hangar-sized structure of brick and corrugated iron had been painted yellow with the word

TRAMPOLINE spray-painted in red over the door. Karl knew from the journals that they were a project founded by an ex-Transition protégé. Trampoline was a charitable organisation that renovated urban spaces. It had turned the old factory into a drop-in centre and a community vegetable garden. Karl walked around and helped himself to a paper cup of water. There were even twelve dorm-style bunk beds in one corner, a porridge cafe and pop-up gallery space which was currently showing large canvases of extreme close-ups on human fingernails.

In the rough patch of land around the building an anarchist movement called Class Ceiling were picketing the factory. A group of twenty, variously aged, some in balaclavas, clustered around a black banner decorated with graphic bloodstains and the legend TRUSTAFARIANS OUT.

A woman with a purple metal ring in her lip stood to the left, drinking from a flask.

'Fuck's sake,' she said to him. 'I don't even know what a trust fund *is*. I've tried talking to them, but whatever.'

The day spread out ahead of him with an emptiness that made him frightened. He went to the cinema. A sequel to an action comedy Karl hadn't seen was starting in fifteen minutes. He checked the running time and bought a ticket.

When he left the cinema it was dark. He started to walk home, then realised he wasn't far from Keston's neighbourhood. Keston's flat looked similar to his office at Edson Hinks – blue wallpaper, dark wood. Keston loved furniture – he was always saving for something. He spent his days off trawling the intoxicating bricolage of antiques centres. By the window he had a Hepplewhite chair of which he was particularly proud. He also had some old leather armchairs and a big floor-standing globe-shaped liquor cabinet – something he always used to talk about. Tell you what I want, he would say, once or twice a week, one of those globes that opens out into a liquor cabinet. If I ever get one of those I'll die happy. Sometimes it was a donkey, but mostly it was a globe-shaped liquor cabinet. Karl sat down next to the globe.

'I feel partly responsible for all this, K-mart,' said Keston.

'Oh, right, rather than solely?'

'Yep. Partly. Take it or leave it.' He poured Karl a gin and tonic which was mostly gin. 'Because you have to. I'm not being generous –' he added a drop more gin. 'I'm trying to use it up because it's terrible. What do you want?' said Keston.

'Gin and tonic's fine.'

'No,' said Keston. 'What do you want?'

'Oh. This.' Karl shivered. 'I need to be with Genevieve.'

'Right.'

'They've separated us, they've persuaded her to come off her medication. I'm going out of my mind with worry. She does whatever they tell her. Or, you know, she *seems* to. I mean it's like they've found the weak spot in our marriage: the fact that I have to look out for her, and the fact that it makes me kind of overbearing sometimes. And they're using that to … I need to, like, kidnap her …'

'That's not a good idea.'

'Kidnap her and drive into the sunset.' Karl drained half his glass and started pacing around the globe-shaped liquor cabinet.

'Then what?'

'Flee the country?'

'With your £20 allowance?'

'Can you lend me some money?'

'*Gosh* no,' said Keston.

'Whose side are you on?'

'Nobody's. It's an institution. Institutions have their flaws, Karl, but ultimately they're just tools and structures. There's no right or wrong, there's no morality whatsoever; it's irrelevant. Genevieve isn't in anyone's clutches, she's enrolled on a self-improvement programme and doing rather well at it.'

'And what if it's being used, the system, for … for … a kind of social cleansing?' Karl sloshed some gin and tonic out of his glass. 'What if it's actually a system to find the right kind of people and throw the rest of us on the shit-pile? *I'm* not the right kind of people, I know that! I *pride* myself on not being the right kind of people, but what if they decide Genevieve isn't either?'

'You're becoming demonstrative. Stop getting excited. Let's be goal-oriented about this,' said Keston. 'Have you heard of Clovis? Jim Clovis?'

'No.'

'American. Extraordinary. Came up with this thing – you break the task down. You make a list.'

'You check it twice.'

'Your goal is you want to rescue Genevieve.'

'Not *rescue* her. She's not a storybook princess, Keston.'

'A man needs a narrative, K-Jung. That's something you feminists never seem to understand.'

'Then I'll be the Mother. Or the Flood.'

'Great – perfect! Clovis's principle is simple: no heroes. Nobody ever achieved anything by trying to be heroic, not really.'

'This sounds like it's in my wheelhouse.'

'It's a bit self-helpy. Bear with me. You have to – this may sound odd – it's a visualisation technique as much as anything. You have to see yourself as the villain. Or not even a villain. A problem. Any sort of problem. It's so easy to mess things up. That's your mantra. What can I do to mess things up?'

'What can I do to mess things up?' said Karl.

'It couldn't be simpler,' said Keston. 'Do you master the subtle art of the endgame or stand up and sweep the pieces off the board? Do you enter into complex negotiations or do you blow up the whole building? It's the main advantage terrorism will always have over the rest of us. So however bleak the situation, there are going to be some easy, stupid, destructive things you can do to get a little closer to your goal.'

'Makes sense,' said Karl.

'See yourself as a virus,' said Keston.

Karl had spent too much money on the cinema. The walk home took him an hour and a half, but it was a purposeful hour and a half and by the time he reached the service entrance to Janna and Stu's house his feet felt flat and virtuously achy. At the top of his concrete stairwell five stems of a weed, dead and blackened by persistent drizzle, pointed to the sky. Four heads had been lopped off, but one still had an attempted budding, halted at the seeding phase, the white fluff of its parachutes visible but arrested.

This, Karl thought, might make a good first paragraph for his Why I Hate The Transition thesis.

# 36

**SHE CALLED THEM** conjugal visits and laughed. For one hour every other day. Can you believe this shit? Karl wanted to know.

'Meh,' said Genevieve. 'Maybe some couples go for days together without ever really spending an hour in each other's company.'

'Maybe.'

'Maybe this will help you appreciate what a catch I am.'

'I'm keenly aware of that,' said Karl.

The scarcity of her presence intensified Karl's longing for Genevieve. The days felt so blank that even before the week was out it was all he could do not to spend 6:30 to 7 p.m. sitting at the bottom of the spiral staircase which led up to the ground-floor cupboard, whining like a Labrador. Until the trapdoor opened and Genevieve descended. His brief sessions with her felt like a tiny window onto a foreign esplanade, a static live-feed of a single field in a disputed territory where the passing figures were – huddled citizens? spies? militia? What did she do on the days he didn't see her? What was her job? Was she getting ill? Of course she was getting ill. *How* ill? At the end of the second week she came to see him wearing a smart grey dress and black heels with pointed toes. Her hair was up as if she were attending a wedding.

'Wow,' said Karl. 'I think I have a thing about business-women.'

'You have a thing about everything.' Genevieve sat on the school chair. 'What do you want to talk about?' she said. She crossed her legs and raised her eyebrows, professionally.

'Well, listen,' said Karl. 'I want to talk to you the way we used to talk. We used to talk about things that had happened to us and listen to each other.'

'Oh, I used to love that,' said Genevieve, wistfully. 'We'd sit up all night talking.'

In fact, when Karl had responded to Genevieve's plaintive email (in which she told him nobody would ever take care of her again, and that he probably didn't even remember her, *her*, the woman whose expired railcard he'd been using as a bookmark since he'd finished university), she'd turned up at the tiny bedsit he was renting the very next day. It was the Easter holiday so she wasn't teaching, and Karl was in too much of a state of bliss to pay any mind to his professional engagements. It didn't seem possible that someone he had silently pined after, daydreamed about, longed for and written off ever seeing again could just show up like that; it was like visiting a ruin and finding it new and never fallen. When she fell asleep next to him in the single bed he pressed himself against the cold wallpaper, not daring to move in case he touched her. After two nights like this Genevieve groaned, muttered that he was an idiot, grabbed his arm and rolled into him.

They lost all sense of day or night. Every five or so hours one of them would leave the room for the shared kitchenette to make coffee or fry eggs with diced red and yellow peppers, which was the only food in the cupboard. He remembered the urgency of their conversation, as if he'd walked into his room to find a complete stranger sitting on his bed and she had two minutes to explain what she was doing there, except that two minutes had sprawled outwards into a lecture series, a song cycle. She was the same person he'd met at university: here was someone who burned clean, who asked you how you were and genuinely wanted to know the answer. She stood out like a foreign-exchange student from another era.

'But isn't that just what people do?' said Genevieve. 'When they're getting to know each other?'

'Well …'

'I mean that's the point of it, isn't it? To get to know one another.'

'Except …'

'It's like you don't just carry on screwing each other like you did at the beginning.'

'No,' said Karl, 'apparently not. I mean I'd be pretty amenable to that, but …'

'It's the same thing.'

'Except I don't really feel like I know you,' said Karl, his voice unexpectedly thick. 'And now it feels like all I do is snap at you and criticise you.'

'Yes, *exactly*, that's what I've been trying to tell you!' said Genevieve.

'Don't gloat.'

'I'm not!'

'I thought it might help … I thought maybe we should make a conscious effort to start talking to each other again. Seeing as the time is limited anyway.'

'It'll be like going to the gym,' said Genevieve.

'Well …'

'I don't know if you can fake that. It's like: you can't *make* someone laugh.'

'Yes you can.'

'It's like …'

'You can absolutely make someone laugh.'

'You're not …'

'I think you're fundamentally misunderstanding the whole function of laughter.'

'It's usually you who hates organised fun. You don't even like public footpaths. Can't we just be natural about it?'

'I've tried natural. My natural state is complacency and boredom.'

'I don't see why these hours need to be consciously *used* for anything.'

'What is it you're frightened of?' said Karl. 'That I'll get to know you and realise that I don't like you?'

Genevieve leaned forward and kissed him on the lips.

'It's eight,' she said. 'You're smitten with me and you always will be.'

Two days later Genevieve was wearing a fitted tartan trouser suit which looked strange but not unattractive. He didn't ask where she was getting all the clothes and shoes. He assumed Janna was taking her shopping. Like a divorced dad trying to curry favour.

'It *was* crying, you know,' she said.

'What?'

'That sound in the attic every night. You thought it was pipes or something.'

'How do you know it was crying?'

'I knocked on the door,' said Genevieve. 'Our neighbour. His name is Dragan. Poor old guy.'

'Why is he crying?'

'Long story,' said Genevieve. 'I've told him I can visit every now and then. Help him get the garden sorted out. And he said he'd stop sleeping in the attic. He didn't know it was disturbing me. In fact that was exactly why he'd chosen the attic to cry in every night – because he thought it wouldn't disturb anyone. I gave him a hug and told him not to be ridiculous.'

'You knocked on the door,' said Karl.

'That's exactly the tone of voice which would have stopped me knocking on the door,' said Genevieve.

'So now you have two sad men to visit,' said Karl.

'Do you want to start the Talking To Each Other project today?' she said, putting a hand on his knee.

'All right,' said Karl. 'I think you should tell me something you've never told me before. Something you've never told anyone before.'

Genevieve sat in silence for a little and then said she would tell him a story about when she was seventeen and living with her aunt. A temporary set-up for eighteen months after her grandmother died and before she went to university. Genevieve had the guest room, which was peach-coloured and had a box of tissues in an ornate metal case as if it were a Byzantine icon. Shelly had divorced her husband earlier that same year and they were both heavily medicated, according to Genevieve, and would drift around one another in a sort of chemical haze.

'We'd take turns burning the toast every morning. We'd raid the wine cellar and watch the news, taking in precisely nothing. At night, though, I would just go. Shelly always left her car keys in a silver bowl by the front door and I'd wait until she was asleep. I'd get to the motorway at about 3 a.m. so it was quiet, and I'd be in the fast lane—'

'The second overtaking lane.'

'– and it was an Audi, Shelly's car, Steve, her ex-husband's car, and those things can move, you know? It still smelled of cigarettes and Steve's aftershave – a heavy, medicinal smell. And as soon as I was past junction four I'd put my foot down and I'd just *drive* as fast as I possibly could, 80, 90, 100 … Tears streaming down my face—'

'Stop it, you're turning me on.'

'120, 130, just bawling, openly. And I'd stare at the horizon and it felt like I might be a pilot, that the car might just take off, fly off the planet with me in it. I'd scream. And then, junction eight, I'd slam on the brakes, shoot up the exit, swing round the roundabout and drive back to Aunt Shelly's in the slow lane—'

'It's not called the slow lane.'

'– and I'd park the car right where she kept it, in front of the garage – Steve's table-tennis table was still in the garage. I remember he used to say, *I'm no socialist, but I draw the line at keeping a car indoors.* He had a conscience, you know, for a banker. I'd park it right there and drop the keys back in the little metal fruit bowl and she was never any the wiser. Or if she was, she never confronted me.'

'Distracted by the whole divorce thing.'

'You know, I never even considered that she might have known …'

'Didn't have the inner resources to deal with an out-of-control Genevieve on top of everything else.'

'I wonder.'

'So she just let it go.'

'So anyway, one night,' said Genevieve, 'maybe the eleventh time I'd been on one of my little drives, I'm just breaking a hundred where the Novotel meets the abandoned warehouses, about half three. And the road is just abandoned as usual – I passed two lorries about five minutes ago, apart from that not a soul – and by this point I'm used to that; it's like my own abandoned playground. But then I see, in my rear-view mirror – I'm nearly sick with fright – I see red and blue spinning lights and I go all dizzy so that I think I might faint and just barrel straight off the motorway. My first reaction is to slow down as quickly as possible, as if I can get away with it – is *that* how fast I was going, officer? And of course he nearly goes right into the back of me. Then he undertakes and I can see him frantically waving me over. I pull in to the hard shoulder. He parks behind me and slams his door so hard I jump in my seat. I sit forward, like, braced, until he raps on the window. I'm trying to anticipate what he's going to say, starting with *Young lady* … And I'm not insured on Shelly's ex-husband's car, so that's kind of worrying me too. And also I'm a *little* drunk.'

'You're *what*?'

Genevieve looked at the floor.

'I snuck a few drinks from Steve's single-malt collection. Not enough to get drunk. But I'm almost certainly five or six times over the limit, you know?'

Karl said nothing.

'And this is the funny thing: I remember hearing something about how sucking a penny neutralises the alcohol on your breath, so a breathalyser can't detect it. I don't know who told me, but it's all I can think of in the seconds that pass as the policeman approaches, after slamming his door like he wants to slap me, and I reach into the little dashboard compartment and I pull out a handful of loose change – 5ps, 10ps, coppers – and I just shove them all in my mouth. I can still feel it. Taste it. I'm terrified. But then he's standing over the car and he doesn't knock at all, just waits for me to open the window, and I look up into his face lit only by the half-moon and some residual light from our headlamps – and his red and blue lights still spinning – and he's smiling down at me, kindly, not even raising an eyebrow, and he has a well-trimmed beard and oh my God, Karl, it's my father.'

'*What?*'

'I mean obviously it's not my father,' said Genevieve, 'but my God, separated at birth, okay? And I'm sitting there like this –' she did chipmunk cheeks – 'with my mouth full of coins. And what do you think he says?'

'I haven't the faintest idea,' said Karl.

'He says, "You need to stop doing this." That's all. Calmly, pleasantly. And I start crying, and there's money falling out of my mouth. He puts his hand on my shoulder. Then that's it. He walks away. Slams his car door again. He leaves me sitting there on the hard shoulder. And as the car passes I see that it's a sort of boxy old Ford, with POLICE written on the side in big blue letters, but none of the – the fluorescent markings it should have. And the next day I do some research and it turns out the last time the police used a car of that model was over thirty years ago.'

'Oh?'

'So what the hell, right? Some kind of guardian angel.'

'Or something,' said Karl.

'And I never drove at 130 miles an hour at three in the morning ever again. Okay, your turn.'

'I don't know. I sometimes wear your underwear.'

'Really?'

'No.'

'Because, I mean, feel free. I can bring you some.'

# 37

**KARL WAS WOKEN** up by a heavy knock on the glass. He staggered around looking for the key. When he opened the French windows he recognised the Transition driver.

'Hey.'

'Karl. Sorry to wake you.'

'What time is it?'

'Six.'

'Ugh.'

'They've got you your placement. Six weeks. Starts this morning.'

'Oh,' said Karl. 'That's good. Where is it?'

'An orchard. Few miles out of town. Idyllic.'

Karl had time to splash cold water on his face and put on some jeans before meeting the driver in the road.

'I never asked your name,' he said, when they had been travelling in silence for five minutes.

'Izzy,' said the driver.

'Izzy. Have you seen much of Genevieve?'

'I take her to The Transition every day,' said Izzy.

'How does she seem to you?'

'Fine. Little bit stressed. But it's a big chance, the leadership programme.'

*Leadership?* Karl cleared his throat.

'She talks to you?'

'You know,' said Izzy, 'I think I've probably told her more than I've told my therapist.'

'She talks a lot?'

'She's great, isn't she?' said Izzy. 'Treats everyone like a long-lost friend. She's like a female Jesus.'

Karl wasn't sure whether that was really the point of Jesus, nor whether it was an accurate analogy for his wife, but he felt almost chastised and didn't speak again until they reached their destination.


Roderick's Orchard covered twelve acres of scruffy dry land. The self-drive dropped Karl off at the muddy driveway. A tall man with a slight limp walked towards him.

'So you're the intern,' he said. 'Ha!'

'Ha,' agreed Karl.

'My name is Mr Roderick. If you don't mind, you can call me Mr Roderick – it's what I answer to. I was a teacher and I barely remember my first name.'

Mr Roderick was a thin man, either a well-preserved late sixties or a worn-out early fifties, Karl couldn't decide. But he had a dense, black, decidedly unironic beard that made Karl feel itchy just looking at it. He wore a straw hat whose jollity only served to make his expression more sour by comparison. He showed Karl two of the fields, picked him an apple and took him to a newly built barn which smelled strongly of second-hand books. Next to the barn, a concrete bunker containing a cider distillery, where Karl would be working. Next to that, a bar in a good-looking prefab wooden hut, designated *The Apple Core* on a smartly illustrated sign. A chalkboard listed three varieties of cider. The dark floorboards were scattered with straw and a wedge-shaped stage in the far corner held a pair of mic stands, a single speaker and a dusty bass guitar.

'This is a great set-up,' said Karl. 'So many people dream about having their own bar.'

'Good for them,' said Mr Roderick. 'I hate it. It's a necessity.'

'Do you open every night?'

'Weekends. Ceilidhs.' He said the word with a rictus of disdain. 'And we do weddings for people who want to demonstrate how unfussy they are. About twenty a year.'

'Sounds good.'

'To be honest with you, Karl, I don't even like apples very much,' said Mr Roderick. 'But running an orchard beats the Neoliberal Free State of Education. I was a teacher for twenty years and for twenty years I was planning my escape. This was my father's land.'

Mr Roderick's father had run a ropey pick-your-own fruit farm and had left half of his land fallow. So when he inherited, Mr Roderick did some research, sourced a variety of dwarf apple trees and spent everything he could spare on them. He took an evening class in pest control and maintenance. Dwarf trees – they might start producing a small crop after three years, but full productivity, you're looking at seven or eight, he told Karl. And then it takes another year or two of harvests before you admit to yourself that you're barely breaking even.

'And so,' Mr Roderick nodded at the bar, dug his thumbs into his belt and did a joyless little dance. 'But enough about me. What did you do to get relegated?'

'They didn't tell you?'

'Oh, I've got the paperwork,' said Mr Roderick. 'But I like to hear it from the protégé and judge for myself.'

'I didn't write my journals; I threw lukewarm coffee in my mentor's face; I embezzled money from a fictional portfolio and spent it on booze.'

'That all?'

'Apart from that I was just being myself.'

'Oh, you must always be yourself,' said Mr Roderick. 'You're here for six weeks, yes?'

Karl nodded.

'All right. You clean the machines. You wash the apples. You pick out any bad ones and throw them in the skip. You clean again. Everything. You spend more time cleaning than making, that's the reality of the situation and it's the only way you get a consistent and industry-acceptable product. That's it.'

'Sounds good.'

'It's wet, cold and miserable,' said Mr Roderick. 'That's the second time you've said "Sounds good". Is it your catchphrase?'

'No.'

'I'll get you started disinfecting the presses. Sound good?'

Neither the two large presses nor the big kettle-shaped tanks nor any of the other machines seemed particularly dirty, so cleaning them inside and out with a series of chemical sprays and a pressure hose wasn't a satisfying experience. But three hours later Mr Roderick popped his head through the factory door, looked from wall to wall, nodded twice and walked away. This was sufficient encouragement to keep Karl buzzing with approval for the entirety of the 45-minute drive back to Janna and Stu's.

'Tomorrow at six, then,' said Izzy.

Karl walked around the row of houses to the back alley, picking his way over brambles and a pile of disintegrating half-bricks before descending the stairway at the back of the house. He pricked his finger on the wire key ring and, with some difficulty, managed to turn the key in the lock and force the French windows open onto his basement flat. It smelled of cat pee.

To his surprise Karl found working at Roderick's Orchard therapeutic for the first week. It was cold and exhausting and he woke up in the morning in Janna and Stu's basement not wanting to go to work, dithering in the shallows of sleep, harbouring some fantasy that he might not have to. But once there he enjoyed the isolation, the finite tasks interrupted only by the occasional gnomic utterance from Mr Roderick. The exhaustion of physical labour turned the mere act of sitting down into an intense pleasure, and this alone felt like a new and important discovery: life was a matter of contrasts, and all of his unhappiness and unfulfilment related, it seemed to him now, to the similitude of his work and leisure. Sitting in the same position, staring at the same screen that spewed out duties or entertainment depending on which way the sluice gate was open. The life of a battery hen. After each of the nine-hour shifts Mr Roderick would produce a boulder of hard bread and an oblong of crumbly cheese so mature it stung the roof of

Karl's mouth. They'd sit at a picnic bench and eat while swigging from a plastic jug of cider from the previous year.

That evening preceded a wedding party and Karl swept the floor of the barn with a useless but beautiful broom. The walls were hung with nine large collages of apocalyptic and mildly pornographic images over enlarged, yellowed pages from old novels. A price guide by the door valued the works at £4,000–£6,000. Mr Roderick was clearly a patron of the arts. Karl wasn't into art, so he liked it when the artist included words. It gave him something to read while everyone else was appreciating the art. He made the rounds and didn't recognise any of the titles until he came to the fifth:

## T. PIVEN – THE TRAPEZE

so the world ended more than 2,000 years ago,' said Katya. The dark shape gave her to understand that this was true by undulating gently. In so doing it inadvertently absorbed some of the light within the walled garden, which dimmed significantly, and conversation among the other guests temporarily hushed.

'The Entity fashions us the opportunity to start again.' The portly gentleman took her elbow as if it were a bird to be set free. 'Only imagine – the population of the world capped at 500,000,000. A farewell to misery of every category, to poverty, to war and violence. Disease eradicated, famine and hunger a distant memory. The free migration across every border and the celebration of every culture for their distinct qualities, and all shall have a plenitude! A surfeit of land and wealth.'

Katya watched The Entity shift forms so that it appeared to look like a spiky ball. And then she wasn't sure whether she might only have been looking at the sky, a trick of the light to the left of the moon. Had the gentleman said 'The Entity' at all or had she merely misheard him?

'But what is his name?' she asked.

254

The canvas was dominated by a topless woman with a binary galaxy instead of a head.

'Who's the artist?' he asked Mr Roderick.

'I'm sorry?'

'I like the art. Who's the artist?'

'Oh. Nobody. They're computer-generated.'

Karl looked at the canvas. 'They can't be.'

'Project by one of my former students. You set a few sliding scales – surreal to naturalistic, monochrome to Fauvist, heart to head – make a few category choices and it generates some attractive but hard-hitting concept work you can print onto any surface you like. Then she signs them and we split the printing cost and profits.'

'This novel,' said Karl, 'The Trapeze, do you know it? Do you have it?'

'Ha! That thing's still doing the rounds?' said Mr Roderick.

'Another protégé gave me a copy,' said Karl. 'They said it was supposed to be the book The Transition is based on. I fell asleep reading it and then it was gone when I woke up. I assume Janna or Stu took it.'

'How would you describe your relationship with your mentors?' said Mr Roderick.

'They're very upfront about everything,' said Karl. 'Janna always second-guesses how uncomfortable and stupid you're going to find something before you have to do it.'

'And then you do it. Any mind games?'

'Well, yes,' said Karl. 'But Janna always says that they're mind games before they start.'

'It's *all* mind games,' said Mr Roderick. 'Every conversation you have has been worked out in advance.'

'Even this one?'

'*The Trapeze* revolves around a radical reduction in the world's population: The Winnowing. It's a potboiler. Politically it's somewhere between Fascism and radical environmentalism. Wouldn't it be heaven on earth if there were fewer of us, and if those who remained lived sustainably and in peace, gradually curing every known disease?'

'It would for the survivors,' said Karl.

'Would you expect to be one of the survivors?'

'Not remotely,' said Karl.

Mr Roderick regarded him coolly.

'Good man,' he said.

'So the point of *The Trapeze* is that The Transition is in favour of mass extermination?' said Karl.

'In *The Trapeze* the radical reduction is to be achieved over a generation through total birth control. It's paranoid conspiracy-theory guff, and the book is a hoax.'

'So why'd they take it? Janna and Stu, I mean.'

'I don't know,' said Mr Roderick. 'Poe's Law implies that the parody and the actuality gradually become indistinguishable.'

Karl looked at the signature in the corner of the nearest work: Alice Jonke.

# 38

**THE WEEKENDS WERE** the worst. No work at the orchard – although Karl had offered to help out at the bar – and no Genevieve until Monday. It was incredible to Karl how quickly the loneliness had set in. He talked to himself, walked in circles. He went to town and tried to read in the library but kept abandoning things after a page or two – something had happened to his focus. He ate nutritionless snack foods and stared at the wall. He thought about his dad alone in his chalet and felt terrible. Maybe his dad had more of the essential qualities required to take on the great labour of loneliness. Karl feared that he lacked them entirely.

'You look ill,' said Genevieve. 'What are you spending your food budget on?'

'I'm doing fine.'

'There's a McDonald's straw sticking out of your pocket.'

'How's it going with Mutt and Jeff?'

'They're really pushing me – I've already worked with three different teams – PR this week.'

'And you're enjoying it?' Karl unravelled the straw sheath and started to tear bits off it.

'Karl, it's *great*. I can't believe how long I put up with being a fucking teacher. The only thing they get neurotic about is food. I passed by the kitchenette and, get this, there were three vegans all competing to say the worst thing they could about soya milk.'

'Soya milk is bad?'

'Your body can't digest it. It causes precocious puberty in children. It's destroying the rainforest.'

'Wow. What did you say?'

'I told them it also inhibits the absorption of protein. We're going out for cocktails tomorrow. I'll have to bone up on what's wrong with quinoa.'

She kept kneading the palm of her left hand with the thumb of her right.

'Bone up?' he said.

'Do you think there's anything screwy about herbal tea? Reckon I can get them on an air-only diet by the end of summer.'

'You look beautiful.'

'Janna showed me your browser history.'

'She what?'

'She felt it was her duty.'

'What browser history?'

'It's funny because I never really thought of you that way. I mean, it's sad.'

'What are you talking about?'

'Does it actually make you feel good?'

'What is this?'

'It was the type of material that I found a little upsetting—'

'You believe some list that Janna produces?'

'Karl, you've been using someone else's internet to look at porn. You've even been using the tablet to look at porn, which is fully networked and accessible by your mentors. That's just a verifiable fact.'

'Maybe a couple of times,' said Karl.

'Exactly one hundred and nineteen times, up to four times in a single day.' Karl felt his face flush. 'I checked through the links. You have a very particular type, Karl.'

'Actually I was trying to find women who looked like you.'

'Oh, that's so romantic,' said Genevieve.

'I'm serious. It's actually a thing. Facial recognition stuff. You can create a kind of surrogate—'

'Please stop.'

'It got a little out of control. But the point is, why are they sharing this with you? They're trying to discredit me,' said Karl.

'You don't make it difficult.'

'Little things here and there to erode what you think of me, what we have together, and our obligations to one another. If they can make you believe I'm some kind of sexual deviant you'll find it easier to leave me.'

'Oh wow,' said Genevieve.

'Look,' he said, 'this isn't a big deal.' He put his hand on her knee. She looked at it and then into his eyes. 'I don't mean it isn't a big deal. You're maybe thinking why did I keep it from you, but really why would I tell you? I don't even think about it. It's a process. Like brushing your teeth.'

'Ha!'

'You don't seem to understand what it's like having a sex drive.'

'What?'

'You can withstand long periods of time without any intimate contact. Like a sex camel.'

'Sex camel!' said Genevieve. 'Take that back. It brought a lot of things into focus, actually. This is all you do all day – you work from home so you can just … I mean I'm not saying you don't do any work, but whenever you want to …'

'This isn't who I am.'

'Yeah, but it kind of *is*,' said Genevieve.

'It's not the good part.'

'No. But it makes me wonder if The Transition is really even going to improve you in any way.'

'I wasn't planning on letting it.'

'Do you not want to be more than an appetite? Do you just want to slowly turn into Jabba the Hutt?'

'That's not your reference,' said Karl. 'Since when do you use *Star Wars* references?'

'Oh, Karl,' said Genevieve. 'You do realise I carry on existing when we're not in the same room? That I've seen films you don't know I've seen, that I *exist*?'

'Yeah, yeah, of course. Stop it.'

'That I'm not the sum total of the things you know about me?'

'Don't make this about more than what it is.'

'Dad used to say you judge a man by what he does when nobody's looking,' said Genevieve. 'Although God knows what he got up to.'

'Isn't that a koan?' said Karl. 'You can't see someone when they're alone. Doesn't it just mean you can't judge?'

'Maybe it was *when he* thinks *nobody's looking*,' said Genevieve, sliding off the stool and tugging her skirt down to her knees.

# 39

**WHEN THE SUN** was low it picked out the gnarled trees of Roderick's Orchard like exhibits in a museum cabinet, every furrow and knot cast in bronze light. Mr Roderick passed the cheese and took a swig from the plastic cider keg.

'So how are you finding it?'

'The work? Fine.'

'I mean The Transition.'

'Recently? Not so good.'

Mr Roderick grinned. 'But you'll do your stint here, write your paper and then get back on the A-stream.'

'I don't know,' said Karl. 'I'm trying to work out what it is they want with me. You get a lot of interns, then?'

'Two or three a year,' said Roderick. 'It's free labour. I get paid for taking you, actually.'

'I guess that makes sense,' said Karl.

'In fact I make about as much for mentoring B-streamed protégés as I do hawking craft cider.'

'Like a state subsidy,' said Karl.

'If you like. Roderick's Orchard is one of a hundred or so interests The Transition uses for placements.'

'And your past interns,' said Karl. 'They tend to get back onto the A-stream?'

'That's up to them.' Mr Roderick leaned back. 'When I left teaching – I taught Information Technology, and I was very good, which was the problem – when I left I thought I might take a job in the commercial sector for a while and one of my former students was working for a new firm called The Transition and she tipped me off that they were hiring data managers, paid a good wage, and they promised absolutely cutting-edge stuff: DNA storage, the frontier. And for a while it was a good job. But I didn't like what I was seeing. I think we're quite alike in that respect. I didn't like the pattern in the data I was handling.'

'Which was what?'

'You liked the paintings, did you?' said Mr Roderick. 'If I were to tell you that I loathe The Transition and all it stands for, what would you say?'

'I'd say why are you taking its money?'

'And I'd say why are you compromising and defrauding the top tier of the educational system by writing essays for rich idiots?'

'I make study aids,' said Karl.

'Does it ever strike you that some of the people whose coursework you fabricate might go on to work in positions of responsibility? That you're directly enabling the subliterate to teach literature, for instance? That you're contributing to the victory of the privileged and stupid.'

'They're doing pretty well, either way.'

'And you've got to make a living, right? Look at this. I've been waiting for the right moment to show it to you.' He took from his pocket a crumpled sheet of paper and gave it to Karl. It was a list of names and full addresses. 1 The Plaza, 2 The Plaza, up to 18. Number 1 was occupied by Ms Da-Xia Shih; 2 by Harry and Lucia Syverson; 3 by Richard T. Potter; 4 by Donna Weston.

'I'm giving you this because you're a deeply compromised person and because I trust you. This is a small, selective estate where graduates from your programme live. Notice anything?'

Karl scanned the rest of the list. Cino Padovano; Valerie Philips; Nora Keisjers; Soren and Sophie Guertin. He felt a chill.

'They're mostly single occupancies.'

'She said you were brighter than you seemed at first.'

'Who? Thanks.'

'Alice, my old student, the one who made the art – she lived there too. I think you met her. She's the one who sent you my way.'

'*Alice* chose my placement?'

'She volunteers for The Transition. Organises auxiliary placements and such.'

'She sent me here.'

'She's a good judge of character. Gives me people she thinks I'll get on with. I've known her a long time. We were in love. I say that. It wasn't right. I lived my whole life hating men who do that – say that they've fallen in love with one of their students. It's pathetic. Exploitative. And then I fell in love with one of my students. You're right to look at me like that. We were close, is the point.'

'I don't judge,' said Karl.

'You should,' said Mr Roderick. 'That it ended so well is down to her grace and maturity. Since then we've been working together against some of the more … toxic elements we've identified on the scheme.' Mr Roderick pointed to the list. 'Alice lived in 14 The Plaza, alone.'

'Yeah,' said Karl. 'She split up with her husband. She told me.'

'You've noticed a lot of single occupancies on the list. What does that tell you?'

Karl said nothing.

'A lot of things mean the exact opposite of what they appear.' Mr Roderick topped up Karl's glass. 'It's always worth reversing them; check the fit. What does it mean when someone says, *That's a very good question*?'

'I don't know.'

'It means: *That's a stupid question, you berk*. Get into the habit of reversing things. So The Transition – what do you get if you reverse it? What's it s'posed to stand for?'

'It's a helping hand for the younger generation.'

'Mm, but who exactly? Why did you even hear about it?'

'Tax evasion, fraud.'

'Because you broke the law.'

'Right.'

'So it's a rehab programme.'

'I guess.'

'Turn it around …'

'I'm sorry,' said Karl. 'I'm feeling sort of blank.'

'There's a very obvious thing you're missing here,' said Mr Roderick. 'The Transition is for couples. Always has been. Basic building block of society. Very couple-oriented.'

'Sure.'

'But only one protégé in every couple was the screw-up who landed them both in The Transition, right?'

'That's me.'

'Meaning that their partners are not only completely innocent of any wrongdoing, they're also people with some pretty admirable qualities: loyalty, hope, patience. People who don't walk out, however shitty the situation. This is basic psychology, Karl. They're people who work hard, who don't say no, who make sacrifices. Tends to extrapolate to the workplace. They're a *very* valuable human resource. The good apples. You could start a stellar recruitment agency if you wanted to, but that's not how The Transition works. It's a winnowing fan, sifting the best candidates out and chucking the rest on the heap. People like your wife. Adaptable, diligent, honourable; exactly the sort of people The Transition wants working for it. And it's a broadhead contract; you're part of it for life, one way or another. The entrepreneurs pay their dues – The Transition automatically owns twenty-two per cent of former protégés' businesses. More likely is you'll be offered an entry-level job with decent prospects. The failures, and there are failures …'

'Hang on,' said Karl.

'The failures can be used for plenty of things. The dead-end work. Depending on your personality you could become an enforcer – someone who rounds up the run-aways. If you plotted a graph of how many protégés are B-streamed against how many of those B-streamed were the original offenders …'

He took Karl's tablet from the picnic table and started making some adjustments.

'So what I did, when I noticed what was going on, I set up a little piece of code to boomerang all of the data back to me and dump it in a personal file and I've been collecting it ever since. It's encrypted, which blocks me from moving it from that file en masse, but I'm working on that. Actually I've been working on it for two years, and I'm very nearly there.'

'But what *is* it exactly, this data you're talking about?' said Karl.

'You know you get to read the best diary entries from the last decade?' Mr Roderick entered a number and pushed a few more sliders on Karl's tablet. 'Only the good ones, curated for a satisfying personal journey: mild peril and disenchantment ultimately overcome. The ones who make The Transition look as if it works. But once I've cracked this, you'll have the losers, too. The lot. About 28,000 journals in total. Every failure's sorry self-published life story. A libraryful.'

'Sounds awful.'

'I have a feeling it'll be quite a page-turner. So what do you think, Karl?' said Mr Roderick. 'You happy to be the editor?'

# 40

**THAT EVENING GENEVIEVE** was fifteen minutes late, and when she arrived, she couldn't sit still. She kept getting up and pacing around the basement, avoiding the cracked tile, clenching and unclenching her hands.

'What's wrong?' said Karl.

'What?'

'You're full of nervous energy.'

'I *know*,' said Genevieve, irritably. 'Are you trying to make me more self-conscious? I'm just pacing. Do you want me to stop? Here,' she sat down on the bed and started tapping her foot. 'Happy now?'

Karl sighed. 'If you want to pace, please do.'

'God, Karl, make up your mind,' said Genevieve. She stood up and started walking from room to room again.

'Is something wrong?'

'No. I had to pull an all-nighter. Well, one and a half all-nighters. Important deadline. I'm doing hospitality – we've got a group from Toronto and a group from Chicago coming. I've got to present. Most of the information is provided for me, that's the great part, but I need to put my spin on it. And I need to be able to rattle off the statistics when they ask me. This is happening, Karl. The thing is –

Janna said this – the thing is, all the skills I've been using as a teacher, the public speaking, keeping the attention of thirty-five children, some of them very difficult, the clear communication, it's all, it's all, it all makes me better at this job than most people who've taken degrees in it. I'm a natural. God, it's *cold* down here.'

'I'm glad,' said Karl. Genevieve walked out of the room and he waited until she returned. He wasn't glad at all, but the only advice he had ever been given on how to cope with Genevieve, once by her aunt, once by a book, was that it was very dangerous to challenge her. 'You're under a lot of pressure.' He spoke in a flat but cheerful voice as if reading the same book aloud to a child for the hundredth time. 'It's good that things are going well.'

'I'm not the only one, of course,' said Genevieve. 'It's almost like a job interview – a secondment for a handful of the protégés who show potential. But Janna says I'm the best one by far.'

'That's great,' said Karl, and tried to mean it.

'You sound gloomy. You don't sound happy for me.'

'Genevieve.'

'What?'

'Could you try and lie down with me. For a minute.'

Genevieve re-entered the bedroom. She was frowning and smiling at the same time, as if he had asked for something strange.

'Okay,' she said, and lay down beside him on the single bed. The bed was so small that they rolled into each other. 'Hello,' she said.

'I miss you,' said Karl. 'I miss holding you.' He kissed her neck. She laughed.

'We've been living in each other's pockets for so long,' she said.

'Living in each other's pockets?' said Karl. 'We're married.'

'Exactly, Karl,' said Genevieve. 'We're married, not kangaroos. I've been talking to the doctor – the one Janna put me in touch with. The good one. I know you don't approve.'

'I don't *approve*?' said Karl. 'When have I ever been the kind of man who … Genevieve, when have I ever …'

'But you *don't* approve,' said Genevieve.

'All I want is for you to be well.'

'You want someone you can control. You're frightened of me having my own life.'

'Oh, I'm frightened of everything,' said Karl.

'*Good*,' said Genevieve. 'Good that you can admit it. I look back over the last four years and, honestly—'

'Please stop talking.'

'This is what I'm talking about. You're closing me down.'

'You look back and what? Everything is my fault?'

'I think I'm going to go back upstairs.'

'You've only just got here.'

'You're being really weird,' said Genevieve. 'And that's quite insensitive when I've got an important job to prepare for.'

'No. Look. I'm sorry. Just stay,' said Karl.

'What do you want from me?' said Genevieve. She sat up and shuffled to the edge of the bed. 'You want to talk? You want to get to know me?'

'I'm worried,' said Karl. 'You're talking too fast, you're anxious. These are bad signs. You know that. We have an agreement.'

'Okay, look,' said Genevieve. 'I *am* going to go. Stop looking at me like that.'

'What?'

'Like you're about to cry.'

'I'm worried about you.'

'This is so inappropriate.'

'I'm sorry.'

'You're guilt-tripping me. This is emotionally manipulative.'

'I'm sorry,' said Karl. 'Don't go.'

'Come on. Cheer up,' said Genevieve. 'I need to focus. This is such an opportunity and I need you to support me.'

'Of course.'

'And the best way you can support me right now is to give me space.'

'That's fine,' said Karl, sniffing. 'Space, closure, name the fucking cliché and I'll give it to you.'

Genevieve was pacing again.

'I'm so disappointed in you, Karl. I'm so disappointed in you for trying to sabotage this with your ... your neediness.'

'You don't sound like yourself,' he called, his voice thick. 'You don't look like yourself. Your eyes ...'

'I'm going now, Karl.' He heard her flip-flops spank the metal steps.

'Fine,' he said.

# 41

**AFTER A FRETFUL** night Karl fell asleep just as the sun was rising and dreamed of being very thirsty on a boat.

He owned three pairs of jeans but tended to wear them for month-long stretches, so that when he rotated it tended to be to a pair of jeans – the faded black pair, the dark indigo pair or the bleached pair – which he hadn't seen in a year and which had cleaned themselves through a kind of osmosis at the bottom of a pile of other things. It wasn't unusual to find something in the pocket – old train or bus tickets, scribbled variations on a new product review, occasionally a five- or ten-pound note, which was a joy, and which went straight on coffee and pastries. He felt something against his left thigh and pulled out a pink card with a phone number on it and the name Samphire. The girl with the long white hair. Samphire was seventeen and starting university – it was, he remembered, why her mother had given him the number – and she had a ridiculous name. He fell back onto the surprisingly solid bed and looked up at a crack in the plaster of the basement ceiling. He thought of Lorna reading his voice at the party. *Some thoughts belong in the basement.*

He reached for his tablet and entered the number. He could spare a couple of his daily texts.

- Hi, it's Karl from Janna and Stu's party. Don't
  know if you remember. Your mum wanted me to
  talk to you about university. Free after work?

Karl tried to clear his sinuses. He tried to find a tissue but
only had a folded piece of toilet roll in his pocket which
disintegrated when he blew his nose on it. He lay back and
massaged his eye sockets. He wished that his nose could be
replaced with a ceramic, flushable nose. He would happily
walk around with a tiny urinal in the middle of his face
instead of a nose if it meant an end to sinusitis. He stared
at the ceiling. The cobwebs in the corners annoyed him
suddenly and he stood up to find a duster, a mop, a stick
even, though he knew every square inch of the basement
and that there was no such thing. A bluebottle, bright as a
piece of costume jewellery, was nutting the French
windows. Karl sat on the yellow tiles and stared at its shiny
carapace as it threw itself over and over again against the
glass. He got very close to it, so close that he thought he
could feel the vibrations of its wings against his nose.

"'I throw myself down in my chamber,'" he said. "'And
I call in, and invite God, and his Angels thither, and when
they are there, I neglect God and his Angels, for the noise
of a fly, for the rattling of a coach, for the whining of a
door.' That's Donne,' he told the bluebottle.

His tablet purred. Samphire's reply.

- Ha. You're so weird. Sure, why not? I've finished
  my exams. I have literally nothing to do x

* * *

262

When the self-drive stopped to pick him up after work Karl had swiped a jug of cider for Izzy.

'Mate,' said Izzy. 'That's lovely.'

'Izzy, Mr Roderick needs me to stop here,' he said, pretending to shuffle through some papers: '10 Boar Hill. On the way back. To drop off some, uh, casual labour forms. Is that okay?'

Izzy snorted. 'I'm running errands for a cider farmer now.'

'It's a favour. For me.'

'Oh, well, in that case.' Izzy punched some buttons on the display. 'It's ten miles away. Shit, Karl, you just say yes to anyone?'

'Yes.'

'No matter who has to do the actual job?'

'I thought it might be nice to see the countryside – see how the self-drive handles it.'

You have to promise not to judge, Samphire had texted him. It's not very salubrious. Karl wasn't sure if she really meant salubrious or whether she thought it was a synonym for luxurious, but when he arrived at 10 Boar Hill, which appeared to be the only thing on Boar Hill apart from rams, dry-stone walling and moss, he decided it could be either. The static caravan sat against a mossy stone wall, wild grass around its base. A permanent wooden stepladder led up to the front door, frosted glass like a bathroom window. The sweet tang of silage. It was a bright day and the last blushing yellow leaves cast shadows on each other and flickered when the breeze got up. Karl was dizzy from the swift self-drive's precision lurching, mostly uphill through lanes corridored by trees embracing on either side.

'Here?' said Izzy.

'This is the place,' said Karl. 'Some colleagues of Mr Roderick – he just needs me to go over a few forms.'

'Yeah, all right,' said Izzy. 'Don't take all night.'

Karl knocked on the glass and it made a flat, insubstantial sound. A form appeared behind the door which opened inwards.

'You found us, then,' said Samphire, with the breeziness of a well-worn phrase. Her long white hair was frizzier and bigger than he remembered. 'You look bad,' she added. 'What happened?'

'Not sleeping,' said Karl.

'Awesome.'

'I've been stuck in the basement. My wife's not talking to me.'

Samphire raised an eyebrow.

'Just born lucky,' she said.

Karl sat on a thin cushion against the static caravan's fibre-glass wall. He took in the room: a Formica table with built-in seating. A wooden clock with Roman numerals and a plastic gold pendulum, tocking but not ticking. An unframed print of a wolf jumping over a gate. A shelf up against the ceiling was full of old leather-bound books. A thin corridor also served as the galley kitchen with closed doors to the left. The place was clean, and smelled antiseptic, so actually quite salubrious.

'You're probably wondering,' said Samphire, pouring boiling water from the kettle into two chipped Denby mugs, 'who's their interior designer?'

'It's like being on holiday,' said Karl.

'I like you, Karl,' she said, kneeling to fetch a glass bottle of milk. She was wearing a kind of raffia-work poncho; headshop stuff. 'You didn't say *what's with the hair?* at the party. You're not saying, *what's with the shitty caravan?* now. Lack of curiosity is a rare virtue.'

'Well,' said Karl. 'Prepare to be disappointed.'

'Ha. Most people,' said Samphire, placing his cup of tea on the Formica table, 'are like chewing gum.'

'Disposable?'

She sat down opposite him, her legs crossed.

'No. Gradually less interesting. Go on then, disappoint me.'

'Where's your mum?'

'Lorna? Teaching. Then playing.' Samphire sneered. 'Folk,' she said. 'Then drinking. She gets back late on Tuesdays. There is –' she smoothed her skirt and looked Karl in the eye – 'a marked lack of progression in her Wednesday students' fiddle playing.'

'You said she used to teach Janna.'

'Oh, okay,' said Samphire. '*Talk about university* indeed. I figured you either wanted to sleep with me – I mean the way you were staring at me at the party—'

'I was high.'

'– or that you were digging for information. Which is in fact the case.'

'They've basically kidnapped my wife and locked me in the basement,' said Karl. 'Janna and Stu. I'm sorry to turn up under false pretences.'

'Oh God, no, I'm relieved,' said Samphire.

'I don't get to see Genevieve. She has visiting hours to

come and visit me. But she doesn't show up. She's not well. I'm going out of my mind.'

'So you thought, *I know, I'll go and visit a seventeen-year-old girl I met when I was off my face at a party.*'

'I want to know what you know. I want to know what The Transition is. You seemed to be old friends with Janna.'

'I don't think I'm going to be much help,' said Samphire. 'Lorna was surprised we got invited. I was a little girl when we last saw Janna.'

'Little girl with white hair?'

Samphire blew him a kiss.

'I'm going to find you something.'

After Samphire's bedroom door clicked shut – a light, plastic click like the capsule from a Kinder egg closing – Karl stood. It started to rain on the caravan, a lovely sound which got heavier and made him want to curl up in a ball. The door clicked.

'Look at this,' said Samphire. She rifled in her poncho and handed him a small, polished stone. Its markings and layers of minerals made it resemble a Japanese painting, with valleys, mountains, sky, a branch with blue blossom in the foreground bisecting a pale moon. Then you looked again and it was just a trick of the eye – a random pattern. Then you turned it and it seemed impossible that someone hadn't carefully painted a landscape on it with a single-hair brush.

'It's lovely,' said Karl.

'It's jasper,' said Samphire. 'A picture stone. It's just a polished stone you can buy from a gift shop for a pound. I can't remember where I even got it. Hold it up to the window.'

Karl did as he was told. He looked through the window to the horizon. The hills, one symmetrical and topped with pines, one with a sharper precipice, rolled into one another to the east. The skyline was uneven but for a perfectly flat area to the west. Then he looked at the stone, which depicted exactly the same scene, the lines a perfect match to his eye, differing only in colour – the stone was a yellowish brown. The world could look like that too in certain lights. He looked back at the landscape. Right in the centre, an oak tree in the middle of a hedged-off field appeared to be missing some of its branches, as if a bite had been taken out of its top right. He looked back at the stone. Was he imagining a tiny mark in the middle of its 'field' in exactly that shape? He laughed, half in disbelief, half to shrug it off.

'Even the farmhouse,' he said.

'I only noticed yesterday,' said Samphire. 'I absolutely freaked. To be honest, it's why I asked you over. I wanted to show someone.'

'It's not painted?' said Karl, examining the stone closely, its pits and seams of mineral.

'It's a natural formation,' said Samphire. 'Weirdest thing.'

They stood looking out of the window until a flock of starlings passed overhead.

'Why won't you tell me how you know Janna and Stu?'

'Why this obsession? I've told you.'

'They're trying to separate me and Genevieve. They've got her on this high-powered corporate scheme. But it's like they're grooming her for something else. They stole a photograph I have of her, long before …' he trailed off.

'What?' said Samphire.

'You know something,' said Karl. 'Why won't you tell me?'

'This has been a blast, Karl. I must invite strange men to my house more often.'

'You're scared of something.'

Outside, but as loud as if it were happening within the caravan, Izzy sounded the self-drive's horn, one short, one long.

'It's your chauffeur,' said Samphire. 'What a pity.'

'Give me something,' said Karl. 'Just before I go. I promise I'll leave you alone.'

'You're *so* annoying.'

'You'll never hear from me again.'

Samphire sat down on the thin cushion and rubbed her eyes.

'Your mentors,' she said. 'Janna and Stu, they're not just a couple who happened to get a job working for The Transition. They *met* on The Transition. They were put together by their own mentors, who were, way back, put together by, et cetera. That's how … That's why it works.'

'No,' said Karl. 'Come on. I don't believe The Transition can just systematically split up everyone who enters the scheme.'

'No, of course, not everyone,' said Samphire. 'Just the right ones. Someone like Genevieve … She's of great interest to The Transition because she's unusual and attractive and smart. There are different categories, different qualities they look for. She'd be highly rated as a 4K, at a guess.'

'Which is what?'

'You shouldn't keep pictures of someone lying around like that – I'd murder you.'

'I didn't tell you anything about the picture. What's a 4K?'

'I don't have time to give you a full briefing,' said Samphire. '4K is very good.'

Outside Izzy leaned on the horn for a long five seconds.

'Somebody worth holding on to,' said Samphire.

# 42

**THE CEILING TRAPDOOR** thudded and Karl heard a heavy footfall on the spiral staircase. At first he couldn't tell what had changed about Stu's appearance. He had a laptop under his arm, a black T-shirt with a white circle printed on it and his head was completely clean-shaven.

'Every leap year,' said Stu. 'Keeps people on their toes.'

'It looks …'

'Takes a while to get used to,' said Stu. 'Janna hates it. Think you're ready to start your assignment?' Stu put the laptop down on the Formica table. 'It's all online, but you've only got two hours before lights out, so don't waste it. Be back to pick it up at eight.'

Karl, compulsively scratching his cheek, was two paragraphs into an intensely lyrical description of the dead flax growing in the stairwell when he remembered, with a start, that he hadn't checked his Study Sherpas© account in some time. He logged in to his profile page to be met with a new one-star review. He felt winded.

ONE STAR. Ruined my fucking life. WHERE is my DISS on ELIPSIS in Henry JAMES? DO NOT USE THIS FUCKING TIME-WASTER, LEARN FROM MY MISTAKE I am probably going to fail my degree now thanks to this cunt.

Karl instinctively started to write a response, but there wasn't even a window to do so. Oh well. He went back to his essay. *Atrophied on a branch already dead at the root*, he wrote. He spent an hour working on his thesis. He finished his cup of instant coffee and went to the bathroom. The shaving light flickered and then settled, alarmingly brighter than before, a fluctuation in voltage.

He inspected the familiar raised red patch on his cheek, which looked angry. Floodlit by the malfunctioning shaving light in the basement bathroom, his face seemed to be visible in high definition for the first time, every enlarged pore and acne scar. He scratched his cheek and tried to focus. His face had bothered him the whole time he was writing – a tingling sensation to the right of his jaw. He craned closer. Something … It was like a tiny stitch or staple in the middle of the welt he had never left alone, the one Janna and Stu had tried to confront him about on the first night. Karl scrambled out of the bathroom to his hold-all and went through the side pockets for some tweezers but found nothing of the kind. The only thing in the kitchen drawer with a sharp point was the bread knife, which had a cheap plastic handle and two fangs at the end of its serrated blade, a throwback to open fires. Back at the bathroom mirror Karl held the over-long knife by its very point like a dart, for maximum precision. He moved around until he found the right angle for the light, located the stitch again and worked at it until he hooked it, then lost it, then hooked it again and pulled out a loop of hair. Then he threw the bread knife into the corner of the shower. He was equally nauseated and entranced. He pulled the tiny loop with his fingernails and it unravelled into a single hair, which kept coming until it was almost two inches long. Bells tolled in his head. He wished he could tell someone about it. Instead he ran his finger over the giant hair protruding from his cheek.

'You were there all along,' he said.

# 43

**IT WAS JUST GONE EIGHT.** Karl showered and put on one of his two button-down shirts. Earlier he had walked down to the park and picked some daffodils which now drooped in a jam jar on his bedside table. He hated waiting. He was eager to see Genevieve and explain what had happened last time, or have her explain it, or pretend it had never happened. He walked from the bedroom to the desk room, then to the wet room and back again, describing a figure of eight. He paced like this for five minutes, retracing the path Genevieve had anxiously trodden two days before. Then he climbed the little spiral staircase to the basement entrance and knocked on his ceiling, their floor. Nothing. He knocked again.

After more pacing Karl checked his watch and saw it was nearly 8:30, thus half of his visiting hour was over. This wouldn't do. He put on his shoes, left the French windows open and jogged around to the front of the house. Janna opened the door.

'Oh,' said Janna. 'Hi, Karl.'

'Sorry to disturb you,' said Karl. 'I know I'm not supposed to come to the front door. But Genevieve's late.'

'Is she?' said Janna. 'I thought she was with you. I'll go and check her flat – two ticks.'

Janna closed the front door and Karl took a step back. It was cold. He could see Stu in the living room ironing a shirt. Stu gave him a salute, which Karl returned then tried to be very interested in the honeysuckle climbing the wall on the other side of the front door, which opened again.

'Karl,' said Janna, 'I'm sorry, but Genevieve says she doesn't want to see you.'

His brain felt roughly half the size it needed to be in order to process this.

'Is she allowed to do that?' he said.

'Well, I don't know, Karl,' said Janna. 'I'll go ask the eighteenth century. Look, don't worry. She's really busy – we've got her working with a delegation from Toronto next week and she has to prepare a presentation.'

'That's ... Okay,' said Karl. 'Tomorrow, then?'

'Well, she's not designated to visit you tomorrow,' said Janna. 'But the next day, if she feels like it.'

'Right,' said Karl. 'Tell her I said hi.'

He took the knocker and pulled the front door closed on Janna, which felt like a small victory.

Back in the basement he tried to lie down and tried to pace. He reached for his tablet. There was a message from Mr Roderick. *I've done it,* it read. *I've done it. I'd crack open a bottle of something fizzy if it wasn't cider. Open attachment NOW.*

Karl accessed a long list. Each journal had its own identity code. Some of the codes were in bold, but the majority were greyed out. There was a time when that many manuscripts would have required a vast archive hall. Karl chose a greyed-out code at random and skipped to the last entry:

## JULY 7TH

The life of a glass collector. Skyway is a rooftop bar, which is cool, sometimes you just want to drop a glass over the side but it might hit someone and the glass collector would be first on the suspect list wouldn't they. Two girls in the kitchen – fit – they were like what brings you to Chicago? Are you studying? I honestly didn't know what to say. Nice to know I still look young enough to be mistaken for a student. I wasn't about to admit to failing a remedial life-coaching course was I. So I said I was on an exchange. Then it was like a thousand questions in half an hour while we deep-cleaned the kitchen. was I single? Was I gay? favourite sex position? might sound sort of invasive, but the way they asked it was funny, I didn't mind. On Saturdays I easily find at least $30 in dropped change and am saving up the flight home although what will I do there, my life is here now. This is something I will go more into later. Well this is supposed to be an opportunity but I can honestly say I feel too old for it. Maybe ten years ago, maybe twenty. Weather or not

The journal ended mid-sentence. He tried another.

Ever get the feeling you've been lied to? Jason keeps on at me, but I don't mind where we've ended up – I always wanted to see Japan and this could be a great opportunity if we work our way up. For now it feels a bit like being a typist again, but it's bearable.

He read deleted journals until 3 a.m. and found a similar narrative trajectory in each one. Those who hadn't finished The Transition and gone on to open gourmet cheesemongers or theatre companies for babies or invented a new mouthwash were shipped away to work for numerous Transition franchises and concerns overseas. It was, he gleaned, a voluntary move, at least at first, but then the B-streamed protégés found themselves living in a new city in another continent, with an income that more or less covered their rent and little chance of saving for the considerable airfare if they wanted to get back to England. The broadhead contract, as Keston had called it, presupposed compliance, and most probably it sounded like an attractive proposal. The Transition contract tied the client into the scheme for life, even if they started an independent business. And those who didn't were employed to maintain the organisation in various ways. He read the final journal entries of data-enterers, cleaners, corporate entertainers, waiters. Two of the journals he read concluded with their protégés working in a factory where The Transition's tablets were manufactured.

I am going out of my mind – I never even understood that phrase before now: I LITERALLY feel separated from my mind like I'm watching my body from a wall-mounted camera. Watching my poor little body standing at the counter attaching tiny batteries to tiny sockets. I have never stuck factory work for more than a week as a holiday job and even then I admired the mental firepower of the people around me who'd done it all their lives. god this is hell. Yesterday I heard voices in the hum of the machines. My mother's voice, my EX mentor's voices and Michael's voice of course Michael's voice, god I could kill him. they didn't say much – they didn't even say things I remember them ever saying, but it was like I could HEAR them, actually HEAR them rather than I was imagining them and I had no control over what they were saying.

A later entry read:

Kill me.

And the next day:

Sorry. Struggling yesterday. Things seem brighter today. I had my lunch in the quad and it was cold, but the sunlight hit the giant paracetamol-shaped factory with some kind of force, like an indeFATIGUEable force, like it was god saying there's more than this. God, I don't know, ask a poet.

That was the last entry. Karl spun through the list and picked another.

I feel, like, titanically alone. I'm trying not to think about Natasha. The days pass quicker that way. What the fuck IS this? Which part of the contract stipulated that I was going to end up an actual fucking slave?

# 44

**KARL GOT TO** Roderick's Orchard desperate to speak to Mr Roderick. He felt like an excitable dog, running in and out of every room to find his master. He was crestfallen to find him absent and tried to busy himself. He was sluicing down vat B when the water pressure dropped to a trickle.

'It's a trap, then?' said Karl, looking up to find Mr Roderick standing in the doorway. 'They cherry-pick the best protégés and send the rest of us halfway round the world and leave us there.'

'Late night?' said Mr Roderick.

'They're going to split me and Genevieve up and then pack me off to Abu Dhabi.'

'Travel is the best education,' said Mr Roderick.

'Why are you letting me know all this?' said Karl. 'Why do you want to save me?'

'It's not personal,' said Mr Roderick. 'It's the right time, that's all. It could have been this time next year with another protégé called Mark or Sophie, with Karl Temperley safely at the top of a distant Transition hotel scrubbing toothpaste flecks off a mirror.'

'Look,' said Karl. 'It's not that I think I'm too good to clean toilets – that's probably my natural station in life. I'm a prole with an aristocratic degree and my handwriting and draughtsmanship are appalling. In the nineteenth century I couldn't have even cut it as a minor clerk.'

'Or you'd prefer not to.'

'It's only technological advances that have given me what I have and it's not much,' said Karl, aware that he was talking too fast. 'I don't even know how to repair the tools of my own trade. But what I *do* have is Genevieve and there's very little I wouldn't do to make sure she's okay, and that means being by her side. Even if romantic love is a tawdry invention of twentieth-century capitalism. So whatever you're planning, I'm in. I mean you are planning something, aren't you?'

He searched Mr Roderick's expression for anything other than faint amusement.

'I mean you are, right?'

Mr Roderick put a hand on Karl's shoulder.

'Come to the bar,' he said.

'Every six months for the last few years I've harvested the censored journals,' said Mr Roderick. 'Just on a hunch. At first it was a hundred or so, but it's a franchise now, with branches all over, so we're talking thousands a year. I knew there was something to it.'

'So when do we go to the press?' said Karl.

'We've both seen what's happened to the people who quit The Transition or tried to move against it,' said Mr Roderick. 'It's remarkable how easy it is to ruin someone – nobody realises how very precarious they are. We rely on little electronic transactions, paycheque to paycheque, to keep food in our bellies and a roof over our heads. So the solution: I could just take the story to the press, on my own – I'm sure there are some very good journalists within living memory. But imagine this instead: we send all the censored diaries to every single Transition tablet: Zing! Suddenly every protégé has access to the whole truth. To both sides of the story. Then we walk away. No whistle-blowing, no glory, no victimisation. We put the truth about The Transition in the hands of those enrolled on it and we let nature take its course – an uprising? a mass walkout? a huge news story, with backing and testimonies from hundreds of protégés? It doesn't matter. That's up to the thousands of people like you, Karl, enrolled on this nefarious scheme designed to steal your partners and send you to a tower in the middle of a desert. The touch of a button and all the redacted journals appear on every single Transition tablet in the world, for them to read and digest at their leisure. And then act on. Hopefully.'

'So what are we waiting for?'

'I don't know how,' said Mr Roderick.

Karl's disappointment felt like a stubbed toe.

'The only reason I have the journals at all is because I coded that part of the security system. But the tabs don't like receiving that amount of data in one go – it's taken me two years just to work out how to share it with your tablet as a one-off, but sending so much data to every single Transition tablet is going to be impossible without some-how sidelining their data security from within. But we could perhaps just choose a few choice cuts, a few horror stories if you've picked out any highlights so far?'

'It has to be all of them,' said Karl. 'It can't just be a few disgruntled B-streamers. They'd say it was a regrettable exception they were looking into, that most people are totally happy or something.'

'Here's the thing,' said Mr Roderick. 'The files which have been bouncing back to me the last few years all come from the same location – it wasn't hard to find the geographical coordinates attached to it, so a couple of years ago I drove over there to stake the place out, imagining I'd find a complex with massive fences, warehouses. But what do I find instead? Some sheep. A dry-stone wall. A static caravan with two women living in it.'

'But that's—'

'One of them plays the violin. I watched them come and go for a few hours over a week.'

'But I know them!' said Karl. 'That's Lorna and Samphire.'

'Friends of yours?'

'I met them at a party at Janna and Stu's,' said Karl. 'They're connected; they're—'

Mr Roderick held up a hand to stop him. With his other hand shaking he took out his phone and dialled. 'Alice?' he said. 'I'm with Karl.'

He put the phone on the bar.

'Am I on speaker?'

'Yes.'

'I hate being on speaker. Hi, Karl.'

'Hi.'

'He knows the women in the caravan,' said Mr Roderick. 'I'm an idiot. I thought the archive must be under the ground. I've been looking for some kind of secret entrance. But they're connected to The Transition. They must be … security or something.'

'Why do they need a physical place to store the data at all?' said Karl. 'Isn't it all on the cloud?'

'Karl,' said Alice's voice, 'you *work* online. You do realise *the cloud* isn't an *actual cloud*, right? It's all server farms and underground caves in China full of hard drives.'

'Oh,' said Karl. 'Right.'

'Some of them are really pretty – you should look it up. I mean, did you think …' Alice started laughing.

'It's actually a fair question,' said Mr Roderick. 'A few years ago they'd have used a giant email account to store their data like anyone else. But record-keeping is very important if The Transition is going to keep its funding. The material is sensitive and confidential; it makes sense for them to bring data storage in-house.'

'Plenty of talent on the scheme to help out,' said Alice. 'Plenty of black hats and crackers and, *oh, I hate the names so much*. Plus we lost some data in this stupid grievance case with Sebastian Francis, who enlisted a group of teenage weirdos and managed to delete almost everything to do with himself and almost everyone else.'

'So now The Transition has its own underground cave,' said Mr Roderick.

'And nobody knows where it is. Okay, Karl, listen,' said Alice. 'You on good terms with the women in the caravan? Could you make up a reason to visit?'

'I think so,' said Karl. 'I mean, yes, sure.'

'And you're certain they're involved in The Transition? God. It's not like you can just go in there and take their computer,' said Alice. 'We need to think of a way to get some kind of leverage, get them onside.'

'Um …'

'Take it slowly,' said Alice. 'Sleep on it.'

Izzy took him back to the basement.

The next evening, a Friday, Genevieve was supposed to visit. He tried to kill the hour as efficiently as possible. He opened a book on *Medicine and Hermeneutics in Donne* and read half a paragraph. He turned on the dribbly shower and tried to wash the sticky apple smell off his body, hoping he might emerge with towel around his waist to find Genevieve sitting on his bed, smiling, miraculously restored to her full self. It was twenty-two minutes past seven, his scalp chilled from the water he hadn't dried off, when he gave up waiting, stamped up the spiral staircase and pounded the underside of the trapdoor with his fists. He did so repeatedly, as if working a ceiling-mounted punchbag, until his knuckles began to throb.

'Janna?' he yelled. 'Stu?'

The trapdoor swung upwards. Janna stuck her head in. She had a black cigarette between her lips, unlit.

'Karl? What's all the noise? God, you're practically naked! What's the matter?'

'What do you *think* the fucking matter is, Janna?'

'Something wrong with the placement?'

'Where is she? She's supposed to be here.'

'*Oh*,' said Janna. 'Look, Karl, she's really busy. I don't think she can cope with seeing you right now. She said you'd been arguing. Emotional work is work too, Karl. I suggested she should prioritise, see you in a couple of days.' She smiled sadly at him, tilted her head to one side. 'I'm sorry. I probably ought to have come down and told you. We've got guests. I got distracted.'

'Right.'

'I don't want you to worry about Genevieve.'

'That's thoughtful.'

'She's excited. She's doing very well. She's impressed the board. A couple of the management team are totally in her corner, and she's the main point of contact for the delegation from Toronto.'

'She mentioned something about that.'

'Well, it's going ahead. And it's a big deal, so of course she's anxious and … maybe you're not used to seeing her like that.'

'Anxious?'

'It's a high-pressured job. Honestly, whenever I had to present I was just sick, just throwing up for two days beforehand. Couldn't eat. It affects people in different ways.'

'Okay.'

'And it's not that she doesn't want to see you – she's just got a lot of prep to do, you know? She's very chatty. She's just Genevieve, Karl. Lovely, effusive, slightly bats but, you know. She's Genevieve.'

'Janna,' said Karl. 'She's clearly heading towards a breakdown – you must be able to see that.'

'She's a bit stressed. Honestly, she calms down after a glass of wine and a foot rub.'

'The pacing, the fast-talking, the … There are cues you wouldn't pick up on.'

'Maybe that's significant, Karl. Maybe if there are cues only *you* pick up on, you're the only one with the problem. When it comes down to it, all I see is an ambitious young woman stressed out about one of the most important tests of her life,' said Janna.

'Do you believe there's anything wrong with her at all?'

'I believe you're obsessed with there being something wrong with her,' said Janna. 'If I'm worried about her I'll let you know – deal?'

'*I'm* worried about her,' said Karl. '*I* know.'

'Take a couple of paracetamol. Honestly. It'll take the edge off.'

'If I could just see her.'

'That's not possible right now.'

'I think you're going to regret this,' said Karl.

'I should probably leave you to get dressed,' said Janna. She leaned closer. He could feel her breath on his bare shoulder.

'You'll be out of here soon. You don't need to be afraid. We're looking after her.'

Karl stared at Janna. There was nothing he could yell or scream that wouldn't make the situation worse, but for the first time in his life he felt physically incapable of saying something essentially placatory. He snatched the black cigarette from her hand, tore it in two and dropped it onto the tiles.

Janna paused for a moment, apparently uncertain what to do next, then she laughed, gave him a friendly punch on the arm and disappeared back through the trapdoor.

*Emotional work is work too.* Karl kicked a wonky Formica cupboard. *Fuck you, Janna.* He sat in a corner and stroked his sore knuckles. He daydreamed about breaking Janna and Stu's door down, an ambush which would leave them no time to retaliate; he would swipe Genevieve's hidden credit card, the one she'd stashed in *The Go-Between* which he'd never mentioned to her, and run to the station, to the airport … The trouble was that even in his fantasy Genevieve didn't want to leave the house. So Karl's imagination kept stalling in the hallway – attempting to reason with her? To scream at her? To give her a fireman's lift out of the front door? He couldn't picture one of those things. And then the fantasy door would close, gently, and Stu or Janna would say, *Karl. Come on.* This went on with minor variations for upwards of an hour.

Karl dressed in a pair of shorts and a Yo La Tengo T-shirt. He paced around the small, cold rooms. It was what everyone said about Genevieve when she was getting ill: they told him she was funny, full of life and creativity; that maybe he couldn't handle her real personality, which was strong and quick and, sure, a little eccentric, but that was part of her charm; maybe he was so used to Depressed Genevieve that he'd forgotten who she really was; and that he was worrying about nothing; that he had to accept her for who she was; that he needed to stop being so neurotic. And this would go on until Genevieve went from saying a lot of things quite quickly to saying a lot of strange and increasingly aggressive things. At the first sign of which the same friends would run a mile before Karl could even say I told you so. There was a thing, a nervous tic he had developed: if she was struggling to be understood, if she was getting tangled up in her own words, he felt personally responsible. This meant that he would frequently start to talk for her, or talk over her and he wondered, as he lay in the lumpy duvet, if she wasn't perhaps better off without him after all.

★　★　★

**THE VOID OF** the weekend was getting unbearable when Karl got a message from Keston instructing him to come over at once. He set off on foot. Maybe he always over-read the signs. He had the unshakeable conviction that Genevieve was in trouble and needed his help. At least in a very simple, practical sense. She had called him on it early, before they'd really started seeing one another. It was pouring with rain and they shared an umbrella on the way back from a restaurant, a small chain which was still using fresh ingredients and employing real chefs. He had lent her some CDs, which she didn't like. He held the umbrella and found that Genevieve was very good at linking arms – she linked arms as if it were a dance.

'Steph used to say her type was *tall men with severe mental-health issues*. And you like troubled girls, don't you?' she said, leaning into him as they walked. 'I remember seeing you with that … what was her name?'

'Emma.'

'Yeah,' Genevieve whistled. 'She still alive?'

'I don't … That's harsh.'

'You like troubled girls because you think you can save them.'

'You flatter me,' said Karl. 'I like troubled girls because they make me look good.'

'As long as you don't try to save me.'

'I think you're probably beyond my messiah complex.'

'We'll see, won't we?' said Genevieve.

When he arrived at the flat, he found Keston sitting in his leather armchair wearing a quilted maroon smoking jacket. He was drinking a Bloody Mary and looked like he was about to introduce *Masterpiece Theatre* or a tale of the unexpected.

'What's happening?'

'I'll tell you what's happening, K-braham,' he said. 'The middle class just died.' Keston's globe-shaped liquor cabinet was wide open in the middle of the room, like the world throwing back its head to laugh. It was empty. All of the bottles, some sealed, some half full, several containing less than an inch, were stacked up around the chair.

'You're drunk.'

'I'm moving out,' said Keston.

'Oh,' said Karl. 'Your place is nice. I'm sorry.'

'Not a big deal. I've been here three years, quite attached to it, but I'm a big boy. Landlord's selling the whole building, as is his right. Happens all the time. Month's notice. I've found a new place already.'

'Okay,' said Karl.

'But this is where it becomes a tale of woe,' said Keston. 'It turns out you need quite a lot of money. Two months' rent in advance, a damage deposit when I don't have the damage deposit back from this place yet. A holding fee of a hundred and fifty. Agency fees of three hundred and fifty. For what? Twelve pages of photocopying and some phone calls. To *me*, most of them, so they can let me know how the twelve pages of photocopying's going. Two days' unpaid leave to find the new place. All in all it's more than I earn in two months.'

'So you're selling the liquor cabinet,' said Karl.

'Selling everything,' said Keston. 'I need to raise fifteen hundred pounds, yesterday. Everything must go.'

'Not the grandfather clock,' said Karl. He could see the shadow of Keston's Georgian walnut-inlaid grandfather clock.

'Especially the grandfather clock.'

'The armoire? The Hepplewhite?'

'I'm an accountant!' said Keston, sloshing the bottle of vodka into his tomato juice. 'I work fourteen-hour days! I'm supposed to be the, the – the – the leech sucking this country dry, and look at me! I've fallen through the net! I'm the silent majority! Fuck!'

'It makes you wonder,' said Karl, 'how people on minimum wage get by.'

Keston thought a while, took a draught of cherry brandy straight from the bottle and said, 'What would you bring in a month, on minimum wage?'

'Uh, like seven-fifty?'

'Jesus.'

'Wouldn't even cover a week's rent,' said Karl.

'So how do you get by at all if you're on minimum wage?' said Keston. 'Tell you what –' taking out his mobile phone, an early series model which he insisted was a design classic – 'let's ask someone, shall we?'

Karl watched as Keston picked up a slim blue manual by its corner and leafed through it like a card dealer.

'What's that?'

'I got it because it went with the phone cabinet,' said Keston. 'But believe it or not some people still have landlines.'

Keston stopped on a page and fumbled with his mobile before putting it to his ear. He raised his eyebrows at Karl, who shook his head.

'Ringing.'

'Who?'

'Yes, hello. Yes. No, actually, we're not interested in that at all,' said Keston. 'I wanted to ask you – I work for the government, you see – I wanted to ask you if you're able to survive on your wage. I hope –' he tried to conceal a burp – 'I hope you don't find this an infringement. I'm with the government. A think tank.' Keston rolled his eyes. 'We're called, uh, Cloaca. No. Yes, we're calling twenty people a day from a – a – a sample list and your number came up. So if you … Yes, that's right. Thank you. Thanks. Cheers. So it's just three questions, really, and it won't take more than a minute or two. Firstly, if you wouldn't mind telling me your net monthly income. Right. That's. Right. Okay. And could you tell me your monthly rent or mortgage? Hmm.' Keston sipped his cherry brandy. 'So how the fuck does that work, if your income is less than your rent?' He cleared his throat. 'They hung up. Well, that doesn't explain anything.'

'Some people get help, don't they?' said Karl.

'But that's, what, like sixty quid a week?'

'When I was on Jobseeker's for two months,' said Karl, 'I'd have had my rent paid for me. If I could have found anywhere that accepted DSS tenants. Which I couldn't, so I used a credit card.'

'This doesn't make any sense,' said Keston. 'How do you live on negative one hundred pounds a month?'

'It's interesting that you're suddenly developing a social conscience,' said Karl.

'You think an accountant can't have a social conscience?' said Keston. 'I give away a third of my salary every month to homeless charities.'

'Shit,' said Karl. 'That's amazing.'

'It's not true,' said Keston, 'but how would you know if I did? And I can tell you, if I *did*, I certainly wouldn't *tell* people about it. Even what I'm saying right now could be a double bluff.'

'I've known you for fifteen years,' said Karl.

'I just think it's beneath you, K-dog, this pigeonholing. People who care about stuff run theatre companies and eat flax, is that it? One of my clients runs a theatre company and he's a monster of complacency. Look at my shoes!'

Keston swung one of his legs onto the table. The sole of his black, well-polished brogue was flapping loose.

'Middle-class revolt,' said Karl.

'This is the darkest of days,' said Keston, and closed his eyes. 'Maybe I should enrol on The Transition.'

'What you *could* do,' said Karl, 'seeing as you've nothing left to lose and all, is you could help me bring The Transition down.'

'Oh, Karlsberg,' said Keston.

'Don't you care that you've been pushing people into a programme that systematically ruins their lives? Don't you care that they've made you one of their … their *beagles*?'

'Beagles?' Keston screwed up his nose. 'Huh. All the good it's done me.'

'So why not help me stick it to them?'

'What's the story here, though, Karl? Idiot Fails Self-Improvement Course? Hold the front page.'

'We're planning a subtle but devastating coup. A big information drop, then we just let everyone make up their own minds.'

'*We* being?'

'Me. A cider farmer. Girl with white hair. A woman who makes computer-generated paintings.'

'The Fantastic Four,' said Keston. 'And what do you need from the dark accountant over here?'

'I need you to blackmail a cash-in-hand violin teacher,' said Karl.

Keston looked at the ceiling.

'Are you there, God?' he muttered. 'It's me, Margaret.'

# 45

**IT WAS AN HOUR** before his alarm was set to go off, but Karl lay awake thinking about Genevieve's body. The lightness as she drew away from him, the force as she drew towards him. He thought about her laughter. It was over a week since he'd seen her. He edited their marriage down to a highlights reel. He wanted to write her a letter. He wanted her to appear on the spiral staircase, to climb into the single bed, to roll on top of him. He wanted to say sorry for his ingratitude, his callousness, but already this felt like something he couldn't tell the actual Genevieve. Actual Genevieve rarely behaved in the same way as his inner Genevieve. She told him, after a year of marriage, you have an *idea of me* that you're in love with. When Karl protested, she told him that it was fine. She had an idea of him too. Nobody really wants to know anyone. We have an idea of someone and we get upset when they don't behave in accordance with it. Karl told her that seemed kind of sad. Oh Karl, Genevieve said, and lit a cigarette.

But he acknowledged, had always acknowledged, that he was a man who instantly idolised his wife the moment they parted. Actually it was worse: Karl idolised *everybody* when he wasn't with them. He longed for reunions, but as soon as he was actually in the same room as his friends the only thing he could think to say or do was to organise the next reunion. *I wish we saw more of each other. What are you doing in February?* It was a wonder anyone ever wanted to see him. Once at a dinner party in a house Keston briefly shared, Genevieve drank too much sparkling wine with the starter and had to go upstairs to lie down. She slept through the rest of the meal and ensuing party. Keston had found Karl after dinner gazing at an old photograph framed on the wall – a student production of *Shopping and Fucking*, Genevieve as Lulu. He looked at nineteen-year-old Genevieve, her tied-back hair dyed a shade lighter, a silly self-conscious grin she didn't really do any more. They hadn't been getting on for a while and had rowed before the party, but looking at her in the photograph Karl saw a sparklingly charismatic, intensely pretty woman who had inexplicably elected to spend the rest of her life with him. He felt a clap on his shoulder, a squeeze on his collarbone. 'Oh come *on*,' Keston had said. 'You're like a monk staring at an icon. Karl, she's *upstairs*.'

She was just upstairs now, of course, in Janna and Stu's house but further from him than ever. When he had finished dwelling on his love for his estranged wife, Karl rolled out of bed, kicked the square of red carpet which had corrugated in the damp and went to unfasten the drawing pins that held his makeshift curtain over the French windows. His untrimmed nails made this easy. He felt morose. A manila envelope stuck out from under the door.

The letter was addressed to Mr Karl, no second name, and was pamphlet-thick. He tore it open. There was no covering letter, just a corner-stapled document of several pages. An attached handwritten note read: *Karl, I'm doing what I can, okay? I have confirmation that she's safe and will try to get you an address for the ward. Meantime you need to do what we discussed if you want a bargaining chip. See you tonight. Be strong. Alice x*. Karl's hands shook as he read the report.

## B17 – INCIDENT REPORT

The alleged took place on the night of _____ and concerned myself, three further delegates from Toronto and the respondent, whose role was to entertain/relax us after a busy and challenging day. Dinner was consumed at an upmarket bar and grill. Two large glasses of IPA were consumed. A wooden plate of beef ribs and skillet of potatoes dauphinoise were consumed. Eight bottles of champagne were consumed. A white, bile-like substance was vomited and a severe episode of the hiccups began which continued for the rest of the night, mocked tirelessly by my party. Hiccups were mimicked, sighed at. An illegal substance offered by the respondent as a 'pick-me-up' was refused. Said illegal substance was accepted by two of my party, and one made his apologies and returned to the hotel. A collective level of intoxication beyond the usual was reached and a suggestion of adult entertainment was made in jest but seized upon by the respondent, who suggested a 'crawl'. A cash withdrawal was made using a company credit card. A turn for the worse was taken. A private dance was purchased in the first club and several comments, commensurate with the party's relative lack of experience, were made, to the dismay of all involved. Such comments, offensive and taboo in nature, reflected what might be termed a naïve sense of having already transgressed and therefore nothing being, as it were, off limits. The party was ejected from the club and sought another. Eighteen Long Island Iced Teas were consumed. Substance was proffered again and accepted. A further private dance was purchased from three dancers, followed by an unprovoked but not unwelcome level of intimacy between myself and the respondent. The bar was visited but on return to the table the respondent was found to have vanished along with one of my party. The club was searched by myself and a second member of my party. The streets in the immediate vicinity were searched. The second member of my party returned to the hotel. A pulled pork burger from a street van was consumed. Subsequently the respondent was found lying in the road with her feet up on the curb. Horns were sounded by passing cars as they manoeuvred around the respondent's head, and epithets were shouted from windows. The finger was given by the respondent. The respondent was removed from the road by myself and the remaining member of our party. A heated exchange followed and some doubt was felt as to whether anything might be done to help the respondent. The respondent became violent. A passing 'stag party' involved itself in the fray and the respondent was asked if this man (i.e. me) was bothering her. The respondent stated that this was so and followed the group of strangers, linking arms with the interlocutor. At this point the remaining member of my party expressed frustration at the situation and returned to the hotel. Unwilling to abandon the respondent, I followed the group at a safe distance from which laughter, of a somewhat harsh quality, could be heard and these sounds developed in severity such that I broke into a run, finding the group outside an establishment named chicken.com. The respondent had scratched the stranger on the cheek and had been shoved onto the ground. The respondent was helped to her feet by me, following which a punch was taken to the side of the head and the right eye, following which I curled up on the floor and received several light-to-heavy kicks to my sides and back while the respondent screamed. The 'stag party' whooped as they departed. A state of sobriety seemed suddenly to have been entered by the respondent and she supported me back to the hotel and the egg-sized lump above my eye was tended to with ice from the minibar. A mutual attraction was felt in the process. A long-term partner was betrayed. Remorse was felt.

# 46

**KARL FINISHED READING** the report half an hour before Izzy was due to arrive to take him to work. Karl ran around to the front door, rang the doorbell, then struck the knocker, then beat the door with both fists. Nobody answered. He got down on his knees, pushed the letterbox open and put his mouth to it, as if a house could be a giant woodwind instrument and the letterbox the reed.

'Genevieve?' he shouted. 'Janna? Stu?'

The self-drive pulled up while he was shouting.

'Ready?'

Karl climbed into the passenger seat.

'So, Izzy, Mr Roderick needs me to go to Boar Hill again, is that okay?'

Izzy sighed.

The lawn around Lorna and Samphire's caravan had been trimmed severely. It looked scruffy and yellow. When he knocked, Samphire opened the door and he just had time to notice that she was wearing her white hair down or, to be precise, *out*, before she flew at him and shoved him back down the stepladder.

'You motherfucker,' she said. 'You fucking …'

'Ouch.'

'You go after my mother? You fucking piece of shit.'

She punched him several times rapidly on the chest.

'Ow – Samphire, please.'

'Fucking, fucking, fucker.'

'I didn't mean to scare her or alarm her in any way.'

'Bullshit,' said Samphire, hitting him on the chest one last time so that he sat down on the bank, wheezing. 'A court summons!'

'Maybe she'll end up on The Transition,' said Karl. Samphire hit him again, sideways and hard enough to numb his upper arm, then she sat down next to him.

'Tell me what you want,' she said.

'I was confused as to why they'd put an old woman and a teenager in charge of data security, but that was actually pretty convincing.'

'What are you talking about?'

'The reason you're living out here.' Karl could feel the warmth of bruises forming on his upper body. 'I know. The data storage for The Transition. You're …'

'The caretakers,' said Samphire. 'All right, round of applause, Karl. You saw through the whole facade. Except I *am* actually taking my A levels and my mum *is* actually a violin teacher as well. We'd go out of our minds with boredom otherwise. I don't know what you think is so confidential anyone might be interested in it, to be quite honest. But just to be clear, if you weren't extorting my mother I would be tasering you to within an inch of your life right now and sitting on your pathetic unconscious body until the Transition security arrived.'

'But seeing as I am?'

'But seeing as you are, ask me anything.'

'Where are the banks of computers? Not in the caravan, right? I was told The Transition used advanced technology.'

'DNA data storage is apocalypse-proof, and extremely space-efficient,' said Samphire. 'You can fit a petabyte of information on a square centimetre.'

'Where is it kept?'

'You're looking at it.'

'Where?' Karl looked over her shoulder.

Samphire raised her arms and pulled out a single, uneven strand of white hair and handed it to Karl. It was nearly two feet long.

'Every movie ever made,' she said.

'*What?*'

Karl imagined taking the strand of hair back to Mr Roderick, presenting it like a sacred relic, waiting for some kind of result.

He twiddled the hair between his fingers.

'What do you plug it into?'

'You need a DNA reader, silly,' said Samphire.

'So it's all … in … your hair?'

Samphire laughed.

She led him through an invisible gap in the hedge behind the caravan. Once on the other side he saw that a small, partially sunken World War II blockhouse had been encased in the hedgerow, adapted so that its lookouts were inlaid with shiny black metal.

'I'm a side project, a case study. It's completely of my own volition and I'm handsomely remunerated. In the future we'll all have everything encoded in our little fingers, but for now it's in the bunker. All we really do here is keep an eye on the temperature. Dry, dark place at seven degrees Celsius. One of us signs in and checks every three hours and the temperature is constantly displayed in the caravan.'

Samphire drew a wire from a box mounted on the door. She appeared to touch it to her tongue and the door slid open.

Inside, the bunker wasn't quite big enough for Karl to stand up in. The walls were matte black and three flattish square objects, the size of pizza delivery boxes, were bolted to the floor. One wall contained three screens, two blank, one displaying 6.8°. A low hum intensified.

'The air-con takes up more space than the units themselves,' said Samphire. 'To give you some idea, you could store the complete sensory memories of every human being who ever lived in one of those. And we've literally had to do nothing other than dust them in a year and a half.'

Karl bumped his head on the ceiling.

'That's pretty much it. Any questions?'

'What if I wanted to get something sent out to all of the current protégés, to every tablet? Would that have to be done here?'

'Could be done remotely,' said Samphire. 'You'd need one of the parent tabs.'

She opened a slim metal drawer in the wall and took out a square piece of red glass, roughly half the size of Karl's tablet. She went to hand it over, then stopped.

'Karl,' she said. 'You have to get this back to me as soon as you possibly can. Do you understand?'

'My friend is a really good accountant,' said Karl. 'He can make the tax thing disappear again overnight – I promise you.'

She looked him in the eye then turned and walked back to her caravan and muttered, 'Fuck off, Karl,' without looking back.

# 47

**KESTON WAS OPENING** and closing the yellow capsule from a Kinder egg. Alice was screwing and unscrewing the horn of a small blue plastic unicorn. Mr Roderick sat at Keston's desk, the red tablet scrolling through numbers and locations. He was wearing a small pair of spectacles and tapped a larger, standard tablet and, occasionally, Keston's laptop which was linked to both. Karl was pacing from Keston's office to the kitchenette and back again.

'This shouldn't take long, Karl,' said Alice. 'I know you must be going out of your mind with worry.'

'After a while you get used to being out of your mind with worry,' said Karl.

'You must want to just run to her straight away. I've got eyes on her,' said Alice. 'She's in a private ward, she's resting. Honestly, once this is done you'll be compensated for the shit you've been through. You'll be able to name your price.'

'Twenty-two thousand, four hundred and eighty-six users, internationally,' said Mr Roderick. 'We can access any individual tab or we can make a global alteration to the system.'

'And then our faces melt,' said Keston.

'How long do you think you'll need?' said Alice. 'There's a garage round the corner and I can go and get some supplies if anyone's—'

'I've just done it,' said Mr Roderick, sitting back and putting his hands behind his head.

'Oh.'

'No fireworks?' said Keston. 'Not even, like, an emoji of fireworks?'

'How do we know it's worked?'

'Check your tab,' said Mr Roderick and hunched forward in anticipation.

Karl took out his tablet and handed it to Alice. They watched a list cascade from the *Past Journals* section, a waterfall of disgruntled B-streamers, their identity codes and a red RESOLVED against each entry. Karl hit one at random: a short video diary of a young woman in a surgical mask fastening the glass back panel onto an identical-looking tablet with a tiny electric screwdriver. She placed the tablet in an indented tray of six. Then they opened a document by a man who had been employed to clean rooms at a conference centre in Columbus, Ohio.

'It's done,' he said.

'Ha!'

'A party popper, even,' said Keston. 'Nobody thought to bring a party popper.'

'What do we do now?' said Karl.

'We wait,' said Mr Roderick.

'For the uprising,' said Alice Jonke. 'Which could take some time. Maybe I should do a snack run now?'

'I'll come with you,' said Keston.

'Hang on,' said Mr Roderick. 'The parent tab gives us an alert when the file is accessed. I've had confirmation that someone in Albuquerque has opened the journals.'

'Oh God,' said Alice. 'This is going to be like a general election.'

They sat in silence for a full minute.

'That's it so far,' said Mr Roderick. 'What I meant by *waiting* is that we go back to our lives and we wait for the truth to filter through and we never speak of this again.'

'Fine by me,' said Keston.

Karl started pacing again. He made a lap of the kitchenette and Keston's desk and then stopped in the doorway.

'The red tablet,' he said. 'We need to get it back to Samphire before she gets into trouble.'

Alice drove them, at lurching speed in her small bubble car, Karl in the back and Keston next to her.

'I'll stop before we get there and you can walk the last bit,' she said. 'No point in us meeting her.'

'That's sensible.'

Alice forced an estate car into a hedgerow as she overtook.

'We need to start thinking about any little nudges we can make,' she said. 'Roderick's playing it down, but this is huge, guys. This is like a kettle on an ants' nest and all we need to do is ... That's not a good analogy. Karl, do you have friends on the programme? Anyone you got chatting to at the meetings? You need to contact them right now – just be like, oh, hey, have you noticed this? You tell a handful of people locally, it'll spread. Within the hour the map'll be lighting up.'

Karl remembered his university friends – Pavel and Sumita – who had given him the copy of *The Trapeze*. He took out his tablet to compose a suitably breezy message.

He could hear owls as he walked away from the theatrical glow of Alice's headlights into total darkness. He looked up and followed Orion's belt, up and right to the Pleiades. When he reached the gate he momentarily felt that Alice must have driven to the wrong address. But it was clearly the same approach, even in the dark, the same overhanging tree and wedged-open double gate. In the moonlight Karl could see a long, oblong patch of pale, sun-starved grass where the static caravan had been. It reminded him of the area left by the trampoline they had in their garden as kids once his sister broke her arm and their father sold it. To the left, timber and tarmacked canvas had been stacked in a neat pile. Karl made for the hedge and found the gap between the branches which Samphire had led him through. The bunker had been gutted, the metal windows removed. He wiped the red tab with the sleeve of his jumper and dropped it through the rifle slit.

'When did you last see her?' Alice sat with her legs out of the car, several files open on her tablet.

'Three-ish?' said Karl.

'Samphire Randles, Lorna Randles,' she said. 'Been with us a long time. They've been relocated … to … Derby.'

'Oh.'

'Plenty of worse places.'

'They're safe?' said Karl.

'I'll check up on them. Of course they're safe.'

'But won't they get blamed for the breach?'

'Well, it *was* their fault,' said Alice. 'They'll be fine.' She slipped her tablet back into her jacket.

On the way to the city Alice stopped at a petrol station and said that she would buy them both the worst breakfast ever. They watched her walk across the floodlit forecourt and waited in silence until she emerged with three square pastries, tossing one each into Karl's and Keston's laps.

'It contains everything,' she said.

As they drove around the corner from the petrol station the valley plunged into total darkness and Alice flicked on the full-beams. The pastry was too hot to eat, so Karl checked his tablet to see if Sumita had responded.

'Oh, hello, what's this?' he said.

The screen displayed a large blue-bordered message, pulsing gently.

PLEASE READ

'What?' said Alice.

'Oh dear,' said Karl.

'Karl? What?'

Karl read the message out loud.

A glitch in the system occurred last night which temporarily flooded your tablets with unnecessary data in the form of every single protégé's journal from the past decade. This appears to be the work of a hacker and, while motive is unclear, of an essentially harmless 'nuisance' nature. We are happy to confirm that none of your personal data was compromised and that the surplus data has been removed. We would like to clarify that all journals are available for your perusal under the Freedom of Information Act should you wish to consult a specific document. In the interest of full disclosure, we will allocate twenty minutes of next week's general meeting to any concerns or issues arising. In the meantime we would like to thank our security team for heading off the issue before any damage was done.

'That was quick,' said Keston.

'Oh God,' said Alice. She punched her steering wheel and the horn emitted a brief, pathetic meep.

'This is bad, isn't it?' said Karl.

'Oh God,' Alice said again.

'Is it that bad?' said Karl. 'All for nothing?'

'We're all going to die,' said Alice, speeding up. 'I'm just going to drive us off a cliff – it's simpler that way.'

'You can drop me at the, uh,' said Keston.

'Fuck,' said Alice. '*Fuck.* Do you think anyone saw the redacted files before they got taken down?'

'That guy in Albuquerque?' said Karl. 'Trouble is, you need to read quite a lot of them before you realise the pattern is systematic. And that must have been, what, twenty minutes?'

'Gah,' said Alice. 'You're right. It's completely fucked.' She crunched the gears.

'Thing is,' said Keston, 'the B-streamers, as I see it … I mean, nobody *wants* that, right, but what makes us think we deserve any better than most of the world's population throughout most of human history?'

'Ha!' said Alice.

'Isn't the real lesson here that we're not very nice and we don't give a shit about each other?'

They drove on in silence for a few minutes and then Alice pulled into a lay-by. She got out of the car, leaving the engine running, and walked to a low railing, bathed in its headlights. They watched as she took her head in her hands.

'Well, this is an enjoyable interlude from all the things I urgently need to attend to,' said Keston. 'Sorry. You must be disappointed.'

Karl lay back so that his head touched the cool glass of the bubble car's rear window.

'I'm just sorry for wasting your time,' he said.

'One way of looking at this,' said Keston, 'is that I could potentially get an awesome girlfriend called Alice, who works in PR but also makes computer-generated art, which I kind of always wanted. So thanks, Karl.'

'I'm very happy for you.'


Karl saw Alice check her tablet, stand and walk back to the car. She got back in and rearranged her hair.

'Sorry about that,' she said. She turned around to face Karl. 'Your mentors are looking for you. I'll drop you off.' She spun the steering wheel.

Karl blinked his eyes in time to the passing lamp posts. Riding in the back seat always made him regress.

'It's actually not that bad,' said Alice. 'We'll rethink, regroup. Roderick will be gutted. But we'll *get* them. T.D.F. Like in chess. Trap, dominate, fuck.'

'Are you just going to carry on working for The Transition like nothing's happened?' said Karl.

'I know you wanted to do this to help Roderick bring The Transition down completely, Karl, but you might have noticed my position on it isn't quite as simple. It does a lot of good work, a lot of things I'm very proud of. What it really needs is a regime change. Get back to its roots.'

'You mean radical population control?' said Karl.

'I mean helping people realise their potential,' said Alice. 'It doesn't have to be the exploitative social-engineering experiment it's become. I'm finding enough people who want to turn it around.'

'Your ex-husband,' said Karl. 'Jonathan. Did he get sent away on the B-stream?'

'God knows where he ended up,' said Alice, quietly. 'I'd rather not talk about him if it's all the same to you, Karl.'

They drove in silence a moment.

'You're not worried about them tracing the leak back to you?' said Keston.

'They won't. They trust me. And Roderick's always said he'd take whatever flak comes our way. He's a sweetheart. A weird old socialist crank, but a sweetheart.'

'This regime change,' said Keston. 'Would it involve some measure of power going to you?'

'*Me?*' said Alice, indicating left. 'I suppose I hadn't thought that far ahead.'

'Little old you,' said Keston.

'Well,' said Alice. 'If it does happen, you want in? You're already well thought of.'

She pulled up outside an industrial estate.

'We're about a mile away from Janna and Stu's,' she said. 'Best this way, if you don't mind the walk.'

She and Keston got out of the car. Karl's seat belt stuck in the socket and it took him a moment to join them. Under the white glow of a security light Alice took his shoulders and gave him a kiss on the forehead.

'I'm really sorry about what happened with Genevieve, Karl,' she said to him. 'I'm sorry about everything. What you experienced, what all protégés are experiencing now – it's not what The Transition should be. I know you probably think I should abandon it, stop trying to work from the inside. I know Roderick probably thinks so too. I expect there are debt collectors who think they're going to bring down the system from the inside right after they've broken down the next door. But this is honestly the best chance I have of changing things.'

'Karl,' said Keston. He was looking at the half-moon. 'Remember when I first met you, you hadn't even eaten blue cheese.'

'What does that have to do with anything?' said Karl. 'Are you drunk?'

'Only place you'd ever dined out was a Little Chef,' said Keston. 'He'd never had blue cheese,' he said to Alice, who was already getting back into the driver's seat.

'I'd eaten it,' Karl protested. 'I just didn't like it.'

'And I said, what did I say?'

'You said I *had* to like it.'

'I said you have to *try* it, Karl. I said you were probably eating it wrong. I put some on an oatcake, I ordered you a port.'

'I think this was maybe more meaningful for you than it was for me.'

'And what's your favourite food now?'

'Keston,' said Karl. 'Nobody's favourite food is blue cheese.'

'Tell Genevieve hi from me,' said Keston.

# 48

**A SINGLE GOLDEN** high-heeled shoe had been placed in the middle of Janna and Stu's coffee table. The two-inch heel was snapped and lay to the side, thin as a cigarette.

'She was getting out of control,' said Janna. 'It was all a bit sudden.'

It felt like a hospital waiting room. Nobody could make eye contact. Either Janna or Stu had put the Goldberg Variations on quietly in the background.

'She was like a complete stranger, mate,' said Stu. 'Never seen anything like it.' He blew, as if extinguishing a candle, and almost smiled.

'What have I been saying,' said Karl, 'the whole time you had me shut in the basement? What did I tell you?'

'We understand you must be upset,' said Janna.

The shoe's patterning had the suggestion of alligator skin and the finish was iridescent, even under the warm side lights of the living room.

'But you'd decided I was holding her back. As if that never occurred to me before. Of course I'm fucking upset. I'm very good at worrying. It's one of my core skills.'

'She's safe now,' said Stu. 'I mean obviously she's not well enough to face the consequences, and getting a doctor's note was fairly important there. But you don't even want to know how long I've spent defending her today. To levels of management I've never even met before. You don't want to *know* some of the things they've said to me and Janna.'

'She caused a lot of trouble,' said Janna. 'And it's been very expensive undoing the damage.'

'I don't give a shit,' said Karl.

'No, well,' said Stu.

Karl was no judge of shoes and it could either have been from a European catwalk or a fancy-dress shop, but he suspected the former, and that Genevieve had borrowed them from Janna for her night out with the foreign contingent. The buckle, for instance, looked as robust as a miniature horseshoe, but had the elegant shape of a hatpin.

'I'm curious,' said Janna, 'and please don't think I'm prying, but what kind of support do the two of you have, out there? How did you manage?'

'We get a psychiatric appointment every four months,' said Karl.

'Karl,' said Janna. 'Are you honestly telling me that you don't have medical insurance?'

'You're honestly asking me if we have private health-care?' said Karl.

'But how can you …' Janna took a sip of her coffee and frowned at the shoe. 'You can't put a price on your health,' she said. 'You can't put a price on your wife's health.'

'Well, somebody did,' said Karl. 'The *vast majority* of people can't afford to go private. We're part of the vast majority. We always have been. Most people are.'

'And what we've been offering you,' said Stu, 'all we've ever been offering you, is a chance to escape that.'

'A chance,' said Karl, 'to live out the delusion that we're in some way special, that we deserve better than everyone else. Why?'

'Because you *are*,' said Janna. 'You *do*.'

'Karl,' said Stu, looking up, 'you have the voice of someone who just stepped out of a Spitfire. Don't tell me you're worried about being a class traitor. If there's a broken system you try to improve yourself so that it no longer applies to you.'

'That's rich,' said Karl, 'considering you were in the process of estranging me from my more promising spouse and marooning me in a distant land with a bucket and mop. Do the B-streamed protégés get healthcare? Share options?'

'They're well looked after,' said Janna, slowly, looking at Karl for the first time and narrowing her eyes. 'Who have you been talking to?'

'The diaries all appeared on my tablet last night,' said Karl.

Stu massaged his face hard and groaned.

'Probably the worst security breach we've ever had,' he said. 'It's just as well we own several PR firms. Alice was working through the night. You met Alice, right?'

'I don't remember.'

They listened to the piano a while.

'Why did you take my photo of Genevieve?' said Karl. 'I mean, what the hell?'

'It's a very lovely photo,' said Janna. 'I'll get it for you.'

'We have to inspect the possessions that come with protégés,' said Stu. 'That's just how it is. Security. It fell out of a book. I picked it up.'

'And you took it. And it's mine,' said Karl.

'We didn't think you'd notice,' said Janna. 'And then, of course, you did, but naturally you didn't say anything. I thought that ...'

'This idea of sexual ownership is very dated,' said Stu. 'A consensual expression of your sexuality needn't be any more emotionally complicated than going to the gym or reading a book. It's an optional, but I think actually pretty important, part of being honest with yourself.'

'Sure,' said Karl. 'Whatever. You're swingers.'

'Ugh,' said Janna. 'That's such a horrible word. We're not even a couple, Stu and I, the way you understand it.'

'No, I understand,' said Karl. 'You were engineered by The Transition.'

'Who told you that?' said Stu.

'It's nothing controversial,' said Janna. 'The Transition encourages couples who are in good partnerships, relationships which nurture and inspire, but sometimes it's the case that there might be another person who makes a better match for you. A better mentoring partner. A better business partner. It depends. And if that's the case, this is the ideal scheme to find them on.'

'Transition-funded studies into social and sexual well-being have shown that people having frequent, high-quality sex with similarly enlightened partners are more productive and higher earners, so it's actually—'

'Look, if we thought you were both game and we misread, that's a pity and I apologise,' said Janna. 'When someone goes through your underwear drawer and spies on you through a keyhole it's easy to get the wrong idea.'

Karl blushed.

'Of course, it's also unethical and legally questionable to take and keep an intimate photograph of someone without their knowledge in the first place,' said Janna. 'If you want to moralise.'

'Okay, okay,' said Karl. 'I'm a pervert and a creep.'

'You're not, Karl, that's the point,' said Janna. 'Bloody hell.'

'So if a situation had arisen where you might have needed to blackmail me,' said Karl, 'or cause more friction between me and Genevieve, the photo could have been useful.'

Janna laughed.

'Didn't cross my mind,' said Stu.

'*The Trapeze*,' he said. 'You took my copy of that, too. Why?'

'It's a book of nonsense,' said Stu. 'Harmless, really, but there are some disgruntled former protégés who use it as a calling card. We didn't want you falling in with them. Who gave it to you?'

'Nobody,' said Karl. 'An old friend – they happened across it.'

'We wanted you to have a fighting chance of not screwing this up, Karl,' said Janna. 'It was your own actions that put you in the basement, that separated you from Genevieve and that, eventually, *eventually* made us start to think that perhaps you weren't really cut out for The Transition after all.'

'What we're going to suggest is this, Karl,' said Stu. 'You move back into your room, forget the basement, you carry on with your work until Genevieve's back to herself again. I mean obviously we can't really let her back on the scheme in an official capacity. But she won't face charges.'

'You're dropping her?'

'Pardoning her.'

'B-streaming her?'

'She can live here, of course.'

'Essentially a clean slate,' said Janna.

'God,' said Karl. 'I'll ask her. But I was thinking more along the lines of never seeing you again.'

There was a silence in between tracks 20 and 21.

'There's no such thing as leaving The Transition,' said Janna. 'We've never, ever let anyone down.'

'Or go?'

'It's a broadhead contract,' said Stu. 'You know that. The most we can do, Karl, is to grant a leave of absence, B-stream both of you, then, once we can't roll the leave on any further, keep appointing and firing you from an endless succession of jobs we won't expect you to turn up to for not turning up to them.'

'This is ridiculous,' said Janna.

'I'll do the paperwork myself,' said Stu.

'Yes, okay,' said Karl. 'As long as Genevieve agrees, it's a deal.'

'But, mate, where are you even going to *live*?' said Stu. 'You're honestly choosing to be homeless. Are we – is the whole thing *that* bad?'

'I'll stay with my sister for a while,' said Karl.

'And Genevieve?'

'She can join me when she's well enough. She'll go back to teaching or she'll do something else. Whatever she wants.'

'You've made up your mind.'

Karl was surprised to hear that Stu's voice was thick and almost tearful and felt a rush of affection for them both.

'When I was a boy I remember my dad started a business,' he said. 'It was a good idea and he was going to be self-employed. It was to do with funerals. Burials. All the people who died with no insurance, no plans, whose families couldn't afford a proper send-off. From a variety of different traditions and religions – that was where his expertise came in. It was dignified. He'd applied for charitable status. He worked on it at night, after he'd finished his marking, his lesson plans, after he'd read us our stories and we were all asleep. He stayed up most of the night working on it. But something went wrong. The numbers were out. Or one of the backers dropped him at the last moment. He'd already quit his job in good faith. But he lost a lot of money. We defaulted on our mortgage. We had to move.'

Karl looked at Stu, who shrugged, then at Janna, who seemed to perch weightlessly on the sofa.

'It's actually a really good idea,' said Stu. 'I mean, shit, Karl, it's something you could have pitched to The Transition as your start-up. You still could.'

'That wasn't why I mentioned it,' said Karl. 'Ugh. If there are ten people in a race, ninety per cent of them don't win. You only ever make a profit because someone else is making a loss—'

'Let's run with the sporting analogy,' said Stu. 'If you watch a tennis match, a long one with lots of deuces, back and forth, back and forth, there comes a point where the players are exhausted and you can *see*, even on the TV screen, that one of them *wants it more*. That's what it comes down to.'

'Okay,' said Karl. 'Well, I'm sitting down and playing with my shoe while the ball bounces past me. I'm questioning the very purpose of tennis.'

'Right, well, we've been more than generous,' said Janna. 'Let's get you and Genevieve out of here, shall we? Sooner it's done the sooner we can bring in your replacements.'

'Janna,' said Stu.

'Do you remember the couple who absconded, Karl? Of course you do – you've been digging for dirt ever since you arrived. Ed and Jess Anderton. Well, they came back and we've been asked if we'd take over their mentorship. And we said not until we'd spoken to you. In spite of everything you've done we're still held in fairly high esteem.'

'Let's keep it civil,' said Stu. He handed Karl a white square of card with a handwritten note.

'The address,' he said. 'The hospital where Genevieve's staying.'

'Thanks.'

FIVEACRES. A 'sanatorium', Karl thought. He turned it over. It was his Polaroid of Genevieve, sleeping. His heart beat fast as he tucked it into his inside pocket.

'We'll get the paperwork,' said Janna, springing to her feet. 'Stu?'

They left him on his own. Karl looked around the room. The thick grey impasto of the seascapes, the coffee cups with drips of coffee painted on. Wedged between the speaker and the wall he saw the thick spine of the weathered *Mentor's Edition* and, without thinking, pulled it out and slipped it into his bag.

**KARL BOUGHT A** bacon sandwich and a mug of tea from a grim little cafe and sat at a plastic table. He thumbed the *Mentor's Edition*, then opened it at random and read, the way his mother used to do with the Bible.

### 182

A man lived at the top of a hill in a town that suffered frequent floods. Because he lived at the top of a hill, his house was never damaged when the river burst its banks. He watched from his attic window as human chains passed sandbags; as men waded through the stagnant water to rescue those too stubborn to abandon their homes; as family cars submerged until their roofs looked like keys on a laptop. What could he, a small and timid man, do to help that wasn't already being done better by others? Surely nobody seriously expected him to open the doors of his tiny cottage and take in the needy? And yet the uncomplicated solidarity he observed from his outpost confirmed something he had suspected all his life. Even as a child he felt that those around him were party to some secret tranche of hopes and fears he neither shared nor felt any curiosity about. Music, art and sports did not engage his attention: he had no natural proficiency and no real desire to address what seemed, to him, relevant only to those who did. He achieved B and C grades in his academic studies with little effort or curiosity about the Magna Carta, the GDP of Brazil, relative formula mass. Sometimes, after school, he would be dropped at the houses of his contemporaries and they would play computer games or watch television while their parents made supper. But one day nationalistic slogans were daubed on the side of the school sports hall. While few had strong feelings either way about what had been written, the entire student population was in trouble. Because nobody would come forward everyone had to sit in complete silence in the assembly room for an hour and a half after school each day for the rest of the term; a state of affairs which would cease only when the perpetrator made themselves known, or when someone with information leading to their identification spoke up. He had no idea who was responsible and resolved to take the group's punishment with the sense of complete detachment he felt for most other activities. But to his surprise, during those ninety-minute vigils, supervised and shushed by a rota of staff who resented the encroachment on their working day as much as the student body on their free time, he felt at peace. It seemed right and fitting to him that he should, in some small way, be made to suffer, that *everybody* should, and he with them; that in the interminable wait for someone to come forward and admit to the crime, there was justice, there was dignity, there was meaning.

Karl slipped the worn paperback into a Jiffy bag and went through his pockets for a scrap of paper. He had to ask at the counter to borrow a pen. He wrote his email address and then he wrote *Dear Mr Roderick, I'm sorry things didn't work out as we'd planned. I hope that you don't give up and that* – he paused and chewed the end of the pen, then remembered he'd borrowed it from the counter – *the collapse of the system will prove inevitable. If I can help please get in touch. In the meantime, I wonder if the enclosed might be of interest to you. Make of it what you will. Karl.*

He paused before sliding the note between the pages of the book and added an 'x' after his name, just to annoy Mr Roderick.

# 49

**FIVEACRES WAS AN** oddly shaped building – it looked like a pile of children's building bricks – with a distorted set of manor-house gates and a long driveway. At its door a green plaque commemorated the ward being opened by a Sir. Beneath this a smaller black metal panel was embossed with the legend BURSARY FOR INNOVATION IN FACILITY DESIGN, followed by a familiar little circled T. Karl gritted his teeth. He was buzzed in and an orderly showed him through three sets of double doors, the locks of which automatically shot open as they approached. Karl swallowed.

'My, my partner,' he said. 'Genevieve. I'm here to see her.'

The assistant nurse beamed. They were expecting him. She showed him around the locked ward. It was a large semicircle with communal areas and twelve individual rooms with glass doors.

'You can stand anywhere in the semicircle and see into every bedroom.'

'The Panopticon,' said Karl.

'Makes observations easier. Less invasive.'

A teenage boy sat at a table with a partially completed jigsaw puzzle of Magritte's *Le Fils de l'homme*. A woman with bandages on her forearms sat opposite him, her mouth open.

'Do you ever have anyone come in to read or anything?' said Karl. 'Like a volunteer? Or a poetry group or something?'

'I don't know,' said the nurse. 'We try to keep excitement to a minimum.'

'It could be, like, a boring poetry group?'

'I'll talk to the doctor.'

'If there's something I can do,' said Karl.

He stroked her hair.

'This'll pass,' he said.

'Where? Thistle Pass?'

'It will.'

'What?'

Genevieve lay across his lap. She was wrapped in a cellular blanket. A male nurse kept walking in and out of the area. He pretended to adjust the window.

'You can take her for a walk if you like.'

The hospital stood near the airport and had a little yard which overlooked a disused landing strip. Karl and Genevieve were in the centre parting between the sun lounge and the fence of the distant second runway.

'The apple-thick quadrant,' said Genevieve.

'The what? Don't go all avant-garde on me.'

'It's just words.'

'What have they done to you?' said Karl. 'I love you. I'm so sorry. I love you.'

Genevieve said that she was fine. At first Janna and Stu had told her she didn't need anything, that Karl was keeping her pacified because he couldn't cope with her creative energy, that if she could really commit to an alternative treatment like Calibration she'd be a new woman within a matter of months. Then there was a bad misunderstanding with a visiting group from America or somewhere and she wasn't entirely sure what had happened. Now they were trying some new pills. She said it was like playing a carpeted piano. Maybe if you hit the keys hard enough there was a faint sense of which note had been struck, but really it was just going through the motions.

She smiled sadly. She said, 'Have I told you about how Dad used to take us to the airport? He'd make a flask of hot chocolate and we'd buy croissants with jam from the cafe. Then we'd just stand in the wind and eat cold croissants and watch the planes take off.'

She took Karl's hand and said it was kind of him to visit. He instinctively squeezed her hand and drew her towards him, putting an arm around her. He thought of images of amoebas bonding. Overhead a plane the size of a toy climbed higher with a roar that sounded like victory or agony.

'So,' she said. 'Tell me about yourself.'

# Acknowledgements

I am indebted to Anna Kelly and Lottie Fyfe at 4th Estate. To Georgia Garrett, Matthew Turner and Emma Paterson at RCW. Your advice and attention to detail is greater than I'm worthy of. To those who read and discussed early drafts with me, especially Abi Curtis, Richard House and Luke Brown. To my former professors at the University of Exeter, Andy Brown and Philip Hensher. Also to my English teachers at secondary school, Paul Coffman and Clare Morris, who used to read my short stories – outside of their innumerable official duties – expecting nothing in return other than some later emulation of their generosity which I can only try to live up to. Thank you.